DANCING
EYES

PALMETTO
PUBLISHING
Charleston, SC
www.PalmettoPublishing.com

Hardcover ISBN: 979-8-8229-4552-4
Paperback ISBN: 979-8-8229-4553-1
eBook ISBN: 979-8-8229-4554-8

THE DANCING EYES

MARGUERITE FUSCO

This book is dedicated to my father and my mother.

You were the perfect parents for us.

I am thankful that my children knew you and were
loved by you.

I love that you lived your lives free of possessions.

I am saddened that you were tortured souls.

TABLE OF CONTENTS

INTRODUCTION

C harlie lived a simple life and loved to extraordinary measures. The world around him did not know the extent of his integrity but judged him instead for the unusual appearance of his and Alice's situation. Alice had unprecedented will and perseverance. She would overcome the obstacle of total blindness while succumbing to the psychological reality that was forever looming and would take control of her life. She and Charlie met as children and shared what would seemingly be stark differences but proved to be surprising similarities of personality and inner conflict. Their paths would cross in more ways than one, as he would protect her and their children throughout their lives. All the while, Charlie would go almost unseen and unheard with never-ending dedication to his one and only forever love.

CHAPTER ONE

CHARLIE

The Aldridge children woke to the pitter-patter of rain on the attic roof as Mother called up to the third-floor attic from the bottom of the steps, which were on the second floor of their pencil-shaped house. Rich, Rob, and Charlie slept like soldiers, lined up in their queen-size bed that was situated on one side of the room. Young Gertrude, who everyone called Gertie, and Delilah on the other side of the room. An old flannel sheet with strings tied to the ceiling rafters served to separate their quarters. The temperature was quickly changing from feeling like being in a heat box to suddenly needing to wear an extra pair of socks at night as the summer came to an end.

The children were awoken by their mother's calls as she was still standing at the foot of the attic steps. She banged her metal spoon against the bottom of her stock pot, which served as their daily alarm clock. Within moments, the three boys changed from their sleeping clothes and into their first day of school attire. Rob fixed Charlie's collar and helped him with his tie. They each poured the hot water into their personal buckets from the pitcher that mother left at the bottom of the attic steps, washed their faces in the wash bowl at the end of the hallway, and rinsed with mother's homemade mouthwash that consisted of water, baking soda, and peppermint. They spit it into the antique cigar tin that Grandfather had given to the family. The boys took turns using the six-inch black comb, dipping it into the hair tonic bottle that was next to the dresser as they peered into the tiny round mirror hanging beside it. They could hardly see one person's face through the foggy glass, let alone check that the hairs were all in place.

The children's things were always kept tidy. Each of the five children had two sets of clothes, three pairs of underwear, and three pairs of socks. Charlie's sisters, Gertie, and Delilah got dressed in the bathroom. Each child had their own drawer, and they were expected to put everything back the way they found it before coming downstairs. The children clamored into the kitchen as Mother scooped the oatmeal onto their plates. Giggles filled the room as Rich jumped around, telling jokes, and making wise-cracking antics with magic tricks and puzzles. Rob had moved to the corner of the room, away from the commotion, to concentrate on reading his new book that Sister Irene gave him on loan, *The Call of the Wild*. The rain was deflecting off the tin roof that covered the tiny back porch steps leading out of the kitchen.

"You are going to be late," said Mother as she handed them all a pair of plastic handmade shoe coverings to protect their feet from the puddles. Rich and Rob were always in charge. They were twelve-year-old twins. The boys were born on the day of the biggest boxing fight of 1924. Daddy wanted to name them after the two heavy weight fighters. However, in those days, he listened to what Mother wanted, and she was allowed to name them Robert and Richard after her two brothers. Rich grabbed seven-year-old Charlie by his sleeve to cross the dirt roads of North Philadelphia. Rich walked in front, sporting his muscles and telling the joke about the priest, the rabbi, and the preacher. He was saying something about what each of them would do with their church collection money. One gave it to the orphanage; another put the money into fixing up the church. And then the last one said that he took the collection money each week, threw it up in the air, and responded that God keeps what he wants and that whatever fell back belonged to him. Nine-year-old Gertie giggled at the punch line. Charlie smiled as if he understood the joke. But the truth was that he would ponder over the meaning of the punch line for the rest of the trip until he figured out his own interpretation of the joke. Five-year-old Delilah was skipping along and already forgot what Rich had said but didn't understand it anyway. She was just happy to be walking with her big sister and brothers. Rob, trailing in the back, didn't hear the joke at all. Partly because he was watching the little ones while at the same time slowly swaggering, as he was still engulfed in the details of his latest novel, which he had not put down since they left the house.

They dropped Delilah off at Aunt Betty's house. She wasn't really their aunt but Mother's very close friend. Mother had to get to work at the switchboard at Gimbels for a few hours that morning, and the boys would pick Delilah back up on their way home from school. Daddy was not to know that Mother took any extra money in. He would be furious, as he boasted himself to be a proud man whose wife did not work. In reality, she always worked on the side and kept her earnings in a crawl space under the kitchen table for when Daddy got arrested or didn't come home with a paycheck. It seemed that he never even considered how they got along during those times without him.

Charlie felt like a big kid now because this was the first year that he didn't get dropped off at Aunt Betty's house along with Delilah.

As they walked, the cross on top of Saint Michael's Catholic Church was moving closer, as Charlie was now lagging behind his twin brothers. Charlie followed his brothers everywhere. He did everything they said, and he knew they would look out for him no matter what. They were probably two of the best friends a little brother could have. But when it came to his absolute absolute best friend in the entire world, that would have to be, hands down, his Irish twin, little Delilah.

She was just thirteen months younger than him, and they took care of each other. She knew everything about him. She always understood him and was able to interpret everything he said. Even Mother could not always figure out what he was trying to say and would rely on Delilah's clarification.

The family moved around from place to place. Sometimes two to three times a year. Daddy was always coming up with a new get-rich scheme. Because of the constant uprooting, there really was not much time to make friends outside of their family. Sometimes the brothers would bring kids around to play, but most kids in the neighborhood learned pretty quickly to steer clear of Rich's temper. Therefore, not many kids wanted to hang around them much.

Still on the way to their first day of school, the children walked down Pennsylvania Avenue. They approached the busier streets with the trolleys rolling by. The people who owned cars were tooting their horns for no apparent reason. The level of noise and commotion tripled after turning the corner of Main Street.

Charlie thought to himself how those grown men probably weren't even beeping at people in their way. They were probably just getting pure joy from pushing on their horns just to show the passersby that they had the means to have a car. He thought that they were acting like little kids that enjoy hearing the squawk of their horns attached to their bicycle handlebars. He started to think about how Daddy was always talking about a car of his own and how he was going to have so much money and would buy Mother furs and diamonds and a house telephone. Mother would look at him with her big brown eyes with such longing. Not pining for herself to have those things but longing for her husband to finally feel worthy. To feel like he was a success at something. Charlie thought maybe Daddy would be less angry if he had a car and money and could give Mother all that stuff.

Suddenly these thoughts left Charlie's head as he became distracted by the church bells tolling. It was the most beautiful sound. One that he never heard before. There were no words being sung, just chimes. It made him feel happy inside. Peaceful.

This will be a good place with good people and love, he thought to himself. *Mother will be so happy to know that her sons are in this new Catholic school that plays such heavenly chimes.*

The parking lot was littered with children in uniforms: the boys all in black slacks with white button-down collars, just like Charlie and his brothers. The girls were in black-and-white jumpers. A lot of the kids had black, shiny, patent leather shoes. But you could tell there were other poor kids too. Charlie's shoes were pretty nice because he was a size for big kids. The shoes belonged to Rich at his age, but he'd grown out of them so fast; he hardly even wore them for two months. Daddy was so mad when he had to get Rich another pair and told Mother how stupid she was for not knowing she should buy him ones that were two sizes too big to give him room to grow.

Charlie's round cheeks were flushed with the first day of school nervous excitement. His jet-black hair was parted to the side, which always stuck in place. It was thick and wavy, and Mother never had to use tonic to keep it from looking messy. His blue eyes squinted, and his thick black eyebrows crinkled as he looked up at the cross on top of the building, which only a few moments ago seemed so much smaller. Now he could hardly see the tip of it with the sun beating into his eyes.

Rob pushed Charlie's shoulders forward, pointed him in the direction where his grade of kids should be, shook his hand, and said, "Be tough," as if they were going off to fight in the war or something. Then, with all the commotion of kids, teachers, bells chiming, and chatter, he didn't even see his big brother protectors disappear into the crowd.

Just when he started to feel his throat get dry with fear, he heard a voice call out, "Roll call!" All children were told to find their grade written in chalk on the blacktop and line up in single file, where they would then be separated into A and B lines. The chatter came to an immediate stop, and the children stood at attention. As he scampered to find his spot in line, Charlie spotted the words "first grade." He drew a sigh of relief at this. He came upon a group of kids who looked much smaller and younger than him. Their faces looked more like Delilah's than his own. Looking behind him, he double-checked the line and took his place. His hands started sweating and he could feel his heart beating loudly in his ears. He tried to muster up the ability to open his mouth to ask if he was in the right place when suddenly he heard another voice in line behind him say, "Is this the line for first grade line A and line B?"

"Yes, it is," said another voice. Charlie sighed in relief again, as at least now he knew he wouldn't have to ask someone himself. *Well,* he thought, *maybe I am just like Rich and Rob, and I guess I am tall for my age too, like people always say about them.*

A proud yet still wary grin slid across his lips to form a crooked smile at the thought.

The entire school recited the full rosary before entering the large building that smelled a lot like the incense that burned in the church on Sundays. He knew the rosary well, as Mother had them say it every Sunday evening before bedtime. He mouthed the words, being careful not to be heard by anyone.

The children were separated in the hallway to report to their assigned classrooms. Once again, Charlie felt the chill of fear as he entered the room without his brothers. After all, he never had to worry about anything when Rich and Rob were around. Charlie accepted his fate with the new journey as he entered the classroom. As he looked around the room, he noticed again that he looked much older than the other kids. The students peered at him. Whispers filled the room. He knew he was too old for this class. He thought these kids looked like babies.

Even so, he felt intimidated by their staring. Why did he feel so insecure in his surroundings? Suddenly, it hit him. Like a bolt of lightning into his stomach. *They are going to hear me talk,* he thought. He wasn't sure how this had not dawned on him prior to this moment. It was probably because he was so excited to finally be able to go to school and wasn't used to the outside world being exposed to his disability.

The sweat started to bead on his forehead. His palms were sweaty, his eyes were growing large, and his mouth was as dry as a desert. Feeling panicked, he tried to come up with a plan. He thought he would just sit in the back and not have to say anything. He felt no one would even notice him.

That was it! That was what he would do, and everything would be fine.

As Sister Claudette entered the room and closed the giant door behind her, the air from the outside hallway was forced into the room, and the papers on her desk went flying all over the floor, scattered beneath desks, and furnishings in the room. Among the paperwork that was now left unnoticed under the radiator in the corner was a note that had been placed on top of her roll book explaining Charlie's unique speech situation.

She introduced herself to the class and told the children that they would begin by reciting the Pledge of Allegiance. All the children stood tall with their right hand on their heart and stated the proud mantra of their country. Charlie knew every word. Standing proudly like a warrior and moving his lips just the same without making a sound.

He could hear a little girl's voice to his right. She was pledging her allegiance almost at the top of her lungs. He felt she was showing off that she knew every word and how to pronounce it perfectly. He felt jealous as he heard her speaking so eloquently. He could feel her looking over at him with admonishment, as if she knew he was just lip-syncing. He could tell by her expression that she was judging him for not stating the words out loud. Finally, he worked up the courage to look over at her.

At that moment, his eyes grew large as he felt yet another piercing feeling in his gut. But this time the sensation was much different. It felt like butterflies mixed with nausea. She was the most beautiful thing he had ever seen. Her brown wavy hair was pulled back in the front and secured with a little white bow clipped neatly just next to her right eyebrow. Her green eyes seemed to look right into his soul. His stomach hurt so badly he thought he might vomit.

After finishing the pledge, the children took their seats. The little girl reached into her brand-new zippered pencil case and passed him a freshly sharpened pencil. He didn't know what he was supposed to do with it, so he just shyly took the pencil and turned away.

At last, the dreaded moment had arrived. Sister Claudette announced that each child must come to the front of the class and introduce themselves, tell their age, and talk about their families. At the sound of this, Charlie thought he might faint. Any saliva that was left in his mouth from the time he entered the classroom was surely gone now. His heart was beating faster than a puma could run. He started to see spots.

Please God, don't let me go up there, he thought to himself. He imagined he would surely have had more time to fake it. He knew Mother would have told the school that he could not do something like this in front of the whole entire class. Did anyone tell his teacher that he couldn't talk like everyone else? Couldn't he have gotten to know the routine a little bit better before having to actually speak? If given more time, he might learn how to speak the right way, like Daddy always said he would.

The children, one by one, took turns. They proudly stood behind the podium.

"My name is Daniel Xavier. I live on 22 Sycamore Street in Philadelphia, PA. I have six brothers and three sisters."

Next...next...next...

He watched and counted, as everyone was seated alphabetically, so he knew just when his fateful moment would come around. Since it started with Z and worked its way back to him, he had some time, as he was the fourth one in the first row. It was happening so fast. Before he knew it, it was almost his turn.

He could run, but he would get in trouble. He could stick his finger down his throat and vomit. But it was too late.

Sister Claudette called out, "Charles Milton Aldridge."

Charlie couldn't move at first, and he just stared at her with longing eyes. She repeated his name again but this time with a sterner-sounding voice and a most threatening expression on her face.

"That is your name, isn't it?" she said. Charlie shook his head and stood up slowly, his hands shaking in his pockets.

"Charles, hands at your sides," she said. Sister stood at the front of the class with her pointer in hand. She had no idea what he was facing, as the note explaining Charlie's situation was still wedged beneath the radiator.

As Charlie approached the podium, he couldn't look at any of them. He knew what lay ahead. He looked over at the door as if Delilah would magically appear and stand at her brother's side to interpret his words.

"Charles, the class is waiting for you to tell them about yourself."

Again, he stood silently. Should he just refuse and accept the punishment of getting beat with that thin wooden yardstick? It couldn't be any worse than when Daddy flew off the handle and picked a kid to whip. It was hard to decipher what was shaking more, his voice or his hands. Sister's voice was becoming harsher with a threatening tone.

He was feeling the pressure build and felt like he might explode. Before he could even hear himself say it, he blurted out, "I-I-I-I-I-I-m-m-m-m-m-m-gammogammogammomomom!"

He kept his head down, then sheepishly looked up at the crowd.

The classroom fell completely silent. The room looked like it was full of wax figures. He had never experienced a greater silence than he felt in that moment. It was quieter than an empty church on a Saturday evening just before it began to fill for confession. He slowly looked up at the children's faces. The startled, shocked stares, which seemed to have lasted a lifetime, were very quickly broken with one little giggle. Then another, then another. Before he knew it, someone shouted, "Bibidigiggitybibityshigs!"

Almost everyone in the room broke out with childish laughter. Daniel O'Malley slapped his knee and fell off his chair. Charlie stood there, stunned, looking at the door and then turning to look at the nun with her pointer in hand, rushing over to correct Daniel.

Before he even realized what his body was doing, he suddenly found himself bursting through the doors to the outside of Saint Michael's school. The doors were flapping open in the windy rain. Charlie ran as fast as his legs could carry him. The tears were stinging his cheeks. He couldn't breathe. Soon his neatly groomed, parted black hair that never fell out of place was covering his sweet blue eyes, so drenched that he could hardly see. He was exploding with anger. The frustration of not being able to be understood. His self-expression was completely retarded, in an all too familiar feeling. There was nothing he could do to control it. No matter how many times Daddy told him that he would learn how to talk and to grow up and stop talking baby talk. Daddy's piercing taunts and slaps in the face didn't compare to what he just withstood. These weren't even his peers. They were kids younger than him.

Mother never told him that she held him back in the hopes that he would learn to speak properly if he just waited a few more years.

As he ran, he was throwing punches in the air. Screaming in his indiscernible babble.

"Alumalumaoomn!" This was Charlie's curse word that he made up that he knew no one would ever understand, so he would never get in trouble for saying it. Delilah was too little to know what any of it meant either. He did always take care not to say any of his made-up curse words in front of her, however.

As he ran, his feet carried him all the way down Main Street. He didn't pay attention at all to where he was. He took the corner of Central Avenue at lightning speed. Then suddenly he was halted by the sound of a group of children singing. It was the same tune that St Michael's school was chiming before morning prayers earlier that day. This time the song was with words. He could only make out some of what the children were singing, as he wasn't quite close enough yet. As he approached the voices, he could hear the words matching the beautiful tune.

"Immaculate Mary, your praises we sing."

He fell back against the stone wall in front of a large building with an iron gate and manicured lawn. It looked sort of like the place where his great grandfather was when he got sick. Charlie looked up at the sign on the gate. Rob taught him how to read and write a lot of things. He already knew how to spell the word "school" but couldn't make out what the other word said. He wondered what "bind school" meant.

Charlie slumped down into a crouched position while he caught each skipping breath as the words from the song resonated and made him feel relaxed and at peace. His tears stopped momentarily as his attention was captured by the bus that was pulling up and around the U-shaped driveway. He was drawn to the doors of the bus. Waiting and watching to see what or who came out of them. As the door, shining like new, opened, the right sided, long pane of glass turned outward, and the left one turned inward. It was like watching a clock tick, waiting for church to be over. Still sniffling and drying his eyes, he was drawn to the contents of the bus. So curious as to what was behind those doors. Suddenly he saw a long white stick appear. It was moving from side to side. There was a boy behind it. He was about Charlie's age, and he stepped down, swaying the stick in front of him. The boy was awkward and stumbling. His body was leaning forward, moving faster than his feet. He was wearing dark glasses. As the boy made the final step, he felt for the side of the bus and took his place in a line in front of the bus. Then another similar-looking lad followed suit. And another. And another. One of the boys fell down the last step. Charlie jumped up and started toward the gate and grabbed hold of the bars as he peered through it. The boy stood up, wiped the dirt off his pants, felt around for his white stick, and took his place back in line just as if nothing happened. Charlie thought about how strange it was that the man standing outside the bus didn't bat an eye to even help the boy. He just let him get himself back together, fumble for the stick, and find his place in line.

Charlie couldn't take his eyes off the group of boys for several minutes. He had forgotten all about his own humiliating plight for just a moment as he watched.

He then put his head back, took a huge sigh, and said a little prayer in his head for them.

He then said a little prayer for himself asking for forgiveness. He wanted forgiveness for his fleeting thought of satisfaction that there were others in the world that had to deal with being different, just like him. Only they seemed to be in a far worse position.

Somehow Charlie was able to find his way home without the help of his brothers. As he stood in the kitchen with rain-soaked shoes and clothes, Mother turned from the stove and their eyes locked. She was shocked to see him standing in the doorway so early in the day. They stared at each other for several seconds. With no words she gently walked over to him, knelt down on one knee, and untied his mud-covered shoelaces. She held back her tears with all her might, as she could only imagine what had happened to her sweet child on this day.

"I mnr onin ack ere," said Charlie in a defeated-like whisper.

For the first time ever, she understood exactly what he said.

"Okay, you never have to go back there," she said.

His mother helped him with his shirt, pants, and socks and left to put them in the wash bin. She closed the door, then bent down in front of the bin as she tightly held onto the rim and sobbed for several minutes. She then quickly stood up, straightened her apron, and returned to where her broken child was sitting at the table, covered in his grandmother's afghan. The stew was bubbling on the stove. The silence was both a relief and a torture for both of them. It felt like too much work for Charlie to attempt to explain what happened at school, and he didn't have the energy to try. Besides, if Daddy came home and saw him crying or fussing about it, he would blow his top and call him a sissy boy. Then his father would probably march up to the school and start screaming at the principal for allowing such a thing to happen. His father would embarrass the whole family if he did that. Even so, a part of Charlie secretly wished his father would come to his rescue.

But Charlie couldn't help himself. No matter how hard he tried to keep them from falling, the tears kept coming. He was completely heartbroken. He waited for so many years to be able to go to school with his brothers. Why did he have to talk to everyone in class today? Why couldn't he just say the words the right way? Why was he so different from everyone else?

The clicking of the second hands on the kitchen wall clock, coupled with Mother's arms wrapped around him, put him fast to sleep. His head was buried in his crossed arms that were resting on the kitchen table. Mother gently lifted his head without disturbing him and placed a pillow between his chapped cheek and the table that he was resting on.

He didn't wake up until three o'clock, when the kids came barreling through the door looking for him. Rich, Rob, and young Gertie were frantic because the teachers told them he had left that morning. Once they saw Charlie's face, they all sighed with relief. The three siblings had a pretty good idea of what probably happened. The older kids stood in an uncomfortable silence.

Then Delilah walked in with her usual unassuming sweetness. The family never even realized her intuitiveness and keen ability to cut through situations of thick awkwardness with such innocence.

She walked directly to the cupboard and grabbed Charlie's favorite puzzle. She dumped the pieces in the middle of the kitchen table. This broke the culture of the moment right away.

Mother made them all chocolate milk as everyone scurried around the table and competed to find the matching pieces first. They all knew that Charlie knew the puzzle better than anyone and that he would get most of the pieces put together before the others. He started right in, and then the normal family chatter ensued.

No one uttered a word about what happened that day. The next day, as if it were the normal routine, Charlie and Delilah were dropped off at Aunt Betty's house together while Mother went to work. He watched, with various levels of ambivalence written all over his face, through the front glass door as the older kids went off to their second day of school. Once his older brothers were out of sight, Delilah called to him to play hide-and-seek, and off he ran. His brothers and young Gertie continued to look back at the door as they walked off, feeling guilty for being normal and getting to go to school like everyone else and having to leave Charlie behind.

CHAPTER 2

"Charlie! Delilah! Come on in now. You two need to get on in here and wash your feet," called Rob.

Mother left some beans in the kettle for dinner before she left for work.

Delilah was the sweetest and most innocent one in the family. She'd somehow walked through her life without compromising her values. She had the gift of simplicity. She was the epitome of someone who looked at the world through rose-colored glasses. What some might have interpreted as naivete, the truly wise understood that Delilah was blessed with grace. Her heart was incapable of accepting anything that was evil. The black heart of the outside world didn't have room in her existence.

All Charlie knew was that Delilah was his best friend and he was hers. Delilah was Charlie's voice.

As Rob drew the bath and the two little ones jumped in, still in their underclothes, listened to the instruction of their twelve-year-old father figure while washing their feet and hands in preparation for dinner. Delilah chatted about, while squeezing the water from the wet washcloth over Charlie's head.

"We ran around and played Cowboys and Indians," she said. Delilah elaborated with the details of how they wore feathers on their headbands. She demonstrated for Rob as she put the plastic wash bowl on top of Charlie's head to serve as a cowboy hat. Charlie let her do it and pretended it didn't bother him at all while he carried on washing his sister's little knees and hands. He left the bowl on his head until it fell into the tub. He knew it would make Delilah laugh as it splashed into the water. Rob watched with one eye open while he read his book to ensure that they both properly washed before dinner.

As Rob was reading, he kept a mental note of the most difficult words he could use for his next word-finding game. The tall, lanky, good-looking bookworm didn't joke his way into the world like his twin brother, Rich. Rob navigated the world with the use of his wit and wealth of knowledge that was collected in his wonderful, curious mind. Rob was the smartest person Charlie knew. In fact, Charlie believed his brothers and sisters were the kindest, most wonderful people that ever walked the earth.

Downstairs, the clamor of dishes, pots, and pans could be heard. They all knew it was their daddy. He was in the kitchen. They could hear that ever-familiar sound of the slurred-voiced bully.

"Gertie! Where is it?! I left it in the jar in the cabinet!" he hollered.

Luckily for Mother, she wasn't home and was working the switchboard at the time. This was the best shift for her, as Rob and Rich could stay home and care for the little ones after school and into the evening. As the cabinet door flew open, Daddy stumbled across the kitchen. His empty liquor bottle fell over onto the metal kitchen table, making a clinking noise. With one swift swoop of his arm, he slid everything off the counter, and it crashed to the floor. Then as quickly as he had burst in, he burst out. Not before pushing over the living room chair by the front door first.

Rob quickly got Charlie and Delilah dried off and ready for dinner, just in case Daddy had to use the toilet and might come back in and find them there. The automatic response was to flee any room that Daddy might possibly enter, as he would grab whatever target was closest to him. They would then wait until he would eventually leave, stumbling down the street to McGreevey's corner pub where he would often be found sleeping in the back parking lot inside the trash dumpster.

The kids knew that his visit to the house was likely to look for stashes of liquor money. They knew it was just as likely that Mother had probably already squandered it on the horses at the Robin State Raceway. She would rationalize taking it, as usual. She would convince herself that she would win double...even triple. Then put it all back. It never worked out that way, and Mother never learned. She just kept on dreaming. She was sure that one day she would hit it big.

Several minutes passed, and it seemed safe enough to make a quick descent into the kitchen to feed the little ones. Once they were downstairs, Rich and Gertie's footsteps came pounding down the stairs, and they all shuffled into the kitchen together. Rob swiftly set the table, and Rich and Gertie prepared the leftover baked beans for dinner. They held hands and bowed their heads in prayer.

"Bless us, oh Lord and these, thy gifts, which we are about to receive, from thy bounty, through Christ, our Lord. Amen."

The bread that young Gertie had picked up from Miss Hannah's house just up the street was still warm. After dinner, they all cleaned up the kitchen swiftly, with such organization, as they had mastered how to leave it spic and span over the years. Just like Mother had taught them, everything had its place.

The five of them cuddled in front of the fire that Rich ignited in the small living room fireplace. Rich had a new joke book that their granddad had given him for his birthday. He had just about every one of them memorized at this point. He started in.

"Three men are working at a construction site. Every day the men eat lunch together. The first guy opens his lunch, and its bangers and mash. It has been bangers and mash every day since he started the job. 'If I get bangers and mash one more time, I am jumping off this building.' The next guy opens his lunch, and its spaghetti and meatballs again. He says the same thing as the first guy. The third guy opens up his lunch, and it's pierogies again. He says the same thing as the other two men. Sure enough, the next day, all three men get the same lunch and jump off the building to their demise. The foreman looks at the scene dumbfounded. A coworker says, 'I wish their wives made them something else.' The foreman scratches his head and turns to the coworker and says, 'I don't get it. The third guy packs his own lunch every day.'"

Rob, who was listening with one ear while buried in his book, let out a chuckle. Young Gertie giggled and giggled at the punch line. Little Delilah, not having a clue what the joke meant, delighted in the laughter just because her siblings were laughing. Charlie, on the other hand, sat thinking about the joke. He couldn't understand it at first and pondered for a moment. His face looked perplexed.

Rich turned to Charlie.

"Don't you get it? That's the punch line. He's stupid and just followed the other guys."

"Ohhhhhh," said Charlie. He just shrugged his shoulders and let out a half whisper, chuckle, still thinking the punch line didn't make much sense at all and wondered why the fella couldn't have just made something different for himself for lunch. The group's giggles escalated, and the girls then fell back on their brothers' thighs. The chattering and laughter went on all evening. The children moved closer and closer to the fire as it dwindled down to the last log.

Then, finally, the room was pitch dark. All that was left was the light of the lantern that Rich was holding, leading the way as they walked in formation up the stairs to the cold attic room.

Charlie tucked Delilah in. Young Gertie put an extra blanket over her little sister. The boys filtered into their queen-sized bed. They snuggled Charlie into the middle to keep him the warmest between his two big brothers.

Six months later.

Tuesday rolled around and Mother told Charlie she had a special surprise for him that day: just the two of them were going downtown. The twins and young Gertie dropped Delilah off and made their way to school. Mother and Charlie took the L streetcar to the local Catholic hospital. She held his hand as they climbed the steps to the large white building.

He saw a cross on the top of the hospital. Every time he saw one on a building, it made him feel like that must be a good place.

The examination room smelled like Granddad's hair tonic. Charlie sat quietly on the cold metal table in his white undershirt and black knickers. Dr Smiley entered the room, walked over to Charlie, shook his hand, and introduced himself. This made Charlie feel like he was being addressed as if he were a grown man. Mother watched intently as the doctor instructed Charlie to take a deep breath as he listened with a stethoscope to Charlie's lungs and heart.

"Now, open your mouth and let me see what is going on back inside there," said the doctor.

"Ummhmmm," said the doctor.

The doctor turned and swiveled his chair around in order to face Charlie's mom.

"Mrs. Aldridge," he said, "Charlie has a deformed area toward the back of his palate. This is why he cannot form his words appropriately—there is a hole that is not allowing him to properly form and annunciate his words so that others can understand. In addition, his uvula, which normally hangs down in the center, is shaped like a 'U' and is bifurcated. I believe this can be fixed with a relatively simple surgical procedure."

He looked straight into Charlie's big, sweet blue eyes.

"You know exactly what you want to say, don't you, son?" said the doctor.

Charlie looked back at him as his eyes started to fill with tears of appreciation for this stranger's compassion toward his plight. It was exhilarating to finally meet someone who knew he wasn't a stupid kid. Charlie shook his head up and down feverishly with an eager expression on his face.

Mother threw her head into her hands. "But we have nothing! My husband will not allow us to take charity. Charlie is so sad. The children mock him; his father mocks him. I cannot bear to let him live like this!" she said.

Dr. Smiley paused. He saw pain and darkness in this little gentleman's face.

"Mrs. Aldridge, every year we are permitted to perform an operative care procedure for a set number of people in the community free of charge. I will have our new surgeon perform the procedure under his allowance. His name is Dr. Bentley. Charlie and his brothers can do some community service in order to pay back the debt. You can tell your husband about this so that he will allow it as a form of payment for the surgery. We will get Charlie set up at Saint Francis Hospital next Thursday."

Dr. Smiley turned back around again and looked at Charlie. "As for you, young man, you are going to have a voice, and you are going to be able to talk like everyone else after we get you all fixed up."

At this, Charlie's throat was depleted of moisture. He couldn't speak even if he were able to be understood, as no words would come out. Charlie knew what a miracle was, and he was shocked that someone was willing to break him from the prison within himself.

Charlie and his mother took a seat in the hallway while the doctor's assistant gathered all the paperwork. They were both so excited. They hugged each other and cried tears of joy.

Suddenly, Charlie spotted a tiny little girl sitting close by. She didn't look happy at all, and it made his big smile turn to a sad grin. He stopped and pulled away from his mom, embarrassed that the girl might see him and think he was acting like a baby. This little girl was there on the same day, in the same place, waiting for the next scheduled appointment with the same doctor. He felt like he knew the little girl from somewhere but couldn't quite place her.

CHAPTER 3

ALICE

Alice was a six-year-old girl who lost her sight just about six months prior in an accident on her front porch. She was there to see Dr. Smiley because her temper tantrums had been getting out of control over the past several weeks. Her family wondered if the fall had caused brain damage or something. Alice's mother decided to take her to the doctor to see if there was anything that could be done. He was the general practitioner in town and was loved by all.

Alice was unusually well behaved during the car ride. As they stepped onto the elevator, Alice felt her stomach sink as it ascended the floors, all the way up to the tenth floor. It was a funny feeling. She remembered being in an elevator when she was a sighted person and could see the buttons on the wall labeled with every floor. She thought to herself how sad it was that she would never know what floor was the one she wanted to go to because you had to read the numbers in order to know what floor you were passing. She had been learning her numbers the last time she rode an elevator and remembered reading the elevator levels all the way up to number twenty. She remembered that she and her mom had magically appeared so high up once exiting the elevator and looked out the oversized windows down on the tiny people in the street that looked like ants moving about. Now she had no control of anything. She couldn't see where they landed and where they got off. She couldn't look out any oversized windows. She could only imagine it all. And that scared her. A lot!

Alice sat in the hallway, waiting. She was quietly biting her fingernails and scratching her hands when Dr. Smiley's nurse called her back. The nurse grabbed Alice's arm and picked her up roughly. She placed her on the scale. But the nurse spoke to her rather nicely. Alice had very thin arms and legs.

"Alice, you weigh forty-seven pounds, and you are forty-one inches tall. What a big girl you are," said the nurse.

Alice cocked her head like a perplexed puppy does when someone is talking at them. She was surprised that the nurse was talking to her like a real person. No one had done that in months. Normally people would talk over her and about her while she was sitting right there in the room. Her family felt that they were very attentive, but Alice felt completely ignored by them.

Outside the home, nobody knew what to say to the little blind girl. Therefore, the easier, more comfortable thing to do would be to say nothing at all to her. Her life was becoming increasingly isolated, and no one seemed to realize it.

The doctor's physical exam was pretty uneventful. He asked Alice to recall the day's events and tell him where she lived and when her birthday was. She answered with confidence and as if she were the last standing contestant in a spelling bee. She looked so cute with her wavy brown hair, her bangs parted, pulled back to the side, and secured with a giant white bow. She wore a sailor dress that fell just above her knees, white frilly socks, and black patent leather shoes that made tapping noises as she walked while holding her mother's hand so tightly. Dr. Smiley asked her all sorts of questions.

"Are you happy?" he started.

Alice paused for a moment. Then let out a sarcastic-sounding laugh. One that you would expect to hear from a bitter old spinster.

"No," she replied with a curt yet sad-sounding tone. "I can't use my eyes for anything anymore."

"What brings you joy?" said the doctor.

"Well, I used to look in the mirror at my dresses and bows in my hair. I knew I was pretty. I was learning to read when I was very young, and I was the smartest person in my class. I sharpened my pencils before school every day and practiced my handwriting. I used to swing on swings and jump rope and play with paper dolls," she said.

"But what do you do now that brings you joy?" said Dr. Smiley.

Alice pondered that question for a moment.

"I have a doll. I brush her hair. I sit on the couch and hear the clock ticking on the wall. I like ice cream for dessert after dinner. I can't think of anything else." She shrugged her shoulders matter-of-factly.

Dr. Smiley stared at her in silence. Then he cleared his throat and composed himself, so as not to let his emotions get the best of him. A single tear slid down her mother's cheek at the realization of just how mundane her life had become, and she was still just a child.

After their visit, they walked out into the hallway. Her mom sat Alice down on the bench.

"Alice, I am going to talk to the doctor by myself," said her mother. "You stay put and don't move from this bench."

Alice did not want her mother to leave her there. She felt scared sitting in the hallway all by herself. She grabbed the sleeve of her mother's dress and pulled her down so she could whisper in her ear.

"Please don't leave me. Let me come back in with you and talk to the doctor," she whispered. Her mother peeled the little fingers off her dress sleeve and firmly advised that she would be right back and to sit still until she returned.

Alice flopped back against the hard back of the wooden bench. She started to imagine all the different things that could happen to her in this cold, echoing hallway. What if she didn't stay in that spot and wait for her mother? What if she got up, wandered down the hall, and fell down a flight of stairs? Or maybe walk right into the elevator? It could take her into the clouds or drop straight down to the lobby floor. Her imagination was running wild, and the fear started to take control of her. Alice's eyes started dancing back and forth; her hands were sweating, and her mouth was dry. Her heart was pumping, and she was taking rapid breaths.

Suddenly she was completely distracted from her escalating mental frenzy. There were sounds of giggling and muffled, jumbled words. It sounded somewhat familiar but at the same time unlike anything she had ever heard before. It was the sound of gleeful babbling nonsense. Alice could tell that the sounds were coming from a child. But the talking didn't make any sense. The words, though unidentifiable, were filled with joyful excitement. She could hear a lovely sounding woman's voice responding to the little person. The woman sounded incredibly happy too. She was telling the little babbler to relax and to keep the news under his cap. It sounded to Alice like they were sitting across from her. The woman must have been doing something that the little person didn't like because she could hear him making squirming noises and whining as if he were likely telling her to leave him alone. She could only imagine what the woman was doing to him, as Alice knew all too well what it was like to be primped at all the time. Alice thought to herself that the young person sounded like a boy.

I wonder if he is handsome or if he looks as weird as he sounds, she thought. *He probably doesn't have any friends either.* She felt a little guilty for thinking that and even more guilty for hoping it were true, that someone else might be as lonely as she was.

Alice suddenly remembered that little boy back in the first-grade class who darted out the door on the very first day of school and never came back. Or did he come back? She wouldn't know, because it was the very next day that she had the accident, and she hadn't been back to school since then.

This bizarre speech sounded just like his. Only that little boy had a trembling voice and shaking hands and had hung his head so low you could hardly see his bright blue eyes. She was beginning to forget what blue eyes even looked like. What any color looked like, for that matter. Alice thought about clouds. Are they what she envisioned as white and the sky as blue? Or was it the other way around? The rhythmic nystagmus in her eyes started up again.

Oh, why can't I remember what things look like? Please God, don't let it fade away, she prayed to herself as she held tight to the Blessed Mother medal of the pink rosary that she kept in her pocket. It was nestled between her thumb and pointer finger and was meant to make her feel protected from outside fears.

Her attention was drawn back to the boy and who she presumed was his mother.

I think that lady is probably trying to wipe his face with her spit on a hanky, like Mother always does to me. It makes me feel like such a baby. I know he feels like a baby. He will be especially embarrassed if he looks at me and thinks I'm pretty. Am I pretty? she thought. *I remember being very pretty. Do I look blind? Do I look like an ugly carnival attraction? Are my eyes open or closed? Why can't I even tell? They feel like they are open. Can people see my green eyes with the brown specks? Do they notice me sitting here, and do I look as weird as this boy sounds?*

After the feeling of overwhelming anxiety had passed, Alice reached into the pocket on the other side of her dress and pulled out the yo-yo that her brother had given her and taught her to play. She wasn't particularly good at it and actually didn't understand how it was supposed to be a fun thing to do. However, she kept it with her all the time simply because her big brother, Jack, gave it to her. Since it was so boring just sitting there and waiting for her mother, she decided to toss the round spool of the yo-yo out in front of her and practice drawing it back in. No sooner did she toss the spool out into the hall, a woman walking by stepped right into the string and sent the yo-yo spiraling across the hallway that separated the two benches lined up against each wall.

Oh no! Alice thought. She considered dropping down and crawling around the floor to look for it. But then she realized she couldn't do that. The floor was probably dirty. And she knew she had white stockings on because her sister, Marnie, made such a big deal about Alice having to wear that exact pair to match her blue-and-white dress. She remembered that you can't get white stockings dirty. Besides, she would look like a monkey moving around on the floor.

Her mother would be out soon and would help her find it. But what if that weird-sounding little boy took it while his mother wasn't watching? Maybe he was one of those "sinful" little boys that her mother was always talking about. She couldn't stop obsessing over where the yo-yo was. Her emotions were growing more erratic. She rubbed her hands, and her breathing rapidly became heavier.

She thought to herself, *Here I go again.*

Even at her very young age, Alice knew that she spiraled out of control with her thoughts in her head. It was almost too much to bear already. It was like because she couldn't figure out what was happening in front of her with her sight, she relied on her mind to figure it out. The problem was that her imagination always ran away with her, and the fear of the unknown would get into her head and create horror stories. She imagined that the boy would pick up the yo-yo, toss it into the air, and hit Alice in the head. She would pass out. They would take her to the hospital. Her mother wouldn't know where she was, and she would be lost forever. This and other unimaginable stories always seemed to feel rational to her at the time. Her hands were sweating, and her mouth was dry again as she thought about this inevitable, preposterous, made-up sequence of events. Her heart was still pounding, and she wrung her hands. Her eyes bounced back and forth. There was a picture in her mind of a dark cloud, and she saw yellow devil's eyes for just a moment. It was petrifying.

The boy sitting across from Alice was so preoccupied thinking about what it would be like to have a voice that he forgot she was sitting there. Once his mother got him cleaned up and they were getting ready to leave, the little boy's attention moved to the bright yellow yo-yo as it rolled past his feet. He turned to look at the little lady sitting by herself. She was swinging her little legs, wearing her little shiny black shoes. He noticed the shoes because they looked like the ones Delilah had been asking Mom for over the last year. Delilah's birthday was coming up in June. Charlie had seen the shoes wrapped in paper and tucked under Mother's bed. He knew Delilah would be getting them for her birthday and could hardly wait to see her face when she opened them up.

Now Alice was able to get herself composed again and pretended not to notice that the yo-yo had just slipped out of her hands. She decided to push the scenario of being lost forever out of her head and appear to be patiently waiting for her mother to come out of the office. Alice would insist that they couldn't leave until the yo-yo was retrieved. She rubbed her sweaty hands on her dress and repositioned herself just as she was taught that a young lady should. Sitting with her ankles crossed, swinging them back and forth, trying not to fidget. Though still feeling horrified.

There was something about the girl's wavy brown hair and milky white skin that was familiar to Charlie. Then suddenly his eyes flew open wide, and he waved at her because he had just remembered her. It was that girl...the one in the classroom who had given him the pencil on that first dreadful day of school. But she didn't wave back.

Why does she look so sad? What was she staring at up on the ceiling? he thought.

He noticed her grip on the rosary and that it was making a clinking noise due to her shaking hands. He looked up to see what she may have been looking at. He wondered if there were bugs up there or something. He looked back at her again. He tried to track exactly what she was looking at but couldn't seem to quite narrow in on the specific direction. He stared at her while pulling on his mother's coat sleeve.

"Aaaahhiiissagoingo?" His mother answered back as if he just said something completely normal. Pretending like she knew just what he was saying when in reality, she had no idea what was coming out of his mouth. She always answered him with "mm-hmm" and "uh-uh" to try to make Charlie feel like she was listening and understanding him. Charlie knew this to be true but was happy that she pretended. At least she didn't constantly put pressure on him to speak up and fix his words like Daddy always did to him. Daddy always had to turn it into an embarrassing mockery. Every single time.

Unbeknownst to Alice, Charlie was trying to tell his mother that this was the little girl he told her about on that dreadful day of first grade.

After failing to get his mother's attention, as she was engulfed in filling out the presurgical paperwork instructions, the little boy picked up the yo-yo and walked over to Alice. He kept looking at the blank stare on her face. He waved his hand in front of her, and she didn't blink. The little girl turned her head, as if she knew someone was there, and paused from swinging her feet. Charlie then reached down and took her trembling hand in his. She momentarily pulled back but didn't let go. Charlie turned her palm upward and placed the yo-yo into her outstretched hand. Then he stood there, staring for a moment. Alice froze in place. She didn't know what to do.

"Thank you," she said shyly.

Charlie's mother was finishing her conversation with the receptionist that had come out to the hallway to have her sign some more papers for Charlie's surgery the following week.

"Charlie, let's go," said his mother.

As if snapped out of a trance, he turned, scurried to catch up with his mom, grabbed her hand, and looked back over his shoulder to watch the little girl as he walked all the way to the entrance of the elevator. He continued to stare as the doors shut in front of him.

CHAPTER 4

When Charlie awoke in the hospital, the room was blurry. He felt nauseous. His head hurt. He rolled his tongue across the rough patch on the roof of the inside of his mouth. It felt like little strings were tied together over the hole where his tongue used to fit so snugly into his palate. He tried to speak, but his throat was so dry that it hurt. He swallowed and swallowed in an attempt to create some saliva to wet his esophagus.

"Mmmama," he mumbled.

The door to his room opened and in walked a pretty lady. Her brown hair was neatly tied in a bun smack in the center of the back of her head. She wore a dark green dress that fell just below her knees. He watched as her skirt swooshed from side to side. Her waistline was accentuated by a thick black belt. She wore sensible-looking black shoes and carried a clipboard with a bunch of papers on it. But the main feature of Charlie's focus were her bright red lips. They seemed unusually large, and he couldn't take his eyes off them. Her big smile revealed beautiful, shiny white teeth.

"Good morning. My name is Miss Rose."

Knowing that her name was that of a flower, and watching her smile at him with those lips, made Charlie feel instantly relaxed, and he knew that she must be a nice lady.

"I am going to help you learn how to talk so that everyone will understand you," she said.

She placed her hand on his foot. She looked him in the eye and said, "You will be able to talk in normal sentences, sing like a bird, and maybe even learn to whistle Dixie!"

Upon hearing these words, he breathed a giant sigh of relief. It was like being pulled out of drowning water. As if he was instantly released from a closed space where he was struggling for air. He thought that this must be what it feels like to be in heaven.

Miss Rose got right to work unloading her briefcase of all sorts of cards and papers. She had a bunch of pictures with words on them. He could definitely read pretty well, so he didn't need the pictures. But nonetheless, it didn't really offend him or matter in any way. He used his arms to pull himself up in bed. He took a sip of the ice-cold water that the nurse put by his bedside. As he swallowed, he could taste blood in his mouth but enjoyed wetting his palate just the same.

"Can you tell me what this is a picture of?" said Miss Rose.

Clearly, it was a picture of a baby. Charlie shook his head. First up and down with a somewhat insulted expression. Then, realizing that he had to actually say the word, he paused, then shook his head from side to side, indicating that his answer was no.

Miss Rose said, "Well, let's say it together, then."

Charlie watched as she pressed her top and bottom lips together. He repeated the action.

"Buh…buh…buh…" This word wasn't actually that difficult a word for him to pronounce before the surgery because he didn't have to touch his tongue to the top of his palate to make the "B" sound. However, he knew they were starting out with simple words, and he would, from the beginning, learn how to pronounce every single word with eloquence and appropriateness.

The pair of them repeated the sound over and over again. Charlie beamed, as he knew with that one act, it was working. He started to giggle. It felt so good to know that he would be able to make sounds and form words that he never could before now. In his mind, he already thought that he could talk now. Finally, he was free.

Miss Rose gave him sounds to practice until they were to meet again. He repeated his lessons so redundantly that it became his obsession for two days while in the hospital. The doctor even told him he should calm down a little, for he might tear his stitches out of the roof of his mouth. He didn't know if the doctor was kidding or not, but Charlie didn't care.

After the next couple of days, he was ready to go home. He and his mother stepped on the trolley to make their way back.

On the ride home, he recited, "Bah, bah, bah. Ta, ta, ta. No, no, no. Pop, pop, pop."

People stared at him. Neither he nor his mother paid them any attention.

When they arrived home, his four brothers and sisters were waiting by the door. Daddy wasn't anywhere to be found, thank goodness. They were all so excited to hear the details of where Charlie was. Mother had filled them in somewhat while he was in the hospital. None of them really understood, though, just what a difference the surgery would make. Young Gertie baked Charlie his favorite pumpkin pie and stuck a candle in the center. They all sang "Happy Birthday" and explained they were celebrating Charlie's new voice being born. He laughed and laughed. It was the most exciting time of his life. The simple joy of swallowing that pie and not having to worry about any food getting caught in the hole in the roof of his mouth was another added bonus that he had never even really thought about before, as he had just gotten used to it happening all the time.

While walking all the way up the stairs to his room at bedtime, the phonetics continued. All night, while nestled between his brothers. Rich and Rob covered their ears with pillows to muffle the sound. Rich was even patient enough not to threaten him with covering his face with the pillows because he didn't want to destroy Charlie's joy. The noises slowly faded away as Charlie fell off to sleep. Rich and Rob turned on their sides, toward Charlie, and watched him sleep. He seemed to fade off with an expression on his face that they had never seen before. In the past, they had witnessed Charlie being happy at times, but for the most part, there was always a dark, deep-seated sadness to him from the lack of ability to express himself. Maybe the tantrums that even his big strapping brothers had difficulty with at times would begin to settle down. Even if the outbursts didn't resolve, they loved their little brother with all their hearts and shared in the joy of his wonderful recovery.

Late that night, they were awoken by the usual clamor of pots and dishes. The ever-too-familiar loud tone of Daddy coming home from the gas pumping station. Mother's voice could be heard in a quiet tune, sounding like she was telling him a story about seeing Jesus walk on water. The sullen, muffled tones quickly turned into a loud roar of Daddy yelling at Mother. They could hear sounds of broken glass. Then a thump. Then another thump. Rich ran down the stairs as fast as he could to find his mother on the floor holding her hands over her face. She was curled in a ball. Daddy was kicking, hitting, and punching as if he were taming a wild beast. The table had been overturned and food was smeared all over the floor.

"Leave her alone!" cried Rich as he jumped on his father's back. His father elbowed him off, and Rich fell to the floor with another thump. Daddy grabbed his fifth of whiskey off the mantle, and the screen door slammed behind him. He stumbled down Stone Haven Lane, taking swigs from the bottle, until he disappeared from sight.

Young Gertie tiptoed into the kitchen to help Mother and Rich clean up the mess. As they were kneeling on the floor, picking up the glass, Rob paused and looked into his mother's eyes.

"You fixed Charlie. You fixed him, Mother. That is all that matters!" he said.

Everyone knew that their father had probably lashed out at the news of Charlie's surgery. No one spoke of why their father didn't want Charlie to have the operation. It was likely his pride that stood in the way. Did he actually like having a child with a handicap so that he could feel like a bigger man when he insulted and pushed him around? Charlie was actually his father's favorite, in his own, warped way.

Of course, he enjoyed mocking him and repeating his babble when Charlie was trying to get his point across. However, he often commented on Charlie's good looks. He called them the Aldridge traits. He was proud of his son's tough little physique and bright blue eyes. Charlie hardly ever cried in front of him, and that made Daddy very proud as well. When Charlie got angry, he punched and screamed just like his daddy did. The difference was that Charlie never physically hurt anyone. Daddy believed that real men fought their way out of their troubles, and if Charlie wanted to speak the right way, he would eventually grow out of it and figure it out on his own. Never accepting that it would be a physically impossible task without the help of surgeons. His father didn't like doctors and was convinced that they would butcher his boy if he let them get their hands on him. Nevertheless, he took his anger out on Mother, as usual, and she willingly paid the price. Whatever the reason, it was done now. He couldn't help but notice the good that came from the surgery. There would be no praising Charlie for his mastery of speech, as this would somehow be an admission of weakness on his father's part. Instead, he pretended like the problem, and the solution, never even existed. He turned his sights on ramping up picking on Rob instead. In his eyes, Rob was a scholastic bookworm who needed to "man up". Rob knew that everything that went wrong in the home or wasn't working properly would ultimately be blamed on him by their father whenever he came around. No matter what the situation. And Rob accepted this with unrelenting willingness. Never once did he act resentful of anyone else in the family for not enduring the same type of physical and emotional abuse every time Daddy's wrath came swooping in.

Charlie was so happy with his new voice and so determined to learn how to speak correctly. He continued to recite his exercises over and over again.

"The brown bear chats with short sentences and sells seashells."

He repeated the words incessantly. At breakfast: "The brown bear has big britches. Which sandwich is mine?" At lunchtime…at dinner time…Pronunciation became his obsession. He found this new skill exhilarating. He couldn't stop. At his young age he even thought, in a way, that it seemed to compare to how Daddy must feel about needing his whiskey all the time. Even if someone told him he wasn't allowed to recite his lessons anymore, he wouldn't be able to stop himself. Rich and Rob continued every night with pillows over their heads trying to sleep.

"Charlie, can you please stop until tomorrow?" they would say. Once, Rich actually stuffed a sock in Charlie's mouth to remind him it was bedtime now and that the rest of the house needed a break and to get some sleep. Charlie spit the sock out and began mouthing everything with no sound until he put himself to sleep. Eventually, he got used to his new skills and saved the incessant talking until the daytime. He would take on every new word he learned and practice the elocution of the word until it was perfected.

CHAPTER 5

Alice was always preoccupied with her own determinations. This was the result of the accident, quite honestly. Once she lost her sight, her family didn't know what to do with the little baby girl with the gorgeous hazel eyes who would now have "no life," even before her little life began. She was pampered. Every whim catered to. Not only was she fifteen years younger than her next oldest sibling, but she was also now completely helpless in their eyes. The family mostly told her to sit and hold her dolls, brush their hair, and talk to them. They brought her meals to her. They even started wiping her bottom after she went to the bathroom, even though she'd already known how to do it when she was sighted. She quickly learned that she was the center of everyone's attention toward her physical needs, but no one had the slightest idea of how to foster in her the proper self-confidence and emotional growth that she so desperately needed. Her temper tantrums would escalate. Her mother and Marnie were the most attentive. Marnie took on all the responsibilities that their mother couldn't handle and did anything that their mother asked of her. They transformed the library into Alice's "time-out room." They removed anything that would pose a physical threat to Alice as she went wailing and running about in her fury. Never realizing that they were fueling her anxiety and fear, all the more, with the additional social isolation. Giving her more feelings of having no purpose. But what else could they do? She would at times become so out of control, she would hurt herself or someone else in her rage. This lonely and unhappy child would spend her life trying to grasp the reins of traumatic events. The family's only recourse would be to joke and tease. This made the problem even worse for Alice, as she was too young to understand or appreciate the sarcastic humor. This only added to her frustration.

As Alice climbed into the back of Marnie's Ford Model T that Marnie had bought with the money she saved from her secretarial job at the church, she rolled down the window so she could feel the sun and breeze on her face as they went for their usual Sunday drive. Marnie, no doubt, scored a good deal on the car. She likely walked into the dealership, looking smart and business-like, flashing her flirty smirk, batting her eyelashes, and performing with her quick, humorous banter that was becoming the ever-so-popular style of the 1930s. Women were speaking their minds at this time, and it was quite fashionable. This was all rapidly becoming the wave of the time, and Marnie had aced it!

Their mother was up front in the passenger side as usual. Marnie and their mother were such an oddly matched mother-daughter team. Their mother was tall with a heavy build. And strong. She almost always had her hair pulled back tightly into a bun that rested in the center of the back of her head. She had about eight different housecoats and that was all she wore unless they were going to Sunday Mass. Alice didn't think about what her mother would be wearing today but assumed she was still in her Sunday best since they just came from church a couple of hours earlier, and Alice was still in her church clothes as well. When Alice had her sight, she never saw her mother with makeup or earrings or wearing heels, and she had never seen Marnie without any of it. Marnie had the reputation as being one of, if not *the*, most beautiful single gals in town! Everyone said it. All the time! Including Marnie. Marnie worked long hours as well. After contributing to the family's income needs, she always managed to find a little extra to have nice clothing, lipstick, and jewelry to keep her dressed to the nines. She had men calling on her daily. Marnie this. Marnie that. It was a little sickening if you asked Alice. Marnie rarely accepted any of the male callers because their mother needed her for too much. House chores, bills, raising Alice, or just for general emotional support. Something of which their mother needed quite a bit of. Marnie didn't date much because their mother never approved of any of the boys that came calling. Their mother had an inherent anger toward men and was always telling the girls that boys and men only wanted one sinful thing. She had her girls convinced that if they spent too much time with a man, they would do sinful things too. She made them feel that male relationships were dirty and inappropriate. In later years, Alice wondered how that must have made their only brother feel when their mother talked like that. No wonder he lied about his age and went into the Navy when he was only sixteen years old. Then he rarely came around after his discharge. He shortly moved away to Florida after that. Alice never really knew him well. She would see him on occasion and would get so excited, even for the littlest bit of time she had with him. She likened him to a father, whatever that really meant, as she wasn't sure what fathers actually did.

Alice listened to what her mother said about boys but could never really quite believe it all. She thought about the few nice men and boys that she did know and didn't really know what mom meant by "sinful."

Do they tell lies, not finish their dinner plates, or maybe talk back to their parents? she thought.

The time that Johnny McAndrews put chewing gum on the bottom of Sister Marsha's shoes was surely sinful. *If I played with*

Johnny, would he make me put gum on the bottom of a nun's shoes like that? Alice wondered.

The question would haunt her for years until she finally figured out what her mom was referring to.

Alice enjoyed her car ride, as expected, and turned her face toward the window to feel the sun and wind. She held her bow and hair in place for fear that her mother or Marnie would notice and make her close the window if she looked disheveled. She didn't remember them making this much fuss over her appearance when she had her sight. Was it because they were compensating for the way she looked now, or did they know the world would see her differently, so her presentation had to be set to a higher standard? Whatever it was, she was annoyed by it, and it was just another thing that made her feel imprisoned.

She imagined herself, at this moment, riding a bicycle as fast as her legs could carry her. In her mind, she envisioned herself going up and down driveways and in and out of traffic, trolley cars, and people. The image of people's groceries twirling out of their hands as she recklessly flew by, made her laugh to herself. She wondered if she really would be this reckless if she had her sight. Or did she create this imaginary superpower in her head in response to her unhappiness and frustrations with her blank, boring life?

She began to think about the last time she saw the sun. It was that day. On the swing. Alice's sister Annie was supposed to be watching her, but Annie wanted to try out for the school play and talk to Thomas Whitler after his wrestling match. So, she asked her other sister Helena to watch her. Helena said she would but that she had to finish her math homework, so she could only watch her for half an hour or so. Of course, Annie wasn't back when promised because she ran into Jimmy Miller on the way home and was taking her sweet old time, flirting with the most handsome boy in school. Helena had asked her brother Jack to watch Alice until Annie got back, but Jack was going to Billy Mayer's house to practice target shooting at cans in the field behind their houses. Helena was very annoyed but decided to position herself with her book right in front of the window, so she could have Alice and the Reagan twins in her view as they played outside on the front porch swing. Helena's head was buried in her math book, but she was able to glance out the window every few minutes to see the girls. The three girls started out sitting on the big old swing, moving their bodies to try to make it move to an exciting glide level but to no avail. Sarah Reagan suggested that they stand on the back of the swing. Sarah quickly stood up on one side and her sister Ellen followed on the other side, holding the chains to the swing in one hand. Alice had to climb up onto the middle with virtually nothing to hold on to but the girls' waists. She reluctantly did this. She wasn't really reluctant out of fear but because she felt like it was a bit tomboyish, and she was wearing a dress. She was concerned that someone might walk by and see her underwear if her dress flew up while they were swinging. She took her position anyway and held on tightly to the girls on either side. The girls pulled on the chains and were quickly gaining momentum. Higher and higher they went. The chains that were attached to the old wooden porch ceiling were creaking and rattling. The noises from the chains were getting louder and louder. It was a little scary but tons of fun. As they were swinging higher, Alice's heart was beginning to sink into her stomach. She was starting to lose her grip on the girls' waists. Now it was quickly becoming more frightening than fun, and she hollered out, "We should stop!"

At that very moment, Helena looked up from her math book and spotted them swinging so dangerously high. She jumped up and her papers flew everywhere. She shouted, "Girls, stop swinging so high!"

The next thing Alice knew, she was waking up. Her head felt like it had been hit with a hammer. Not that she knew what that actually felt like, but she remembered Uncle Harry saying it a couple of times and imagined that was what her head felt like at this moment. She wasn't in her own bed, though. And the room was so dark. It reminded her of the time she was in the woods with her big brother when they didn't leave before the sun set. They had to wait there all night until dawn because they couldn't see a thing. Alice remembered being so frightened by the howls of the wolves and hooting of the owls. Her brother Jack held her so tightly and sang to her. She remembered that he sang the words "Dream a little dream of me" until she fell asleep in his arms. This was perhaps her only special experience of spending time with her big brother.

Her thoughts returned again to the memory of that day when she woke up in the hospital. The pillows were harder than the ones on her bed at home. She didn't feel her lace bedspread covering her, and the sheets didn't smell like the lavender soap her mother used on all the laundry. The sheets were so hard they almost felt crispy. Her head was pounding. It felt like she was wearing a hat on the top of her head. How did she end up indoors, on this bed, when the last thing she remembered was being on the porch swing with the little girls? It was so hot outside, but she now felt so cold. Her eyes flew open as she realized something must have happened to her. At least her eyes *felt* like they flew open, but why wasn't she seeing anything? Things looked like they look when her eyes were closed, but she couldn't blink. She couldn't see anything in front of her. And suddenly she felt panicked and started calling out to her mother and Marnie. Repeatedly asking what was happening to her and where she was. Her mother had come rushing in. She remembered how there were hands all over her, and her mother was hollering that she was finally awake. They were pulling up her eyelids and looking in her ears and looking in her mouth and touching her face. Alice had finally hollered, "Get off of me!" as she was trying to grab and bite the hand that kept touching her. Once Marnie was able to get her to calm down, she allowed them to continue their prodding and poking.

They had asked her so many questions about how old she was, when her birthday was, who her brothers and sisters were, and what day it was. She remembered answering all their questions without a beat until she finally shouted, "Stop asking me all these questions and get this foggy stuff out of my eyes! I can't see anything!"

Alice's thoughts now returned to enjoying the car ride. After feeling the sunny breeze on her face for what felt like a very long time, she could hear the sound of gravel beneath the car tires as if in a driveway as the car made its way around. She felt herself leaning to one side and had to grab the door handle to keep herself from sliding over onto the other side in the back seat of the car. Then she heard the sound of the squeaky brakes as the car came to a sudden stop. Alice suddenly realized that her mother hadn't spoken for the entire ride. She was normally always talking about something. Either saying prayers for a safe trip, gossiping about Miss Walnut's daughter—who left her husband to run away with her high school sweetheart—or what Daddy might be doing. For someone who hated her husband so much, Alice's mother sure did talk a lot about him. He had left shortly after Alice was born and she really never knew him. Alice's mind wandered again. Was her dad really as bad as her mother said he was? After all, he was very nice to her that time he came to visit. She was only three years old, but she remembered him. He smelled weird but had the most beautiful green eyes that she had ever seen. He gave her a dollar, patted her on the head, and told her to be a good little girl. That was the last and only time she saw him. After he left the house, she remembered running into her mother's room, climbing on top of her dresser to look into the mirror at her own eyes, and discovering that they looked just like his. Only her eyes were happier.

I bet my eyes look now as sad as his did then, she thought to herself.

She could hear Marnie and her mother's front car doors open and shut. It was so muggy outside; Alice could feel the heat almost immediately, and it was suffocating. She opened her door and turned her legs out to the side, dangling them out of the car to get some air while she waited for her mother and Marnie to get her. She could hear them mumbling. Her mother was asking something about when they could come back and "How will we know she is, okay?"

"Mother! Marnie! Can I get out of the car? I want ice cream! Can we go now?" Alice said.

The murmuring continued for what felt like a lifetime. It made Alice a little nervous, as she could sense that something seemed a bit odd.

Finally, the footsteps against the gravel came close to the car. Marnie picked Alice up into a standing position. She squatted down and gave Alice a giant hug.

"You know I love you, my little Als, more than anything, right? I will always be near you, and I will never let anything happen to you. But right now, you are going to stay with teachers and some other students that are like you. Some can see a little bit, and most cannot see at all. The teachers here will show you how to read and write the way blind children do. You have been asking to go to school every day, and here you are," said Marnie.

Alice stopped hearing what Marnie was saying after she heard the words "stay with the teachers and some students." Everything else was muffled. Alice's eyes started moving back and forth and shaking, growing wider and wider. She wasn't listening anymore; her palms were sweating, and her heart was beating out of her chest.

"No! No! No! Marnie! Please! Where is Mom? She won't make me stay here! I am not staying here! I promise, no more fits! I will eat my vegetables! I will sit all day long and play with my dolls!" cried Alice.

Marnie picked Alice up with tears streaming down her face. Alice screamed with her arms locked around Marnie's neck. Suddenly Alice felt the strongest arms ever wrap around her tiny little body as Marnie was attempting to loosen Alice's grip from her neck. The giant arms yanked her from her sister. She could hear Marnie sobbing. Alice never heard Marnie sob before now. The unfamiliar arms clenched her so tightly that she could hardly breathe. She was so startled by it all that she forgot to scream for a moment. The car doors closed in the near distance, and she could hear the car pulling away. Alice couldn't believe her ears. Her mother and Marnie always did what she wanted. They always gave in to her tantrums. They really were leaving her there. What did she do this time that was so bad that they wanted to give her away?

I will just scream and cry until this person gives me my way and lets me go back home, she thought to herself. Alice then let out the most ear-piercing cry. Fighting, kicking, screaming with all her might. Then she was halted by a most painful feeing. Her ear felt like someone took a scissor to it. It was being pulled and twisted. She screamed even louder and kicked even harder. "You big meanie! Put me down!"

Her shrill cries carried on all through the giant doors of the old mansion. She was carried down a long hallway, then up the stairs, then down another hallway that seemed to go on forever. Finally, they reached what seemed to be the destination. The monster dropped her little flailing body onto a not-so-cushiony surface. The springs beneath sounded like they were breaking. Alice felt around to catch her surroundings. It seemed like some sort of bed. It smelled like fels naptha mixed with must. It wasn't soft and cozy like her bed at home, and it was even worse than that hospital bed she spent so much time in after the accident. She felt around some more while taking in short hiccup-like breaths to calm herself down. The pillow was flat with no fluff. She crawled around feverishly and found a blanket and sheet folded down at the bottom. She was moving around the bed like an animal trying to get out of a cage. She felt underneath and found an empty space. She plopped back on her bottom with her knees together and the bottoms of her legs scissored outward. Her mother always got upset with her when she sat like this. She told Alice that when she grew up, her legs would be permanently stuck in a sideways slant, and she would walk like a monkey. Alice felt satisfied that she was doing something that would upset her mother.

Finally, Alice sat quietly for a moment. *What is this place? What am I doing here?* she thought.

It was silent, cold, and lonely. There were no signs of life as far as she could tell. She fell face down into the pillow, punching the bed and kicking the mattress. The mattress was so hard that it hurt her fists. She pulled her rosary out of her pocket and her favorite lace handkerchief out of her other pocket. Alice recited the "Hail Mary" prayer through her tears until at last, she drifted off to sleep.

The woman who handled her was Sister Gwendolyn. She was a stately woman. She was as round as she was tall. Her nun's habit was pristine. She wore a giant oversized rosary that wrapped around her waist and hung down past her knees. Although who knew if she even had knees. She could have had wooden legs for all anyone knew. The rosary made a clinking noise when she walked. It was different than the bells that the children had to wear on their shoes so other blind children knew if they were among their peers. And it was different than the taps that the nuns and teachers wore on the bottoms of their shoes to let the children know when the adults were present. It took months to get permission from Father Alfred to put taps on the bottoms of the nuns' shoes, as it was not in the Catholic nun's rulebook and would be very difficult to change. However, Sister Gwendolyn argued her case, which was that the children needed to hear her for security and obedience purposes. She eventually got her way.

Sister Gwendolyn stood outside the girl's dormitory room and watched Alice. She observed her through her temper tantrum and while she crawled around the bed like a newborn cub trying to figure out her surroundings, scurrying up and down, then finally soothing and comforting herself.

Sister Gwendolyn knew this may have very well been the first time that Alice ever self-soothed and used self-reliance to conquer an emotional obstacle. As Alice began to settle down, she put the edge of her hankie in her mouth and sucked away. It was so hard for the nun to watch. Alice cried herself to sleep, and the echoes of her sobbing eventually disappeared until the dormitory room fell into dark silence once again.

Sister clutched the crucifix of her rosary and said, "Dear Jesus, please guide us in our endeavors to help this challenging, tough little girl become a happy, independent warrior of yours. Guide me in my discipline and love. Help me to never lose sight of our mission."

Sister then bowed her head, turned, and walked away.

CHAPTER 6

The next morning, Alice was awoken by the sound of whispers and giggling. There was chatter among the giggles, but she couldn't make out what the voices were saying. The whispers started to turn into arguing. She heard the little voices saying something about shoes. They were escalating, and now Alice could hear much better what was being said.

"Give me my shoes!"

"This is my left shoe!"

"No, it isn't!"

Alice sat up in a dash. *Someone is here with me,* she thought. *Thank God! I thought I was in this jail all alone! Forever! Mom and Marnie will be back anytime now,* she said to herself.

Alice knew that they normally caved into her wishes way before now. She sat back and thought about how she would make her mother and Marnie feel so bad about themselves for what they did to her. One time she went an entire day without eating because her mom gave her strawberry ice cream instead of butter pecan. This time she thought she would starve herself for two days, and they would be beside themselves with worry. A slight grin ran across her angry, bratty, sweet little face.

"Who is there?" she said.

The chattering and arguing came to a sudden halt.

"Well, who are you?" a soft little voice answered back from across the room.

"My name is Alice. Where am I?"

There was silence again. Then whispers that she couldn't make out. Her curiosity was getting the better of her, and she had to know who was over there. She leaned her body closer to the voices, as if that would satisfy her curiosity any sooner.

Alice tumbled off the bottom of the bed onto the floor. Then sat on the floor with legs crossed as if it was an intentional landing.

"You are at the blind school, silly!" said one of the voices.

"I am Eunice, and this is my twin sister, Augustine. We call her Tina."

"Hi," said Tina.

Alice was so excited to hear them talking to her. Then she reminded herself of how angry she was and suddenly flipped over onto her stomach, deciding that she wouldn't respond to the girls' voices. Alice's eyes filled with tears again. She had so many questions but was too afraid to hear the answers to them. She lay with her face in her pillow, head turned to one side, straining to hear what the girls were saying but too stubborn to allow them to know that she cared at all about their silly little banter and their dumb shoes.

"They are probably cheap shoes anyway. And ugly!" she said to herself in a soft whisper. *I hope these girls don't think I want to be their friend,* she thought, even though she was starving to have friends. It was what she longed for most since the accident. She thought about how the minute she got home from the hospital, she never saw a friend again. It was like she insulted them all by falling off the swing. Like she was now the enemy because of something that was out of her control.

Alice's thoughts turned back to how she was going to get out of this cold, smelly place. She still believed if she cried loud enough and wouldn't eat, she might get her way. Thinking her mother would not be able to stand it and would soon be back to take her home. She hadn't yet understood that no one in this place was going to care about her spoiled actions, and no one was going let her be in control.

Suddenly there was the sound of an ear-piercing whistle blow. It seemed to be in some sort of code. Two short whistles and one long whistle. Alice could hear the pattern of what sounded like an army of tapping shoes and bells ringing on the hard floor beneath her, sending an echo throughout the room. After a few moments, the tapping and ringing of the bells stopped short. In an instant. Then she could hear the louder, deeper tapping of one big set of feet. She remembered the sound of those feet, and they belonged to that big bully who threw her on the bed the day before. Alice turned her head as she knew the beast was probably approaching her. Alice was so frightened by the approaching predator but pretended not to notice.

"Miss Stiller! Sit up!"

Alice wanted to be belligerent, but she was too scared not to do what she was told, as she already realized this person cared very little about her tantrums. She sat up quickly and dangled her legs over the side of the bed. She didn't need to see in order to know that the pair of shoes that were just dropped into her lap were made from cheap patent leather.

I knew it! she thought to herself. *Cheap shoes!*

"Tap shoes? Oh fudge, I must put these things on?" she thought.

Her bitterness wasn't nearly resolved, and she had decided that she would be a brat for much longer than time was allowing her in this dungeon. Alice picked up the shoes and slowly started to unbutton her sturdy, brown leather cobbler shoe that had a raised, scalloped trim and felt like silk on her little fingers. Alice felt that her own shoes from home were far nicer than these plastic-feeling things that the monster was making her put on.

"Quickly, Miss Stiller! Everyone is waiting for you!" said the voice.

The master tapping noise turned, as if to leave her, and tapped away to the other side of the room.

"Roll call!"

Alice jumped out of her skin at hearing this repeated loud announcement. She quickly scurried to get the tap shoes on, and the little bells chimed as she shoved her feet into them. She was relieved to know that they had snaps on the straps, so she didn't need to worry about tying them. She wasn't very good at tying shoes because no one ever bought her shoes with laces on them, so she never really had to learn how. The names were called out by last name, then first name in alphabetical order. She recognized the twins' names.

"Bradley, Eunice and Augustine!"

"Here," each little voice responded.

Alice hadn't realized how many other children were in the room until this process came about. Then Alice heard her name.

"Stiller, Alice!"

She understood the game now and responded in a crackly, frightened, yet stern voice.

"Here!"

Just then, there was a whisper in her ear. "Psst!"

Alice backed away as if disgusted that someone came so close to her ear like that. Still in a whisper, the voice said, "Stand on the floor at the bottom of your bed. Stand straight with your arms at your sides and hold your head up!"

Alice figured she better take heed to the instructions of whoever this was, as it sounded like it was quite serious. So, she scurried to the bottom of her bed, limping in her new, hard, bell-ringing tap shoes. The little instructor continued whispering to her.

"When she blows the whistle again, it will be four short and one long. Then grab the rope and follow it with your right hand."

"But where is the rope?" Alice whispered back.

Just then, four whistle blows were followed by one long whistle blow. Then the sound of an army of marching feet started in. Alice lost count during roll call, but it seemed like there were around twenty names called.

Did twenty little girls fall off a swing and hit their heads just like me? Or are they even blind at all? Was I thrown in this place with a bunch of other girls who have too many temper tantrums at home as well and whose families don't want them anymore? she thought to herself.

A hand that was smaller than hers grabbed Alice's hand. Alice wanted to pull away, but something told her to hold on, listen to this person's instruction, and do what she was told. After all, the monster that threw her in the bed last night would probably come back and do something to her if she didn't follow these stupid whistles. The little hand yanked hers so hard that Alice did a triple skip to try to catch herself from falling but stood straight up and got into line. The little person placed Alice's hand onto a rough, stiff rope that had no give.

"This is Eunice. Just follow the rope. I will stay behind you," said the little voice.

And off they went, walking down what seemed to be a long hallway. The marches came to a halt. Then Eunice told Alice to take her arm as they walked into the girl's lavatory and into the shower stalls. Alice was amazed at how she was already being given things to figure out on her own. *What would happen if my little guide weren't here?* she thought. *Is this girl just being nice? Would anyone have told me where to go or what to do otherwise?*

"Is it your job or something to teach me this stuff?" Alice said. Eunice didn't answer.

This left Alice wondering how she could treat this little girl. If this was the girl's job, then she could boss her around and not talk to her if she didn't want to. But if it wasn't her job and she was mean to the girl, the girl might not help her anymore. Alice decided she better keep her mouth shut for now and go with the seasoned little resident's program.

"Now get undressed and put everything into the little bag hanging on this hook," said Eunice. She placed Alice's hand on a hook on the wall. "You will get a toiletry bag that you will bring in here with you, but because you just got here and slept in your clothes, you can use my stuff until you get your own," she said.

"Wait a minute," said Alice. "I have to un-dress? Right here? In front of everyone?" She was in disbelief. Eunice let out a big laugh.

"Of course! It isn't like anyone is going to see you. Half of the girls in here can't even hear you!" said Eunice.

Now Alice understood why many of the others hadn't talked to her yet. They had seemed to mostly ignore Alice or brush by her. A couple of them had stepped right into her and didn't say excuse me or anything, and then seemed to just keep walking. She realized that they didn't even know she was there.

Alice reluctantly undressed and put everything in the bag hanging on the hook. She washed herself and shampooed her hair with the borrowed little products. She hadn't ever washed her own hair, but she did her best, as she felt the need to pretend that she could care for herself in front of her little preceptor. After the shower, Eunice placed Alice's hand on a hook on the other side of the stalls, where she found a towel and dried herself halfway off. Then Eunice handed her a robe to put on as they made their way to the sink. They brushed their teeth and brushed their hair. It was then that Alice realized how many suds remained in her hair from the shampoo. Then they put the hard tap shoes back on their feet, which were still dew-covered from the steam of the bathroom, made their way back to the line, and marched down the hallway again as they held the rope that led back to their room.

Once in their room, Eunice and Tina went through the entire process of the daily morning routine. Alice learned to make her bed, put away her things, and get dressed and ready for the day.

Alice found herself enjoying this a little bit. It was kind of like playing a game. She started to have fun for the first time in a long time.

I will master this dungeon and find my way through the hallways, rooms, closets, and hiding places, she thought to herself.

She had longed for a new adventurous house to journey through, and now it appeared that she had found one. Not on her terms, but still…

Alice relied on the twins for just about everything while she learned to make her way around the place. Her devious plans to be mean to them were aborted very quickly after she realized that they seemed to be the only ones looking out for her. Alice thought back to when she was the smartest one in the first grade and would have normally been showing everyone else what to do.

The ropes became somewhat of a lifeline. The girls followed them to the bathroom, the classrooms, meals, playtime. Everywhere they went, there were ropes to guide them to their destination. Always in a uniform line. Always wearing the dreaded shoes. There were schedules, rules, routines, and uniforms for everything.

The day would unfold as the 6:00 a.m. bell rang. There was no sleeping in and there were no alarm delays. It was get up, put the shoes on, grab the toiletry bag, roll call, shower, teeth, hair. Then place the toothbrush, soap, and toothpaste back in the bag. You had to leave the washcloth and towel inside your sink after turning off the water. Then follow the ropes back to the dorm room, make your bed, and put the toiletries away. Each girl had a tall, thin, standing armoire next to their bed. In it were two uniforms, one of their own dresses from home (unless the girls were orphans, and in that case, a dress was given to them), and two nightgowns. One pair of everyday shoes with taps and bells, and one pair of dress shoes with taps and bells. In the tiny drawers at the bottom were seven pairs of underwear, seven pairs of socks for the spring and fall days. All the socks were the same color green. And seven pairs of tights for winter.

Laundry day was on Friday. Depending on their age and level of disability, everyone was given jobs and chores. In Alice's dorm room, five girls would gather everyone's laundry. Each child had a number to identify the items that belonged to each of them. Their number was sewn into every garment that they owned. The older girls were responsible for sewing in the numbers, and these were the girls who excelled at home economics. The numbers were raised and somewhat in regular print so the girls could feel and confirm whose things belonged to whom. Each bed had an embossed number that hung at the bottom of the footboard. Each girl's lingerie sack had their number on it and would be washed as a whole. Once returned, its owner was responsible for separating the socks and undergarments and organizing them in their drawers. There were weekly checks by the house mother to ensure that no one mixed up the numbers or belongings. The inspections also included making sure the beds were made properly and their areas were kept neat and clean.

As the days passed, Alice found herself becoming more and more used to this place. The feeling of heartbreak that resided in her stomach began to subside. The longing for home became a little more distant. She missed and loved her family, but the thought of going back there became a little less desirable as she settled into a life with others who were like her, and she began learning how to do things for herself. She thought back to her daily routine at home of sitting, being pampered, having her every whim quickly answered to. She realized how dreadfully boring and non-purposeful that was. Now she actually looked forward to putting on those cheap patent leather shoes every morning and having something to get up for: following the ropes to reading and writing class, learning the braille alphabet and how to use the slate and stylus to form letters, words, and sentences. She began to forget what regular print letters and numbers looked like. She forgot what a lot of things looked like. She would sometimes lie in bed and try to remember what her room looked like at home. She thought about the park, the swings, the sliding board, the chalkboard in class, and the podium that the children would stand in front of and read their reports and tell all about their summers.

These things all started to fade as she plunged into the world of the unsighted. The girls would graduate into the next dorm room and the next schedule as their mastery of the skills dictated. The girls were not separated according to their age, as the students had varying degrees of physical and mental disabilities. Alice quickly learned that she was much more advanced than the rest and with no delay, climbed the ladder to more mature dormitory groups. Eunice was on par with Alice for the most part. Eunice was unfortunately more advanced than her twin sister—who didn't graduate to the next levels with her—but Eunice luckily stayed with Alice through their journey at the blind school. Alice did not realize that since that first night, when she was thrown onto her bed, she hadn't had a single temper tantrum.

CHAPTER 7

For Charlie, Rob, and Rich, it was the first full day of summer. They showed up for the first day of work to make good on their deal to work in order to pay off the hospital debt as Mother had promised in return for Charlie's surgery. The two older boys walked and Charlie rode alongside them on the family bike. He wasn't even paying attention to where they were going to work. He really didn't care. He was content with knowing that he was with his brothers and that they would tell him where to go and what he had to do. The boys were used to working and Charlie looked forward to it as he peddled up the gravel drive. He didn't notice the sign on the grand stone wall that read "School for the Blind." Once they stepped inside and saw the blind children, he remembered that had been there before, on that dreadful day in first grade when he was running from the school and stumbled upon this place. For some reason, he never told his brothers about the experience of seeing the blind boys step off the bus that day. Mostly because he would have to hash out the events of that horrid day that he managed to put out of his mind for the most part. The Aldridge boys were assigned to keep up with various groundskeeping, weeding, yard cleanup, and painting. On occasion, they would have to help with indoor activities like cleaning the bathrooms or helping set up for dinner.

Charlie still didn't have many friends outside of his siblings. He didn't trust anyone else. The fact that he was becoming more handsome, mannerly, and kind by the day still didn't seem to do much for his self-esteem. Although much happier than when he was incapable of communicating, he continued to have a lot of frustration built up inside him from his previous experiences. He was beginning to master his speech and had almost perfect pronunciation of his words. Still, he didn't feel worthy. He remained quiet, introverted, yet with spurts of chattiness and friendliness at the same time. Curious of his surroundings, he would lurk in corners as to not draw attention to himself. He thought his new job was a lot of fun. Charlie liked sweeping floors, painting, and fixing gates and doorknobs. He was intrigued by the blind students and how they went about their lives and did what they were told. Many of them didn't look very happy. He thought back to the angelic-looking girl that day outside the doctor's office who he had remembered from his prior encounter with her on that dreadful first day of school at Saint Michael's. The looks on their faces were a lot like the way he remembered hers.

When they first started working in the summer, the school was kind of quiet, as most of the students went home over break. The only ones that remained were those without families. Those students all stayed in one building over the break, and he didn't see them very much. He did learn his way around the grounds and was quite sure he had mastered every room, corner, and passageway in the building by the time the fall had come around. There were a lot more students now that the fall semester had started.

The Aldridge boys would leave regular school early on Wednesdays and report to work at the blind school, where they would be given their assignments. Charlie started to take more notice of the students. He liked watching the kids on physical education day. After following their ropes out to the track, they would run, jump rope, hop, and skip. Most of the kids seemed naturally uncoordinated. He wondered if it was because they couldn't see their feet or their surroundings.

How can not one of them have any athletic ability? he thought.

He felt sorrier for them for that reason, then for the fact that they were blind. This place made him feel comfortable. Appreciative that he had his sight, and in some strange way, appreciative that they didn't have theirs, so he would never be seen or challenged with being noticed.

By this time, Alice had of course mastered the routines of the blind school. Following ropes everywhere. She didn't want to admit it, but she liked how it offered her a lot more freedom than when she was back at home, sneaking around the little house to explore after everyone else fell asleep. In this place, there was a schedule for everything. In the beginning, it was extremely hard to get used to, and she definitely didn't like that she had to eat whatever they served for meals. Even liver and sauerkraut. Back home, her fussy little appetite got her whatever she wanted for the most part. She used to sleep in and there was nothing to wake up for back at home. Her day consisted of getting up, being dressed up and pampered, getting her hair done, eating breakfast, then sitting on the couch, listening to the radio, eating lunch…repeat until dinner. Then the frequent tantrums just to make her feel alive.

Now she was awakened daily with the morning whistle. Everything the students did was watched and corrected until the task was mastered. The house mothers even watched her wipe her bottom. At least they didn't do it for her like at home. They didn't do anything for her at this place. No one paid attention if she acted like a brat. Her sheets weren't thick and soft, smelling like lavender. No one was poking and prodding and primping at her. The rules were that you did it yourself. You could part your hair in the middle or on the side, but it had to be a straight part and pinned back neatly. If done wrong, you would do it again and again until you got it right. When washing your hands, you used one pump of soap, then said the Hail Mary as you lathered the top, bottom, between your fingers, and under your fingernails before rinsing. The students were responsible for learning to cut their own nails, which were often riddled with cuts from the clippers for those less experienced. The nails were randomly inspected for length and dirt. Shirts were neatly tucked into skirts at all times.

The house mothers and nuns were always talking about appearances and how it was an extra hard job and of significant importance for these girls. They were representative of the school. They would learn to live in the sighted world in complete, impressionable independence. They would become overachieving, productive members of society and would be respected, not pitied. As much as Alice grew tired of this redundant echo of the school's mission, it was instilled into her very soul, and she not only identified with it, but it also became her destiny. She would master it gracefully and confidently throughout the rest of her life.

In the gym or out in the play yard, the whistle alert to stand in line was three short blows. Your place in line didn't change. Then the announcement would come over the loudspeaker with the instructions for the day. On one particular Wednesday, which usually started with running, Alice lined up in her usual spot. Alice, like most of the others, did not like physical education and always dreaded it.

An announcement was made. "Children, start running!" The institution-provided sneakers were the only shoes in her wardrobe that didn't have taps on them. They were only worn for Physical Education class and placed back in each child's locker before leaving the gym and returning to class. Soon after Alice started running, she suddenly realized that her clumsy feet couldn't keep up with her body. She tripped and fell. Flat on her face. Her knees came down hard against the gym floor. Immediately she let out a shrill cry. She could taste the blood that was streaming from her nose onto her lips. Sister Gwendolyn came rushing over with exact intent. But instead of consoling her, she struck Alice on the bottom with her yardstick. Alice was so shocked at this that her cries were stunted.

"Alice, stand up! Wipe yourself off! Rub your knee and pinch this tissue on your nose! You may sit on the bleachers only until the bleeding stops! Then you will get up, take the rope, and run again!" said the nun.

Alice did exactly as she was told. Once her bleeding stopped, she made her way back to the line. She grabbed the rope and started running again. But this time at a much slower, awkward pace, until she got the hang of it. Alice was quiet and pensive for the rest of the day. She had a true, final realization that since no one was going to care about her antics or heed her cries, she was on her own emotionally. She was reminded of the incident for the rest of the day as her knees throbbed, and she could feel the crusted, dried blood in her nostrils. She would have to wait until the bedtime bathroom routine to wash her face and tend to her sores.

Also on Wednesdays, at 10:00 a.m., the children were permitted to play with whatever they wanted or read their braille books. Alice had learned the braille alphabet at this point and didn't really know how to read that much yet but was beginning to write three-letter words. Braille was completely different than sight words. Nonetheless, she was catching on well and was just introduced to the slate and stylus for writing. She found it to be fun, memorizing the dots in formation and practicing how to write them backward. Her thumb and middle finger were always sore from the way she held the rounded head of the stylus and had to push hard through the thick braille paper from right to left to form the words in order for the dots to poke through well enough to flip the page and read them from left to right. She could tell that she was much better than a lot of the other kids at this. She remembered that Sister Ira told her how smart she was when she was in kindergarten and was quickly realizing that she was still smart. Only now she had to learn things differently than when she had her sight. Still, she felt compelled to constantly remind herself of how much she hated this place. Which in reality wasn't true at all.

As she sat on the bleachers, she held the latest doll that Marnie had sent to her and stroked its yarn-like hair. She knotted it with her fingers and thought about how foolish the doll probably looked. She didn't really know what else to do with it. This dumb doll seemed as if it was as sad and lonely as she was. She heard chattering among the others nearby but would not allow herself to join them. She convinced herself that she was prettier, smarter, and better than the rest of them. Although she did feel a certain closeness to Eunice, Alice was beginning to feel as though she was outgrowing her, too. She was listening to them talk and tell stories about their families and how they were practicing tying their shoes. She already knew now how to tie her shoes, wipe her bottom, and every other stupid thing they were teaching her here. Never realizing how much she had grown and learned both physically and emotionally in the past few months that she had been at the school.

CHAPTER 8

For Charlie, the first Wednesday of the month was the day that he was supposed to clean the gutters. The boys were permitted to substitute work for school on this day each month. However, today it was raining outside. So Edward, the master groundskeeper and maintenance supervisor, who was partially blind himself, gave Charlie the job of taking all the dirty laundry out of the chutes and loading them into bags to be carried out back to the loading dock; the truck would be there by 2:00 p.m. Thinking that it would take him all morning, Edward didn't schedule Charlie to do anything else after that.

Charlie took his assignment and made his way swiftly and purposefully to the laundry room, always focusing on getting his job done. There were twenty piles of clothes. The children that went home on the weekends were required to bring their under-shirts and panties home with them. There was a special launder-ing pile for the kids who didn't have anywhere to go home to on the weekends. Everything had a name and a number on it. Every bag had to be packaged up with the room and the bed numbers for the students owning the belongings. He stood for a moment, looking at the enormous piles of clothes. He blushed when he saw the girls' panties. He wasn't sure if he had ever seen that before. He had helped Delilah a lot of times in the bathroom, but she was his little baby sister and not a "real girl." Nevertheless, Charlie went to work. He separated, bagged, and hauled, trip after trip after trip. He was sweating and out of breath. His arms ached but he was having fun. Before he knew it, he was finished the tasks. He looked at the clock on the wall. Charlie had always been fascinated by analog clocks. He was now very proud of himself for mastering how to tell time. It was only 10:30 a.m., and Edward told him it would take until lunchtime to finish the laundry bundling. What would he do with the rest of his time? He remembered passing the gym and hearing the chatter of the blind kids. He thought maybe he would wander into the gym to see if there was any work to be done there. He grabbed a broom from the utility closet so as to look purposeful upon entering the room. And to separate himself from the "handicaps."

Charlie started with the edges of the gym floor. He felt irrationally shy around these kids despite the fact that none of them could even see him, and only the nuns patrolling the room knew he was in there. Still, he carried on as if they all knew he was in the room, and he imagined they would think he was so much more mature and capable than they were.

As Charlie pushed the broom forward, he spotted Alice, whose name he would later to learn, sitting all alone, playing with her doll. He chuckled to himself at the appearance of knots all over the doll's head. It looked so silly. The girls he knew loved to make their dolls look pretty. He could tell by the look on Alice's face that this little girl would probably find more pleasure in stabbing her doll to death than combing its hair and dressing it up in pretty clothes. As he approached the girl, there was an immediate familiarity.

He paused. *Where do I know her from?* he thought. Suddenly it dawned on him. *It's that girl again!*

He wondered if he muttered those words out loud. The girl outside the doctor's office. He now realized this was the same girl that he met on the worst day of his life, when the nun made him talk in front of the class!

Charlie crawled under the bleachers to clean up the crumbs that the older blind kids had dropped while sneaking their peanut butter cookies out of the lunchroom during play period. He looked up between the rafters and traveled over to see where she was sitting.

He directed his voice toward Alice from below where Alice was sitting.

"Hey, can you pick up that piece of paper for me?" Charlie said, placing a small piece of paper next to Alice as he asked the question.

"Are you talking to me?" said Alice.

"Yes, you," said Charlie.

"Where?" said Alice.

"To your left!" said Charlie.

"I don't know which is my left," said Alice.

"You know. Your left. Your left hand," said Charlie.

Charlie reached up through the opening of the bleachers and grabbed her left hand. She pulled back momentarily, then offered her hand back to him with great hesitation. He uncurled the fingers of her hand and spread each finger back. He created an L shape with her thumb and pointer finger.

"Feel that?" he said. "That makes the letter L for left."

Alice's face lit up with this little newfound trick that she just learned. This was great. She suddenly remembered that letter and could picture it from the alphabet list that hung over the chalkboard in the first-grade classroom. She was so preoccupied with practicing the L shape that she momentarily forgot about the boy under the bleachers.

Yes, this is my left hand, she thought.

She ran her index finger along the lines of the L shape of her left hand over and over again.

"Left, right, left, right. This will come in handy with reading and writing braille too. Read with right. Follow with left."

Then she remembered the boy.

"Are you still down there? What is your name, and why are you under the bleachers? You are going to get in trouble," she said.

But he didn't answer. The boy was gone. She felt around for the piece of paper that he wanted her to hand him, picked it up and put it in her pocket. At any rate, he was gone, and she was now preoccupied with her new left- and right-hand game.

Then another whistle blew. Four short and one long. That meant lunchtime. The children exited in normal fashion, holding the rope to the right through the gym. The kids had to find and pick up their toys and dispose of them in the baskets to the left of the door exiting the gym. Once they reached the flags attached to the rope, it was fifty steps to the bucket, and in went the toys. Everything was organized and had a place. Every single activity of their daily living was carefully thought out to teach the children to be as responsible, independent, and productive as possible.

Alice thought to herself, *Let's see. Today is Wednesday. It will be liver and onions. And an apple for dessert.* Sister Mary Jude was going to make her eat the apple, and it was just too much food. She had to think of a way to get rid of it. After eating the disgusting liver, Alice waited until she could hear the distinct sound of Sister Mary Jude's tapping shoes walking over to her. The taps were fading as Sister approached the end of the oblong table. The tables must have seated forty kids at each one. The room echoed as if they were in a gymnasium. Mealtime was very strict, and there was no talking. It was just like another class lesson to Alice. She couldn't understand why there were more rules at mealtime than at any other time throughout the day. She wondered why they made such a big deal out of it.

Sister would say things like, "You will not look like animals when you eat. No gravy on your chin. No dropping food onto your clothes or onto your lap. Sit up straight. Slide your fork under the food with the knife as your guide. Sit slightly forward so that your face is over your plate. Should the food slide off your fork, it will fall onto the plate, and you will start over again." Alice was almost turning nine and she was starting to realize that certain situations were making her feel anxious and panicked. She didn't like feeling that way but could seem to keep these emotions at bay at times.

Each year seemed to have a significant learning theme. By the time Alice had graduated to the third grade, it was, for sure, focused on table manners. She was so sick and tired of practicing table manners, place settings, silverware holding, and the placement of the napkin on her lap. She was sure that these were all the normal things, of course, that everyone learns. But for the blind, it was so much more. After all, mealtime would be the most massive spectacle out in public. There was the task of finding the food on your plate, keeping it on your fork or spoon, cutting your meat without it falling off the side of the plate, food getting caught in your teeth, or getting food on your face.

It was all so daunting and so much to remember. Trying to learn to politely touch the food on your plate for guidance on how much food was left and where it was located on the plate was probably the hardest task of all. The redundant scooping—only to find that half the time, nothing was even left on your fork once it actually reached your mouth—was one of the most disappointing feelings ever. Mealtime could be the most frustrating time of all. And so much was spent on training. She just hated it!

One of the biggest rules was that students had to finish everything on their plate. Alice did not like this, as she was picky to begin with, so to have to finish it all was just too much to deal with. Not to mention the dreaded apples. Every single day. When she couldn't even imagine eating one more apple, on this particular day, she decided that she would slip it into the wide pocket of her apron. Aprons were part of the routine and grading as well. For obvious reasons: to keep the clothing clean and catch crumbs, spills, smears, and drips. Since the students were graded on etiquette, the aprons would serve as proof of which students were passing and which students needed extra training. Once you mastered having a clean apron for eight days straight, you didn't have to wear it anymore. Alice reached four days once and was determined to reach day eight as fast as she could.

Lunch was now over, and the girls made their way to the lavatory. The toilet stall was about the only place where there was complete privacy. Well, at least for the students that passed the test of wiping their bottoms and having clean-appearing underwear. Alice knew she could be inspected at any time, and someone would surely spot the apple in her apron. Frantically, she wondered what she would do with the apple. She wondered how big the toilet drain was. The idea of reaching down and touching it was disgusting. Yet now that she had the apple in her possession and she hadn't eaten it when she was supposed to, it seemed like her only recourse. She began to get nervous because she'd done something wrong. Her eyes began moving back and forth, her mouth was dry, and her palms were sweaty. She was in a terrible pickle. She imagined getting into so much trouble. She was never whipped with a cat-o'-nine-tails, but she had heard about it. What if this happened to her? She couldn't bear it. Of course, the reality of it was that nothing like that ever happened at the blind school, but the anxiety of the situation had Alice's mind traveling far out of rational thought. She decided to just go for it. Her tiny hand reached into her pocket and pulled out the apple. Her hand was shaking. She dropped it into the toilet, quickly turned and rushed out the stall door, washed her hands, and lined up in unison, in regular fashion, and faded into the group. However, she couldn't settle down internally. She began ruminating over and over about the situation. She became obsessed with thinking about the apple floating in the toilet water. She wondered if it was still sitting in the toilet or if it was going to be flushed and then clog the toilet, causing water to flood everywhere. Would all the students be questioned? She couldn't stop thinking about it. Over and over again. She bit her nails, terrified of what was to come. Time had passed with showering, toothbrushing, and fingernail and toenail inspection taking place, and no one approached her about the apple. She climbed into bed and began to say her prayers.

"Please God, don't let me be whipped. But if I am, I deserve it because I should have eaten the apple when I was supposed to and not dropped it in the toilet."

Alice recited all ten decades of the rosary. Once the rosary was complete, she said the whole thing over again. Her fingertips were twitching, and her hands were still shaking. Her eyes jumped all over the place until she finally fell asleep from complete exhaustion. She hadn't realized that it was just before the morning whistle was about to blow. As she was awakened by the five long whistles, she reminded herself that something had sent her to bed with extraordinary angst. She couldn't remember for a few seconds but as her grogginess dissipated, the memory of the apple infraction came rushing in like the ocean tide. It was flooding her thoughts once again and sending her back into a whirlwind of panic. She had to tell someone. She had to fess up to Sister Gwendolyn and accept her fate.

There weren't any announcements over the microphone that the bathroom had flooded or that the pipes burst or that the girl's lavatory was closed for maintenance. Maybe nobody flushed that toilet yet today. She thought maybe it would happen today. What if her punishment were to pull the apple out of the dirty toilet and eat it?

Oh, I would rather die than to have to do such a thing. What am I going to do? she thought.

Just as the house mother walked through the door in preparation for the morning bed checks, Alice jumped to the rope line that led to the massive dormitory room door, grabbed onto the rope, and ran toward the door. She put her hands out in front of her in desperate search for the house mother, Ms. Motley.

"Oh, please take me to Sister Gwendolyn. I have to confess a most terrible deed! I sinned! I sinned! I have to tell her. It's just so awful! I can't live with my conscience. I just can't!"

Ms. Motley reminded Alice of her own mother. She could tell when touching her that Ms. Motley was tall and stately. Seemingly strict and cold when first meeting her, yet very sweet and loving. Alice sensed a little emotional weakness much like what she sensed in her own mom and in herself. Ms. Motley was an older woman who once had a child of her own in the blind school. Only he had died when he was very young from the brain tumor that caused his blindness. Ms. Motley was widowed as well and had no one anymore. She lived in the blind school with the nuns as if she were one of them.

"Child, rest your mind. What could be so awful? Calm down, you're shaking like a leaf," said Ms. Motley.

Ms. Motley caressed Alice's arms to calm her, but it didn't seem to help at all. Ms. Motley reassured Alice that she would take her to see Sister Gwendolyn but to please relax and have faith in the Lord that everything will be okay. She knew, although Alice was spoiled and entitled, she also prided herself on being the best at everything and carrying out the rules to a tee. She wanted to chuckle because she knew that whatever the misdemeanor was, it couldn't have been all that bad given Alice's determination toward perfection.

However, this behavior was none like she had ever seen. It was so bizarrely frantic. She began to feel sorry for Alice, as this was an apparent precursor to an anxiety-ridden life to come for this beautiful, industrious little girl.

Ms. Motley walked Alice down to the main floor and into the headmaster's office. Once through the doors, Alice could feel how authoritative the room was. She almost tripped as she stepped through the doors onto the plush carpet. It smelled like the cedar polish that her mother always used on the living room furniture mixed with incense burning. It was an oddly pleasant aroma but added to the fear of having to appear in front of Sister Gwendolyn and be given her punishment.

"Sit here, Alice, while I go speak with Sister Gwendolyn," said Ms. Motley.

While she was waiting, the minutes passed so slowly. She rubbed her hands and scratched them.

"Alice, you can come in now," said a voice from across the hall. Alice quickly stood up and rushed into the room, felt for the closest chair to sit down, and prepared her confession. Her report of the event was rather dark. It delved deeply into the sinfulness of lying and sneaking, and all the while she was rubbing and wringing her hands and scratching them. She pulled on her lips. This little girl couldn't stand the thought of getting in trouble. Sister watched and soon realized there was no appropriate punishment for this little girl who was already so hard on herself. Sister Gwendolyn looked at her with pity that someone so young would feel so much pressure. She quickly swept over to her and wrapped her in her arms. Sister Gwendolyn looked at this child who prided herself on being perfect at just about everything. The blindness was wearing on her, but until now she was able to still feel like and be admired as a good girl who took on every task and completed it as directed. Sister Gwendolyn carefully considered the situation. She talked to Alice about recognizing her faults and told her how proud she was that she cared so much about committing a wrongdoing. The two walked to see Father Felix, where Alice recited her confession and was given the penance of saying three "Hail Mary" prayers and one "Our Father" prayer. After that day, no infractions like the apple incident ever happened again.

Over the following two to three years, there were other situations where Alice's anxiety was heightened, but for the most part, it was well controlled because the environment they were in was so very routine and predictable that it helped to keep incidences to a minimum.

As the students matured and could be trusted to make their way throughout the buildings on their own, they were given jobs to complete as part of the life skills training. On one particular March evening, it was still quite chilly outside. It was Alice's job to pick up twenty folding chairs that were lined up outside in the courtyard and bring them into the cafeteria. She made her way through the long hall and down four flights of steps to the basement and out the courtyard door. She had not realized that the door had locked behind her once she walked through it. She followed the rope out to the middle of the courtyard, felt around for the first two chairs, folded them up, and made her way back just as lightning struck and rain started to pour. She hurried back with the two chairs tucked under her right arm and followed the rope with her left back to the door. She rattled the door. But it wouldn't open.

Oh no, it's locked! she thought.

An overwhelming sensation of panic rose up through her stomach into her chest. She couldn't think logically. Her heart was pounding. She felt terror as her eyes flew wide open. *No one will know I am out here. No one will find me,* she thought. *I will be late for breakfast.* All she could think about was that she had a book report due the next day and now it wouldn't get done because she would be stuck outside all night long. Her emotions were beginning to spiral out of control. She dropped the chairs on the ground. She started pounding on the door with both fists as hard as she possibly could.

"Help!" she cried. "Somebody help!"

She continued banging and crying. The tears were streaming. It was purely terrifying.

Just then, she felt something being thrown over her shoulders. It smelled like rain and felt like a blanket. A voice came from behind her. Alice wondered if it was that same boy from the gym that disappeared as quickly as he arrived under the bleachers to try to talk to her.

"Hey, it's okay. I have a key. Come on. Don't be upset. I can let you in and everything is going to be okay."

Alice didn't respond. She was in shock over what was happening. She didn't know what to say. The voice sounded kind of familiar and like a young person's voice. She didn't know whether to be thankful, embarrassed, or scared. She knew right there and then that she was probably overreacting. Alice was still shaking, and her eyes were dancing all over the place at this point. But she managed to thank the helpful person and pulled the blanket around her shoulders. The voice went on.

"You stand in here out of the rain. I'll get the rest of the chairs—just hold the door open like this, and we can set them in the rack." Charlie placed her hand on the inside of the door as he propped it open. She didn't answer him but stepped inside to take cover, leaning her body up against the open door. She listened quietly to the pitter-patter of footsteps running back and forth, bringing the piles of chairs in until the job was completed. Once inside, Charlie gently moved Alice backward to get her out of the way while the door slammed shut behind them. She could tell that he was probably a couple of years older than she was. His voice was deeper than she had remembered but still knew that it was him.

"There, it's all done!" he said.

Alice could tell that he was dripping wet from being exposed to the weather outdoors. She felt the water drip onto her feet and realized that he must be standing very close to her. At this, she blushed. Alice was twelve years old now and starting to have all sorts of feelings that she never had before.

Just then, Charlie, opened up Alice's hand, made the L shape with her left thumb and pointer finger again, and placed a handkerchief in the middle of her hand. He suddenly didn't have words either, as he was taken aback by the beautiful girl once again. He folded her fingers around the handkerchief. Alice blushed even more. She paused. Then quickly pulled her hand away and still didn't know what to say, as it was now confirmed that this was the boy from the bleachers. She then backed up, felt for the railing behind her, grabbed it, and spun around, running up the steps as fast as she could. Once she reached the first landing, she stopped, Turned and shouted, "Thank you! By the way, what was written on the piece of paper you gave me on the bleachers that day?" Charlie responded, "I want to see things the way that you see them."

The boy then hollered up the stairwell, "I'm Charlie!" as Alice continued up the steps.

"I'm Alice!" she hollered back.

Now that she was back in her dorm room, lying in bed, she didn't know what emotion to feel. She was riddled with joy, fear, and embarrassment, all the while pressed with the urgency to get back to her studies. She found herself skipping over to her assigned desk area. She rolled the piece of paper inside the handkerchief and stuffed it inside her pillowcase right next to the rosary Marnie had given to her that smelled like lilacs. She then took out her slate and stylus, opened up her notebook, and went to work on her book report about the life and works of Annie Sullivan.

After lights out, she lay in her bed. Her mind wandered to the boy. His hands were rough when he placed the handkerchief in her palm. Yet his touch was sweet, tender, and innocent.

I guess he must be sighted, or he wouldn't have seen me there screaming like a foolish baby, she thought. *Maybe he has some kind of deformity and that's why he is always around. And why does he have a key? Is he like the hunchback of Notre Dame or something? What is he doing here? Does he talk to the other girls or just to me?*

She wanted to ask the other girls but wouldn't dare let them know about her mystery friend. They would probably tell on her, and the boy would get in trouble. Or maybe they would like him too and start talking to him and steal him away from her. Besides, it was fun having the little secret companion that seemed to be showing up when least expected. She couldn't stop thinking of the chivalrous act with the blanket and handkerchief and the way he touched her hands. She began to liken him to the prince from all the fairy tale stories she had read over the years. In the days and weeks that followed, she didn't encounter the boy anymore. At least not that she knew of. She thought that maybe he watched her, and she didn't know about it. She began asking questions about the people who worked there and what they did, but nobody really seemed to be able to give her much information. Everyone just assumed there were "people" to serve the food and clean the dorms and maintain the grounds.

The only people the students normally interacted with were the teachers, house mothers, and nuns. And of course, each other. Alice began to forget a little bit about the boy, or at least she put him in the back of her mind, as she was so busy with schoolwork, piano, dance, and chores.

Meanwhile, Charlie did not forget about Alice. In fact, he would find every opportunity to catch a glance at what she was doing, where she was going, who she was talking to, and who she was with. He memorized every hair bow that she owned, and she had one dress in particular that she would wear on dress-up days. She looked so pretty in it. It was a sailor dress, and she wore it with white knee-high socks and a big red bow in her hair that was parted over to the side. Charlie was impressed how she always looked so neat and clean. She didn't have sloppy food on her clothes or pieces stuck in between her teeth. Her eyes didn't roll off in different directions unless she was scared. She didn't fumble. She moved swiftly and eloquently as if she wasn't blind at all. Only when you got up close could you see the blank stare that was never fixed on just one thing.

CHAPTER 9

Alice was maturing rapidly. Her breasts were beginning to bud. She found herself wanting to read more and more about the great love stories and tragedies. Her book reports focused more on emotional turmoil and overcoming obstacles in life. She had been able to keep her moods pretty much in check again at this point. Her life in this institution was the safest place for her. She knew where everything was and how everything operated. There was rarely a reason for her to get upset. However, she was beginning to cry more often over silly trivial things, like she did when she was very young. She felt herself feeling blue for no reason at all. Alice would feel panicked at times and her imagination would run wild, sending her off into total darkness but at this point in her life, these were temporary situations for her.

Then that dreaded day that she had heard about from the older girls. The house mothers had been preparing them for this all along. There was so much talk about getting ready for it and having the pads and belts tucked away in their purses. The feeling of the warm gush when it first happened. Luckily, Alice was in her bed the first time she got her period, and no one saw it. She often thought of how embarrassing it must be for the girls that get it while they are out somewhere with their brothers or something. She wondered how she would know if she had blood on her clothes. This thought did cause her to do a lot of ruminating. Whenever she would get stuck on this scenario, she wouldn't be able to sleep, and her eyes would start dancing again. She would lie in bed thinking of how she would handle it if she had to get up and go to the bathroom when around sighted people in public.

Thank God that it happened to her while she was sleeping. She got herself up extra early and hurried to the bathroom. She cleaned herself up. Once out of the bathroom stall, she couldn't stop thinking that blood must be on her clothes and that she didn't clean up well enough. She repeatedly went back and cleaned up again, checked herself, left, went back in again. This must have occurred about eight times when the house mother came looking for her. She watched Alice's OCD behaviors with a feeling of great concern, and it stopped her in her tracks for a moment. Almost as if in a trance, Alice didn't hear Ms. Motley coming toward her. She grabbed Alice, and Alice jumped. She cried out at the unexpected jolt of Ms. Motley's hands on her.

"Alice, my dear!" said Ms. Motley. "There is no blood anywhere! You are clean. It's fine now! Off to class!" she said.

The following day, Alice was called down to Sister Gwendolyn's office. She was introduced to Dr. Button. He was a psychiatrist from the local hospital. Alice could tell that he was young by the sound of his soft, strong masculine voice. She imagined that he was probably very handsome. Alice wondered if her mother or Marnie knew anything about this.

Alice wasn't really sure why he came to see her, anyway. She hadn't really remembered or realized her behavior in the bathroom from the day before. The doctor asked her many questions about herself, her habits, what made her worried or scared, et cetera. She answered quite matter-of-factly.

As she was spilling her personal thoughts to the stranger of a man, she realized that almost everything that was out of her normal routine made her scared. Yet she wanted to do everything that sighted women did. She wanted to travel and work and do things independently. She thought routine was such a bore. She wanted to wear fancy clothes and exchange banter with male callers like Marnie did. She talked about her fits when she was younger and told the doctor that she knew she was a spoiled child and super unhappy because everyone did everything for her while she lived at home. She told him how she felt like a real person at the blind school because nobody did anything for her there. As much as she loathed the routine, she talked about how it made her feel safe at the same time. She talked about boys and told the doctor that there was only one boy that she had ever really talked to and told him about how she met him twice at the school but that she never encountered him anymore. It made her sad to think that she may never get to talk to him again.

As she was talking, she thought that she felt safe when that boy was around. She didn't tell the doctor about the handkerchief or about the boy helping her when she was locked out in the rain in the courtyard. She just said that "someone" came along and helped her get back inside. Dr. Button was genuinely nice to Alice. He didn't repeat anything she told him to anyone, and they started meeting once a week. Before Alice knew it, three years had passed. Dr. Button taught Alice how to notice when her thoughts were getting the best of her. They practiced breathing and meditation. He taught her how to cope with her emotions and compartmentalize stressful situations. It was working!

She practiced the self-help lessons, just as if she were learning her times tables, and was becoming good at reigning in her spiraling thoughts.

Alice was now fifteen and becoming more beautiful every day. She started to look forward to her weekly visits with Dr. Button. She started to fantasize about kissing him at their sessions. She began wearing poorly applied pink lipstick and paid attention to her hair to look more grown-up for their meetings. Alice started asking him questions about himself. How old he was. What types of things he liked.

At a more recent session, Alice boldly asked if she could touch his face and feel his hair. He reluctantly obliged but thought agreeing to it could be an advantage to keeping an altruistic doctor-and-patient relationship going. He allowed her to stand in front of him. She ran her fingers around his face and through his hair. He began to notice the expression on her face and felt her trembling hands. He himself felt a moment of near weakness, as she was quite beautiful. Then he quickly realized what was going on with this innocent girl and that she was infatuated with him. He suddenly grabbed her hands in his.

"Look, Alice," he said. "I need you to understand something. I am your doctor, and you are my patient. I am thirty, and you are fifteen. I have a fiancée. We are getting married in a year from now. I am not your boyfriend. You are a child."

Alice froze for a moment. She pulled away and clenched her hands into her chest. She felt the horrific embarrassment and disappointment beginning to swell in her stomach. She wanted to throw up right then and there, and her initial reaction was to have a tantrum. But she couldn't do that in front of Dr. Button. She wouldn't look like a woman in his eyes. Even more, she still didn't really digest yet what he just said.

Not being able to practice in the mirror, she hadn't really mastered how to hide her emotions behind a grin or practice making mysterious facial expressions. She wanted to stay. Stay and say something seductive so he would take her in his arms and kiss her. Just like she read in *Gone with the Wind,* when Clark Gable grabbed Vivien Leigh in his arms and told her she was a spoiled child, but he loved her so. Instead, she turned, fumbled for the back of the chair that was perpendicular to the door, awkwardly tripped and almost fell, swung the door open, and ran down the hall to her dorm room, where she flopped down on her bed and buried her head in her pillow.

Unfortunately, this encounter with Dr. Button had a significant impact on Alice and was a turning point in her life. This had given her a total misunderstanding of her potential to be loved. She resigned herself to the fact that she would never be worthy of having a man because of her blindness. She wouldn't ever be married and would never have children like her sisters were getting ready to do. It was an incredibly sad, predetermined, unrealistic idea for a fifteen-year-old girl.

Although it was very awkward at first, Alice continued to see Dr. Button every week thereafter. Her demeanor was different toward him. She acted almost as if she didn't know who he was anymore. It was like starting all over getting to know him. Dr. Button found this to be a bit concerning. As if her response to the stressful situation gave her amnesia about who he was. Dr. Button decided to start talking to her more like an adult, and this did help her to grow and feel more confident as a woman. She did eventually seem to open up to him again. He had a way of speaking matter-of-factly but made her feel comfortable with expressing herself and her emotions. To properly respond in the appropriate manner given the situation. They would role-play with frightening situations and work on tactics to overcome the flood of imaginary mishaps that would send her into an emotional frenzy otherwise.

Aside from schoolwork, Alice now spent almost all her time reading the braille books in the library and playing the piano.

She wasn't very coordinated and often thought back to the joke her brother made about embarrassing the whole family with her jump rope expedition when the family came to see her. She was repeatedly dropping the rope and tripping over herself. Though she knew it was a joke, she also knew it rang a bit true, as the words "embarrassed the whole family" bit her every time she thought about it. It mostly bothered her because she revered her brother as her only real father figure in her life, and his opinion meant a lot.

Sometimes the books that Alice would grab from the bookshelves weren't interesting at all. She would run her fingers across the introductory pages, decide if it was something she wanted to spend her time on, and move on to the next. She threw herself into her studies and spent an exorbitant amount of time perfecting everything. Spelling, grammar, punctuation, mathematics. She wouldn't accept any grade under an A-plus. If she received anything less, she would challenge the teachers so much as to why she got the grade that she felt she so did not deserve. Some of the teachers admittedly started just giving the A-plus if teetering between that and a "simple A" so as not to deal with Alice's obsession with having to get the highest score. The other children became exhausted by her as well. They began to expect that Alice would be the recipient of almost every academic award, and she always was the one being picked as the representative of the school. Quite honestly, she was a natural, and they knew that nobody else cared as much as Alice did or put in the same amount of work. Even so, it was dreadfully annoying to the others, and Alice often found herself alone with her books and music without many friends, as she had less and less in common with the others as the years went by.

Alice went on to graduate with honors after the twelfth grade, left the blind school, and was accepted to Saint Mary's College. She was the only blind student in that school. Alice was determined at this point in her life to become integrated into the world of the sighted. She now felt she had the tools to make it in the outside world and was able to adapt to changing routines. For the most part.

She moved into a dormitory with a room on the first floor closest to the bathroom. She was diligent in ensuring that all her things were kept neatly in her room. She woke up earlier than the other girls to make sure she had plenty of time to not only bathe and brush her teeth, but more importantly to Alice, to be sure that she didn't leave a speck of dirt or hair behind. It was driven into her from her days at the blind school how blind people were not to look sloppy or leave a trace, as they were to have a clean, appropriate appearance at all times. Many of the other blind students back at school had given up on being concerned about appearances, as they didn't have the same level of determination and weren't able to accomplish such daunting tasks day in and day out.

Marnie was able to locate a volunteer braille interpreter for Alice's studies. The woman's name was Mrs. Bloomberg. Mrs. Bloomberg's son was blinded in a car accident, and she had learned to read and write braille years before. She became very dedicated to Alice and translated every single one of Alice's textbooks into braille.

Alice longed to be part of the group of girls that seemingly "had it all" in the college life.

The girls were very nice to her and liked to hear her stories and watch her navigate her world of the unsighted. Nonetheless, she knew she wasn't like them. They didn't invite her to the parties that they were attending, nor did she have any dates like the rest of them. They ran back and forth, in and out of the dormitory, juggling their student and social lives. Sometimes this got her very down and sent her into near-spiraling panic. The skills taught by Dr. Button still proved to be quite effective at that time in her life, and Alice really didn't have much time to think about her loneliness with her busy schedule of studying, tidying, and perfecting her daily activities in her darkness, which was surrounded by a world of the sighted. Needless to say, Alice graduated magna cum laude from Saint Mary's College.

CHAPTER 10

Charlie's life, however, evolved quite differently than Alice's. In the years prior to Charlie and his brothers being sent to work at the blind school, the family had moved into a home so that they could be closer to their grandmother and grandfather, Uncle Victor, and Uncle Vinny. Their dad had opened up a Pay-and-Go lot next to the house. This made it easy for Mother to help out, if needed, and the three bigger children were old enough to look after themselves and the little ones. Charlie could now go to a school with kids that knew nothing about his prior speech handicap.

Mother had a way of spilling her woes and knowing the compassionate hearts to prey on. No better place to have mastered that than with the Catholic Church. She met with Father O'Malley at Saint Christopher's School. She told the pastor about how they didn't have enough money to send their five children to a private school but needed them to attend so they could avoid following in their father's evils. Father O'Malley was touched by her sadness and before they knew it, the children were all members of Saint Christopher's Catholic grade school. She talked of her need to repay the debt that was promised to the doctors that helped Charlie and asked what she or the other children could do for the community service to repay not only the hospital but the free education being offered to her children.

Therefore, it was Father O'Malley who was responsible for getting the boys their jobs at the blind school. Mother was elated with the offer and made certain that the boys understood what their responsibilities would be. As always, they did exactly what their mother had requested and showed up for work three times a week every single week. The boys would do anything and everything that was asked of them without complaint.

While growing up, after school and work and on the weekends, the five siblings would play in the yard, play street ball, and run around the neighborhood. For a brief time, it appeared that their father was trying not to drink as much, and he and Mother seemed to be getting along much better. Rob and Rich never left Charlie behind. Delilah was normally trailing along. In turn, Charlie never left Delilah behind. Young Gertie was now a teenager. Her slanty eyes mirrored her beautiful mother's. She loved nice things. She was naturally popular and spent a lot of time with school friends.

When night fell, Charlie and Delilah would watch as their parents crossed the street to the local Irish pub for some cocktails and dancing. Their parent's original attraction was all because of dancing, as they were both very good at the Charleston, and the Jitterbug was becoming popular. They both enjoyed the party life and even indulged a lot more than they should have in the gambling arena. It was exciting for them both. Gertie was always sure she would win big one day. As she grew older, she would put her last cent down on anything that she thought would make her rich. Gertie's parents' roles were quite defined and backward for the day. Grandmother Riley was strict, bossy, and smart with a penny—tight with it as well. Granddad Riley on the other hand, was carefree and somewhat foolish. Grandmother Riley certainly thought so and made no bones about frequently reminding him of this. Granddad would rather spend his days taking the boys to the movies and baseball games. He liked to take them for long walks and adventures. Grandmother Riley never forgave her husband for retiring from the water company and quitting nearly three years before his thirty-year retirement. Not that you could blame her. He had lost his full pension. After all, her financial decisions were the reason why they had food on the table and a roof over their heads.

The grandparents' home was filled with constant noise. They fostered children that ranged from two through sixteen years old. These kids were part of the family and the neighborhood. They would come and go at times but mostly once placed, they stayed.

Grandmother never seemed to be happy. She cleaned, cooked, taught prayers, and hollered at anyone who dirtied her floors.

Baseball was always the buzz about the house. It was the most exciting pastime for Charlie, his brothers, and Granddad. Going to the game at the Baker Bowl was the highlight of the year. If they were lucky, they might get to go to two games in a season. Granddad bought the tickets with the money stash that he kept under the porch, hidden away from Grandmother. Little did he know, she knew it was there all along but turned a blind eye, as this was his only source of extra money. After all, she needed to act a little mean to keep things in check, but she secretly loved to watch everyone's faces when they got their special treats of going on their adventures. She kept her pleasure tucked away under her stern grin, like it was a stolen muffin hidden in the pocket of her apron. At the game, Rich would buy the Pepsi with the money he made working at Harper's pump station and the blind school. Rob would buy the peanuts, and everyone bought themselves a hot dog. Granddad was gentle and kind. He made all the kids feel safe and important. He scanned his audience of grandkids and foster kids when they sat in groups with him. He looked each and every one of them in the eye when he spoke and when they spoke. He made them feel like he was listening to the greatest story on earth when they had something to say. Did he know how this made them feel?

To Charlie, up to this point in his life, this man was essentially the only grown-up to actually "really" hear him. Taking his young words in like they were spoken with the wisdom of a seventy-eight-year-old man, Granddad was the only one who never asked him to stop talking when he rambled on about things such as Mr. Madison at Mr. Madison's Market and how he walked with a wooden leg, and how he would pick up trash with a point on the end of his metal carrying stick, et cetera.

They would do crossword puzzles together and go on nature walks. Granddad loved discovering things and showing his discoveries to the kids. He would make it feel like they were the first and only people in the world to fish and see turtles. Like they were the first ever to swing from vines into the lake on a sweltering hot Saturday afternoon. Granddad would play with all the kids like he was one of them, carrying on, telling stories, sharing his muffins and peanuts with all of them. He would fetch water right out of the creek, filling up his leather flask. He just knew how the kids would love drinking out of it and sharing germs. After all, that was part of the fun.

Charlie thought back to when the boys made good on their deal to start working at the blind school. He thought back to when they arrived, standing out front, looking up to the top of the building at the giant crucifix. The building looked like a castle. Charlie stood and watched the blind students line up in the walk, holding on to the ropes. He remembered this place from that dreadful day when he was stripped of his dignity, when he ran out of the school, not knowing where he was going and was soothed by the beautiful music and church bells that brought him peace on that day. He remembered looking so forward to starting his first real job, and of course, for the opportunity to work with his big brothers. The boys would remain employed at the blind school for the next six years. It was during this time that he would watch Alice almost daily and look out for her in case she ever needed something. The last time that he saw her at the blind school was shortly before his fifteenth birthday. He and his brothers were asked to leave after Charlie managed to get the temporary principal fired for watching the girls in the shower room through a peephole in the wall. He thought he would never see her again.

CHAPTER 11

The Aldridge family seemed to have settled into somewhat of a normal life for several years living with their grandparents, working, and going to school. Still taking care of one another.

The Park-and-Go lot did not work out because Daddy was once again unable to control his drinking, and he had lost the lot to a gambling debt a few years back. Now they hadn't seen him for quite some time.

Soon after, Granddad died, and then Grandmother passed on as well. Charlie's mom didn't have the support anymore, and the last that anyone heard about their father was that he was in jail after throwing a rock through a store window to purposely get arrested, so as to receive a hot meal and a place to stay.

It was time to move on.

Charlie was so proud that he got to unhook the latch on the moving truck and help move all the furniture from the house up the truck ramp and load it into the back. As he lay the giant mirror up against the inside back wall and covered it with a blanket, he turned and suddenly saw his father standing on the walkway. He looked like a wax figure. Staring at Charlie. Charlie was startled at first, as his father was almost unrecognizable. Daddy looked like he had aged forty years since the last time Charlie had seen him. His clothes were dirty, and his face was drawn.

Mother and Rob were carrying the couch out of the house. Everyone paused at once. They gently set the couch down on the sidewalk and stopped and stared as well. Nobody knew what to do or say. Mother's facial expression dropped. She had a look of pity on her face, yet it was mixed with love.

However, she quickly composed herself as the reality of who he was and what he had become set in, and her expression quickly changed to one of anger and disgust. She then walked by him and acted as though he wasn't even there. Rob kept his head down, as he couldn't look at him.

Rob remembered the last time their dad left the house. Nobody had spoken about that day. Daddy had just finished beating him up just because he looked too skinny. He would make Rob stand up to the old man who was going to teach him how to be a fighter. Just moments after knocking Rob down for the tenth time, when Rob could hardly catch his breath—his eyes swollen, lips split, and ribs broken—his mother had finally snapped. She jumped on Daddy's back to get him to stop picking on her fragile son. Daddy then turned on her in a rage and threw her up against the wall. He choked her as if he never planned to let go. Rich wasn't home at the time. Upon seeing this, the girls and Charlie fled upstairs.

Young Gertie ran to the top drawer in Mother's dresser and grabbed something before she bravely made her way back to where the commotion was. This inspired Charlie and Delilah to creep quietly down the stairs behind her.

Suddenly, BANG! It sounded like the Fourth of July fireworks. Only closer than anyone had ever heard. Charlie instinctively covered Delilah's ears with his hands.

There, at the bottom of the steps, with a pistol in her hand, stood young Gertie. Her hands were steady. Her arms were outstretched. She was quiet, focused, and determined. She was looking at no one but her father.

"Get off my mother and leave this house!" she said with a quiet, trembling, yet forceful-sounding voice.

Daddy stood up ever so slowly. He was as shocked as everyone else. He turned and looked at Gertie. Then he slowly scanned the room, making eye contact in the eerie silence one by one. First with Rob, then Charlie, then pitifully, he looked at little Delilah. He watched Delilah's face as a tear came streaming down her freckled cheek with a terrified look as she clutched Charlie's waist.

There was complete silence as he bent over, picked up his whiskey bottle, and left the house. Rich walked in just as their father was walking out. Rich looked at him as they passed each other, with no verbal exchange. Rich walked through the door to find the rest of his family still in complete silence and young Gertie still standing in the same spot, holding the gun, as if frozen in place. Rich slowly approached his sister and gently removed the gun from her stiff hands. She then fell to the floor, shaking uncontrollably.

It had been two years since that incident. Their father stood in front of Charlie now, a completely broken man.

As Charlie stood on the ramp at the back of the moving van, he stared at the frail old man. He thought that this must be what people looked like in those German camps that Gus at the gas station told him about.

His father looked desperate and starving. His hand shook as he reached out to take Charlie's. Charlie hesitated for a moment, then slowly stepped off the ramp and shook his father's hand. It was like a slow-motion movie. Gertie then approached Charlie from behind and put her hands on his shoulders as they watched the old man. Rich, with his shoulders back and fists tightening, came closer to him. Rob was slouched over but was able to lift his head ever so slightly and look up at him over his eyeglasses. Young Gertie and Delilah weren't there, as they had gone ahead a few days earlier to get things started at the new house.

Daddy spoke to them in a whisper. His speech was pressured.

"I-I-I thought I would come and say goodbye. I saw you packing up," he said.

Charlie couldn't think of any words to say but wanted to say so much. It touched Charlie deeply to know that his father had been watching his family from afar.

Charlie then responded, "Do you need something to eat before we go?"

Rich plunged forward and Rob held him back. Rob then reached into the front seat and took one of the sandwiches that Mother packed for their trip and handed it to their father along with a cold bottle of cola. Their father graciously bowed, as the tall young man standing in front of him, who he once battered almost daily, now looked down at him with such disappointed sorrow in his eyes.

Charlie then turned to Rich with an expression of pleading.

"I know what you're going to say, and the answer is NO, Charlie!" said Rich. "He is not coming with us. We can't afford to feed ourselves, let alone this drunken fool," he said.

Rich finished hooking the latch on the back of the truck, and as he walked by their father, his shoulder shoved into him, and the skeleton of a man stumbled back and almost fell to the ground.

Charlie shouted, "But Rich, he's going to die here! We have to take him with us! Come on! We gotta take him! We just gotta!"

Suddenly, and for the first time ever, Charlie experienced his big brother's rage that he had only witnessed with interaction with outsiders before now. Rich grabbed Charlie and threw him down onto the hard floor of the van. His fist was raised, like he was going to beat the compassion out of Charlie for caring about their bum father. Charlie stared up at him with an expression of utter disbelief, then the expression quickly changed to a look of confidence that his big brother would never actually hit him. Rich looked back in Charlie's eyes and lowered his arm. He stood up, picked up his little brother by the front of his overalls, and brushed him off.

Rich then said in a soft, almost-whisper of a voice, "No talk about bringing him with us again. Let's go."

Charlie didn't say another word as he, Mother, and the boys finished closing things up and piled into their vehicles. Rob drove the van, and Charlie, Rich, and Mom pulled away in their used, faded black 1935 Chevrolet.

Charlie watched through the side view mirror as his father still hung around in the street, as if waiting for an invitation as they were leaving. The old man then unwrapped the sandwich and sat down on the curb, drinking the cola in the hot August sun. Charlie thought about how Mother rarely talked about their father's younger years but knew his parents must have been happy at one time, because on occasion she would mention how they would dance and go to the speakeasies before they had children. She told them that he had great dancing moves and when talking about their history, a huge smile would run across her face as she would pause and think back while telling her reminiscent stories. She had a closet full of flapper dresses and hats. Many of which she sold over the years. But Charlie thought they must have had a magical life and found some solace in knowing that at least they laughed and loved at some point when they were first together.

As Charlie grew, he was always the first to help others move from one dwelling to another. He thought about how this would relate to showing their father that everyone had to leave things and people behind and move on. He felt that the comfortable peaceful-ness of staying in one place could not exist. Charlie told himself that people could not remain in your life forever. It was almost like Charlie's penance to his father for deserting him that day. He decided he would never abandon anyone ever again in his life.

CHAPTER 12

The Aldridges had now been living for seven years in a quaint little house in a New Jersey town by the Delaware River. The whole family pitched in for rent and food. They lived together throughout their teen and young adult years. Even when the twins went away to serve in the war, they would send their earnings home to Mother to help keep everyone fed and clothed and the bills paid.

Charlie was now well into his twenties.

Father McHenry announced during Sunday Mass that the old Saint Christopher's Church needed a new roof. There was no money available from the diocese, and he called on the gentlemen parishioners to help with the gathering of materials and installation.

Charlie was working for the power and light company just across the bridge. He was able to secure the needed roof tiles from a buddy whose cousin worked for Bayard Roofing. Charlie and the other town parishioners went to work on the roof, as it was their duty to help the priest with whatever was requested for the church. The men would think nothing of working in the evenings and on weekends in order to finish the job. As Charlie was finishing up on a warm, sunny April Sunday in the early 1950's, he rushed home to clean up and was able to return for the 12:00 p.m. Mass, as the house that he, Mother, and Delilah lived in was only two blocks up from the church. He arrived a few minutes early to en-sure his availability to usher for the money collection. The church was quiet, with the incense odor from Sunday Mass just the week before still filling the air. Charlie would visit each station of the cross and ponder what it must have been like for the man on the cross to endure such a death. He would kneel in front of the Saint Joseph statue and evaluate his own actions from the week prior. He believed devoutly in Catholicism and tried to incorporate it very seriously into his daily life. He thought about how much he disappointed Rich by not attending his wedding to Darla because they were married in a Presbyterian Church. At the time, Charlie couldn't accept this, as he had been taught and believed that only a Catholic marriage was accepted in the eyes of God. He thought about how Rich forgave him for not standing as one of his ushers and how Rich never questioned Charlie's actions outside of that one time when the family moving van was getting ready to pull away.

Now the silence in the church was beginning to break as people began filing in. Charlie took his usual seat in the middle. He felt that sitting too far back was disrespectful of Christ and sitting too close to the altar was too conceited. He felt that whoever sat up front felt like they were "more Catholic" than everyone else, and he didn't want to be associated as such.

The middle of the church felt just right to him. An ordinary spot for ordinary people. There was the sound of quiet whispers and the soft thump of the kneelers coming down as the parishioners took their spots in their favorite pews. He closed his eyes to spend time in reflection but now was having difficulty concentrating as an unfamiliar sound entered the vestibule in the back of the church.

It sounded like a chain rustling. In addition to the rustling sound, he could hear a pitter-patter in conjunction with the noise of high-heeled shoes. It sounded like the pitter-patter and the high heels were walking in unison. He tried to remain focused in prayer but couldn't help but feel tempted to turn to look at what everyone else was looking at as well. Some of the members seemed uncomfortable. The quiet whispering became louder, and the chains and pitter-patter drew nearer. As he could no longer refrain from turning to look at what was occupying everyone else, he rested his chin on his left shoulder as he peeked behind him and there she was. Coming into vision…

It was like a fast-moving time suck into a tunnel. Like no one else was present around him. Charlie's eyes became locked onto this mesmerizing sight that had just walked through the doors.

Swiftly, she made a grand entrance. She entered through the back of the church. She was walking haphazardly, yet with purpose and poise at the same time. The woman had a dog by her side. She was grasping its harness, and the leash was wrapped around her wrist, as she and her dog walked down the middle church aisle. She was wearing a light-blue tropical silk suit with tan hose and cream-colored pump shoes that had sensible steady heels. Her pillow-top hat was covered with a cream-colored lace kerchief that ended just below her left eye. Her suit lapel had a small cluster of baby's breath mixed with carnations. She had bright pink lips and a touch of blush on her cheeks. Her eyes looked slanted. Or were they half closed? It was difficult to see, as the rest of her presence took Charlie's eyes away from that.

Charlie remembered looking at the show dog appearance of the Weimaraner that was leading the lady and thinking that the creature seemed to know exactly where it was going.

Charlie was sure he would have seen this couple in the past, having spent so much time in the church. It seemed as though all activity came to a halt now. Did it really? Or was it that all time stood still in Charlie Aldridge's world at the sight of this different woman in this different situation?

It became apparent that this was a blind girl as she held tightly onto the brown leather harness that completed the presence of her and the stately dog. What everyone else was looking upon as a pitiful sight, all Charlie could think about was not only how darling and brave she was, but that she had somehow been able to pull it off with class and sophistication. More than he had ever seen in any other woman. Even with the snobby and social-climbing behavior of the women in town, who competed with one another for who had the nicest home, the best dressed, best looking young children, and the finest drapes in their homes. They didn't hold a candle to her.

As the woman made her way to the pew just in front of Charlie, he involuntarily started toward her, but one of the other ushers beat him to it. The usher patted the dog on the head and took the woman's arm to assist her into the pew. The woman quickly pulled her arm away from the gentleman and scolded him.

"Sir, I am blind. I am not helpless! If I needed someone to put me in the pew, I would have asked. And I certainly would not have any need for my guide dog to assist me in finding my seat. Now if you would like to help me, please follow MY cues. Then ask if you can touch me. Then, and only then, please place my hand on the back of the pew so that I can get my bearings!"

As if she wasn't already speaking loudly enough, she then raised her voice and turned her head to address the rest of the parishioners.

"I am thankful for the thought. But since I have just moved here and will be frequenting this church, I would like to let it be known to the rest of the congregation, so that you are made aware, that it is not to be assumed that I need assistance finding my seat. In addition, my dog is not to be touched when she is in the harness, as she is working and is not a pet."

She certainly didn't care to whisper her admonishing words. It was obvious that she wanted everyone to hear her commands for respect, once and only once, which warranted a much louder tone than what was required in the House of God.

The usher blushed with embarrassment. Charlie couldn't help but chuckle to himself as the humiliated man was so taken aback. The man replied, "I apologize for the assumption, Miss. Please let us know if there is anything we can do for you."

She simply replied, "Thank you!"

The woman then commanded, "Tusi, forward!" She lifted the handle on the back of the harness and directed the dog as the pair slid in toward the center of the pew right in front of where Charlie was kneeling.

It didn't take Charlie long to discover that this beautiful young lady was none other than the little blind girl from his childhood. It was apparent right away. That hair and milky white skin. She had the same voice that he remembered. Only now, it was so mature and confident sounding. She even moved the same as he had remembered. The girl that he watched almost daily and only had a few encounters within his lifetime. However, in Charlie's mind, those encounters were among his most treasured memories.

He sat there, shaking his head, and gently whispered to himself, "Boy, oh boy!"

He smirked at the thought of that feisty young girl with the coarse, wavy brown hair, and pearl clip-on earrings with the matching pearl necklace. He put his kneeler, up slouched back into the pew, sighed, and was so relieved that he dodged that bullet and wasn't the one to be corrected by her.

Charlie immediately identified with the fight to be seen as someone to be heard, as he felt the same, all-too-familiar quest throughout his young life. In the same fashion as this lovely girl was unapologetically demanding of others.

He felt his face become flushed, hot red, and his palms were sweating. He could smell the faintness of her lavender-scented perfume. He watched her every magnificent move. The woman placed her kneeler down and pulled out her glistening, ruby-beaded rosary, and a big white paper book from her satchel. She lifted the face of the odd-looking, stretch-band gold watch on her left wrist and ran her pointer finger over the hands, clicked the face back down, and then opened the oversized white book with the only printed words being on the front cover in large black bold type, which read *The Daily Propers of the Roman Catholic Mass in Braille*. He watched as she turned the thick pages, which made a noise like a piece of cardboard hitting a surface. Her fingers ran across the raised dots on the front inside page with deliberate speed. She kissed the feet of Jesus on the silver-plated crucifix of her rosary.

She then grabbed the black cloth bookmark sticking out the bottom of the book, flipped to her page, and prepped for the day's reading. Charlie jolted himself out of the hypnotizing spell he was under as he knelt back down on the kneeler. As he put his head in his hands and bowed to ask for forgiveness for not being focused on church, he felt a warm, moist, light pressure against his thigh. Keeping his head bowed and looking down, he saw the dog's snout resting on his knee with her bright eyes staring up at him as if to ask for a pet on the head. He had forgotten all about this dog, as he was so focused on Alice. The dog wasn't making any of the usual dog noises and disappeared from sight, underneath the pew in front of him once they were seated. He stared back into the dog's eyes and thought that if he pet her, the spirited woman wouldn't know. Yet that wouldn't be respectful of her wishes, as the girl clearly had a path set for herself and a plan. It would be like robbing her of her convictions. Clearly a statement was desperately trying to be made, given her response to the usher's charitable effort just moments before. As difficult as it was to keep his hands away from the soft gray furry friend, he decided he would not give in to the dog's plea for attention. The dog's head remained still on Charlie's knee until the opening prayer, when all parishioners stood, and the kneelers went up. The dog then assumed the same position at every kneeling opportunity throughout the remainder of the Mass. The priest then announced that it was time for offering one another a sign of peace, which in the Catholic tradition meant shaking hands with your neighbor, looking them in the eye, and stating, "Peace be with you."

Charlie pondered what he should do in this situation. How could he get this lovely girl's attention in a way that she deemed respectful? He learned from his earlier observation that he dared not grab her hand. However, if he didn't include her in the ritual, it would also give her a feeling that she was different from everyone else, and clearly the woman would know that there had to be at least one person in her vicinity to offer peace to. He became nervous and cleared his throat. He stretched his neck to the right in a tick-like fashion as he always did when faced with an uncomfortable social interaction. Suddenly, as if God Himself staged the scene, the pretty woman turned, extended her arm, reached out her hand in his general direction, and stated, "Peace be with you."

He looked at her long white fingers. Her nails were shortly manicured and filed to meet with the tips of her fingers. She had a large, square golden ring with an amethyst on the middle finger of her outreached right hand. Just as the girl was dropping her hand, as there wasn't an apparent response to her gesture, Charlie grabbed the tips of her fingers as they fell and gave them a gentle caress with a hold longer than the usual time frame. He watched for her expression. A pleasantly surprised look came over her as her fingers moved into a firm grip, enveloping his fingers, and delivering a relatively strong handshake to Charlie. As the woman gently tried to break free of the grasp, he held on to the ends of her fingertips again and watched as her blank hazel eyes flew open wide. Her eyes were unfocused but seemed to be fixed on something out of the world as they knew it. Her pale cheeks were suddenly flushed pink. She ceased her pull and stood there, startled. She could sense that she was experiencing something out of the ordinary. She could tell that this person was not your run-of-the-mill man. Nor was he a "pity pusher." That was the name she'd made up to describe the people that were always feeling sorry for her and felt the need to take care of her whenever she was trying to accomplish even the simplest task. She was captivated by his touch. Could it be that for once, someone was actually showing the slightest bit of romance to a girl who believed herself unworthy of a man's pure love?

The moment of exchange became too much for her, as she was inexperienced and not at all ready for the one thing she longed for above all else. Everything she ever tried to do in her life was achievable, except for feeling attractive by another. For love. The one experience that she had accepted would never come for her. She knew she was beautiful, as everyone had told her so. And she was smart. She was an industrious and talented musician, dancer, and teacher. She could carry on a conversation on just about anything, as she spent most of her life with books and music. But a woman worthy of a true gentleman's touch? The thought was preposterous. And if so, there must be something wrong with the man that would want her. She paused, as she didn't want to let go of the rough fingertip pads that were holding on to hers. Then suddenly she pulled away swiftly and reset her hand at her side.

As the Mass continued, Charlie felt a sense of inclusion with the mystery couple, and he wore his wet, saliva-stained slacks with pride up through the Communion line like a medal of honor. He had an overwhelming invisible sense of connection to her and her companion. What would she have done if she knew her dog had tainted the theatrical staging of its role as a working dog by resting its head on Charlie's leg? Would she correct the sweet canine? He didn't think so. He knew in his heart that this was a good, loving woman standing in front of him. A woman who looked strong on the outside. But Charlie knew she had suffered and was forced by life's cruelties to make her respond with brat-like conduct to the charitable deeds exhibited by others. He saw straight through and remembered her as a little girl and figured she must have had some degree of sheltering. After all, someone must have helped her pick out her beautiful clothes, taught her how to apply her pink lipstick, and wear her hats so deliberately fashioned to mirror a young Jackie Kennedy. Someone must have told her how to stand upright with confidence and taught her how to tell people off whether they deserved it or not. Somebody taught her how to teach the ignorant, nonblind world about the rights of the unsighted and demand respect for this sector of people. Someone had to be at home waiting and worrying about her safe return from this big venture out to Sunday Mass on her own. *How did Alice wind up here?* he thought. He wondered what the chances were that the little blind girl from his childhood would be here right now. The one who gave him the pencil on that first day of school, whose yo-yo he placed back into her hand. The little girl who he taught to know her left hand from her right hand, and the one who he helped out of the rain that day and gave his handkerchief to. The chances that she would walk through that door with her guide dog, yet again, shot a lightning bolt through his heart.

Following the closing procession, Alice and her dog marched out in much the same way that they marched in. It made Charlie laugh out loud as he watched the stares and awkward door-holding from the others. Some of the most uncomfortable-looking people were the ones that were always so pompous-acting under normal circumstances. But Alice now had them squirming. They were rushing to do the right thing, but to get out of her way at the same time to protect their egos and gain social comfort. After all, since everyone was looking at this girl, it would mean that others were also looking at them, and how awkward a feeling that was. Not knowing what to say but following the manners that were taught to them to help those in need. No one really knew what to do with her. She appeared to be exasperated as she reached for the door to get her bearings to the outside. Only to find that it had already been opened by a well-meaning helper. Not being able to feel the door that would indicate that the steps were in front, she stumbled on the slate step, almost falling, but was able to catch her balance. He noticed that she was about to scold again, but he could tell that she just didn't have another confrontation in her that day. He thought that she was offering that one up to God, as she couldn't spend exhaustive moments of time teaching everyone to understand how to live in a blind person's world. They never took her seriously anyway. They would never be able to get past their own ideas of pity and sadness for her, which showed the outright disrespect for her, and she would probably have to tell them again next Sunday all over again anyway.

He had to see where she was going now. Charlie stayed far behind her as he followed her up Landon Avenue. What was she going to do when she got out to busy Broad Street? Surely her ride was just late and would be pulling up anytime to pick her up. Minutes passed as she and her companion were steadfast on their journey to the end of the road. Still, he watched. The couple stopped like soldiers would at the sound of a halt, as the pair waited at the corner. With head bent and ear tilted, the sound of the tires on the gravel dissipated.

"Tusi, forward!" the woman said. They crossed the street. Once up on the curb, she put her right arm out in front of her, felt for the post of the bus stop shelter, and took a place under the bus depot sign as if she and the dog had done it in their sleep a million times before.

"Boy, oh boy. No fear," Charlie said to himself. This woman would risk her life in such a fashion just to cross the road. What else could she do on a daily basis—that the sighted would think nothing of—that would be absolutely life-threatening to someone like her? She was still the most amazing thing he had ever seen. He stood at the corner watching. He leaned against the telephone pole and crossed his right ankle over the left. The bus headed down North Broad Street. It came to a halt for several minutes. Alice and Tusi climbed up the steps, and she handed the driver her money for the ride. Charlie could see her silhouette inside the bus as she clumsily swayed from side to side, felt the backs of the seats, and walked down the aisle as the bus jolted and shook as it went on its way.

Charlie did not share the story about what he saw that day with his family when he made his way back home. It was just like him to keep anything personal to himself. He would talk incessantly about trivial, nonsensical things, such as the guy up the road who owned Turner's Hardware and how he made keys in assorted colors and sizes for every single type of door. Mundane as his stories were, they weren't always met with sincere appreciation for what he was telling others. This woman and her pretty pet were worthy of a response better than "That's nice, Charlie," which was his family's usual reaction to his fact-filled stories that were of little significance to them.

They would have had to see her magnificence for themselves anyway, in order to really appreciate her.

He didn't know why, but he just didn't want them to know about her. It was his secret encounter. She was so different. So exciting. He didn't feel sorry for her at all. He appreciated her fighting will. It was exhilarating to watch her take the role of victimization and kick it in the teeth. He thought about where she might be going and wondered if she lived with others that were just like her. He wondered if anyone else had captured the wonder of this tiny woman with the pink lips. He wondered if she would tell someone else off today, or if she'd had just enough conflict to put her pride to rest until tomorrow. He thought about who she might be going home to, what she would have for dinner, and who would make it for her. He had so many questions about her. She had grown into a most exquisite young lady. He wondered if another man had ever held onto her thin, soft fingertips. Had anyone had a "love at first touch" encounter as opposed to a "love at first sight" encounter with her? He couldn't wait until next Sunday when he might see her again. He decided he would sit behind her at Mass, and this time maybe he would reach out to her first and not only touch her fingertips but envelope her soft, smooth hand with his callous-ridden palm that had a bruised thumbnail on his finger just waiting to fall off. He watched as she left mass again the following Sunday.

Although clearly the girl didn't need or want anyone's help, he had to be sure she was okay until she got to her destination. After Alice boarded this time, he ran over to the bus as it pulled down the road and banged on the doors, giving the driver no choice but to stop and allow Charlie to hop on. The bus made its way all the way down Broad Street into Riverdale. It stopped at the corner of Washington and Arch Streets. She seemed to know exactly when to stand up but waited for the bus driver to announce the stop. She and her companion exited the bus. She valiantly walked with her head held high all the way down Washington Street and turned right off the main road. She and the four-legged companion stood on the corner, and once again she turned and bent her ear to listen for all oncoming traffic. When all was silent, the pair crossed the street. He thought that surely someone must be coming to get her and take her home this time. Wherever home was. Charlie had taken a middle aisle seat. He didn't want the window seat because he wasn't sure which way she would go after getting off the bus and wanted to be able to see everything she would do following her descent from the bus. The girl and her companion turned left onto the third walkway from the corner up to the door of a row-house style apartment building. She reached effortlessly into her clutch bag's front pocket. She took out a key and, without fumbling or feeling around, unlocked the door. The little couple entered, and the door closed behind them. Charlie sat back in his seat once they were out of sight. He thought about her and imagined what she would be doing now. He was sure it had to be something else very amazing, but he hadn't a clue. He continued riding in the opposite direction of his hometown. He watched out the window, daydreaming and looking at the trees that lined the roads as he watched people walking along the tracks, carrying their Sunday groceries, and going on family walks. He watched as lovers held hands on a stroll. The sun was shining so brightly, and he was taking everything on the bus ride in as if on a sightseeing tour throughout a foreign country. Once they arrived at the next township, he thought he'd better exit the bus and grab another one back home in the other direction to get back for Sunday dinner. He didn't want to disappoint Mother, and it would be unusual if he wasn't home in time. Then she would start asking questions that he wasn't prepared to answer about his whereabouts. Besides, he knew how it would appear and sound if anyone knew he followed a blind girl all the way home.

Charlie, Delilah, and Mother sat around the tiny table with silver fold-up legs as Mother shook open the lace tablecloth to prepare for dinner. She made Charlie's favorite hot dog and baked bean casserole. They buttered their rolls with the soft butter that Mother had left out on the counter for the past hour.

Suddenly the phone rang. It was Rich. He had received his pardon from the Navy and was coming home. Gertie was so happy to hear his voice and to know that she would see her handsome, strong son again. It was wonderful news. Rich told his mom that he couldn't stay on the phone for long, as he was only permitted two minutes to speak. As she hung up the phone, she paused and suddenly an expression of great concern grew across her face. It was as if she was thinking about something that had never occurred to her in the past. Mother didn't speak throughout the remainder of the meal, finished her plate, cleared the dishes, and went into the living room where she kept the money files. She began looking through the pages, making some addition and subtraction formulas. Finally, she put the book down and hung her head as if she were hopeless.

"What's wrong, Mother?" Charlie said. "Aren't you happy that Rich is coming home?"

"Of course," said Gertie. His mother did not wish to discuss further, but Charlie probed her. He couldn't help but think that she had done something that she didn't want Rich to know about and that had more than likely involved Rich's money. His mother took after her father. She was a dreamer, and she took risks. Being enamored by the racetrack was a very dangerous thing for a woman who rarely had a penny to her name. It turned out that she had cleared Rich's bank account and lost all his money from betting on the horses. Charlie watched as she cried, her head in her hands. His heart melted for his sweet, irresponsible mom. As he stood in the doorway, he thought of how he had twice that much in his savings and no sooner had disappeared from the house.

Mother flopped down on the couch, lit up a smoke, and dozed off as she always did when there was too much to deal with. Charlie knew his mother spent much of her time thinking back to her flapper days and remembering her happy husband before the war. Before he lost the farm to his older brother. She'd felt sad that her husband was the oldest in his family and assumed that he was the rightful heir to the farm. However, after going away to war, his younger brother, who had been working the farm all along, felt that *he* should be the rightful heir. Charlie's father had almost lost his life in the fight with his brother, as the bet was that whoever won the battle would be granted the land. Charlie's father lost the fight fair and square, as his mighty younger brother was bigger and stronger than he was. However, not before the two of them almost died in the process.

His father then packed up Gertie and young Gertie and moved to Pennsylvania from Maryland. Her husband had big dreams. He failed at every business venture he ever had. Some were great ideas and did very well at first. Such as the parking lot business in Philadelphia and the general store and gas station. Maybe they would have worked out if he hadn't held on to so much resentment about losing the farm and if he hadn't let the drinking ruin everything.

Later that day Gertie was suddenly awakened by Rich as he walked through the front door. He was whistling Dixie as he threw his things down, picked up Mother, and swung her around.

"Woo-wee!" he said. "I sure am happy to be home, Mother. Did I surprise you by coming home early? I'm taking you to Gimbels and buying you a new dress and anything you want!" he said.

"But, but, but…," she started.

Just as she was about to confess her misdeeds to her jolly but fiercely strapping son, he waved his money and fanned it out to show her all that he had collected from his bank account. She stood there in awe, shocked at what she was seeing. How did he have the money? She had taken it all and lost it on the horses. What could have happened? Oh well, at least he wouldn't be mad, and she wouldn't have to fess up to what she did. Whatever happened, she was thanking her lucky stars. Mother walked into the bathroom, fell to her knees, and thanked Jesus for saving the day. Did she end up surmising that it was Charlie who had set things right? Of course. However, it was never talked about. The next day at dinnertime, Mother stared into Charlie's eyes, trying to find some clue that would confirm it was him who had put the money in the bank. He just sat, expressionless, not making eye contact with her so as not to give himself away. Mother knew as well that Charlie would be upset if it was confirmed that he had put the money in Rich's account, as her boy took considerable pride in doing honorable deeds and not getting credit for them.

The days passed slowly until the next Sunday came around. Charlie reminded himself that he must not fantasize about seeing the beautiful girl while at Mass. He prayed to stop thinking of her and to just focus on work and reserve Sunday for prayer. But his mind kept creeping back to her. He wondered where she went Monday through Saturday. Did she have a mate that was just like her? But then why was she alone that day? It didn't add up. She probably scared away every guy that ever approached her if she talked to them the way she talked to poor Mr. Wilson who tried to help her at Mass that Sunday when she first stormed through the doors and down the aisle. Charlie understood that for him and his odd ways, the ladies wouldn't give him many chances. He was strikingly handsome for sure. But his awkward shyness, neck tick, and lack of education didn't exactly make him a customary catch for the ladies. Not that he really cared much. He marched to the beat of his own drum and liked it that way. He didn't long to be with those type of women anyway. Insomuch as it would appear that he wouldn't be worthy of them, they really weren't worthy of him. And he knew it.

That blind girl, though. She was amazing. He felt he was definitely not worthy of her but had to know her.

Sunday after Sunday, he would see her, sit near enough to shake her hand at Communion, but couldn't seem to bring himself to say or do anything more.

She wasn't there on Christmas Day. He thought that must mean that her family didn't live nearby. Then she was back again right after the New Year.

All throughout the season of Lent, there was Alice and Tusi. Front and center.

He realized a year had passed and he didn't know any more about this mysterious girl than he did on the first Sunday that she walked through those doors and stole his heart again. He sat close to her every chance he got. He would jump ahead to fold up kneelers and move missalettes out of her way to prepare a grand passage as she entered the pews and walked to Communion. He wasn't going to let her look clumsy or foolish. People noticed and smiled at one another as they watched him silently look out for the girl and help her shine at Sunday Mass. It would be dreadful for her if she tripped or fell, as she knew everyone was watching and needed to always put on her performance in public. Following the collection, Charlie emptied his basket in the main drop. As he turned around, the priest was standing behind him. He was looking at Charlie with a stern yet friendly expression.

"Son, do you know what you're asking to get yourself involved in with that young girl?" said the priest.

He looked straight into Charlie's eyes, with his arms crossed and his pointer finger inconspicuously curled up, then extended it out in Alice's direction. He knew Charlie quite well and appreciated his fine character. Charlie was always ready to help fix a broken pipe, clean up the pews, and paint when needed. He and a group of twenty-five other parishioners did finish the roof just the previous summer, and Father McHenry was very appreciative of his help.

Charlie just shrugged his shoulders and said, "I don't know what you mean," with a quick and nervous half-laugh.

Father walked away shaking his head. "Just don't get in over your head, son," he said with his back turned toward Charlie.

Just then, Charlie spotted Jean Collins talking to Alice in the back of the church. He knew Jean from the socials held for the church volunteers. He didn't frequent them much but enjoyed the

Sunday breakfasts after Mass held by the Knights of Columbus, and he knew that Jean was always a nice lady. She had five children, and her husband was away in the military. The kids were a little much for her to handle on her own. He had just read that one of her children was arrested for public misconduct. Everyone in the parish knew about it, but no one said anything because she was such a nice person. Besides, everyone knew how difficult it must be for a woman to handle five growing kids with no father to look after them.

When Easter Sunday came and went again, Charlie decided to attend the church volunteer appreciation pig roast. For the most part, even though the girl of his dreams never seemed to socialize at any of those things, he thought just maybe someone might know something about her or maybe even bring her there. From across the room in the church basement, he saw Mrs. Collins again. He thought to himself that he would just go right up to her and ask her about the young blind girl. He would never have been able to say the words if it weren't for the two cold mugs of beer that he downed on that unseasonably hot evening. After telling Jean about his desire to know more about the blind girl with the guide dog, she took his shoulders and turned him in the direction of the table where Alice was sitting. Her seat was hidden behind the pillar in the basement, so he hadn't seen her previously. She was sitting all alone at a table for eight, as everyone else was up and dancing.

"You wait right here," said Mrs. Collins.

He was surprised that she was so willing and anxious to help him. Alice looked bored and sad, tapping her foot to the big band music that was playing. Mrs. Collins walked over to her first, sat down, and vouched for Charlie. She told Alice about the fine young gentleman who attended daily Mass and had expressed an interest in knowing her. She described him physically to her and told her how handsome he was as well. Mrs. Collins asked if it would be okay if he came over to talk with her. An expression of pure glee mixed with terror ran across Alice's face. Alice had practiced all her life trying not to let her emotions be revealed in her facial reactions, but this proved to be futile, as most would be able to practice this in a mirror in order to master it. However, she tried her best to remain expressionless, even though she couldn't help herself by appearing fearful.

Charlie hoped that Mrs. Collins wouldn't let on that he had been watching Alice at Sunday Mass for almost a year now. After all, that would scare a sighted person away, let alone a girl who hadn't had the opportunity to acknowledge his stares. Mrs. Collins wanted nothing more than to play matchmaker with the two of them and took the task on personally. She was very fond of Charlie and knew he was different too. A little odd, but just as lovely as Alice was.

When Alice first heard that this man wanted to court her, she couldn't help but feel a little like her personal space was being invaded. Her initial reaction was to think that he was probably just someone else who felt sorry for her and wanted to help her. This always filled her with rage, as she was now almost brain-washed into believing that everyone felt pity for her and did not understand blind independence. Little did she know that the show of independence she so magnificently displayed was exactly what attracted this young fellow to her. She half-heartedly agreed on the condition that Mrs. Collins would watch them and not let her remain in his company for too long. Mrs. Collins gleefully walked back over to tell Charlie that he could talk to her, but Charlie had already left. He was still too nervous to approach the girl. Besides, there were too many people around that would watch them and make the whole situation completely uncomfortable. He decided that their formal meeting should wait for a better time.

Alice arrived back home to her one-bedroom apartment. After getting changed, brushing her teeth, and opening up her braille edition of Shakespeare's *The Merchant of Venice,* her mind was now wandering. She was in her twenties and had only one relationship with a man, if you could call it that.

She reflected back on Alan Dooley. He was a well-educated blind man. A psychiatrist. To Alice, at first, their relationship was very exciting. They shared their knowledge about literature and the arts and their mutual love for the great thespian writers. He was the staple of what a successful blind person represented. So, she thought.

Initially she felt that they would have made a wonderful couple. They would have shown the world what blind people could do and how to treat blind people. He was the first man, since she had become a young adult, who had shown any kind of love interest in her. He was also the first man that she would ever date.

Not counting of course, the college prom, when Marnie had arranged a date with a handsome sighted medical student to take Alice to the dance. Alice was so excited. She was briefly under the impression that the young medical student had taken an interest in her, and oh, how she'd cried when he never called her after that night. And how she found out later that her sister had pretty much talked him into taking her.

Anyway, she thought back to how Alan was the type of man that, if she ended up with anyone, he was what she imaged it would be.

He enjoyed the 1940s sarcasm and banter that successful young people used to appear self-confident and witty. Had it not been for that night, they may have continued their relationship. Alice had expected that soon there would be talk of marriage.

The memory of how they stood in his one-bedroom apartment. How she got there she couldn't quite remember. Dinner was amazing. They had braised pork, sauerkraut, cauliflower, and rice pudding. Frank Sinatra was on the record player. The night was perfect. She was feeling nervous yet so excited to be in a man's arms. She'd been in his arms before, sure. But not like this. This felt more intense. It was private and romantic. She could feel Alan's perspiration on his back through his shirt, as he was apparently just as nervous as she was. He sang to her the song *"Stardust"*: "And now the purple dust of twilight time."

She flashed back at how it had only been about seven weeks since they had met at the Seeing Eye when they were both new students training with their first seeing eye dogs. He seemed to have everything that she grew up wanting and fighting to have for herself. She wondered if he was handsome. She thought he probably was because he seemed so sure of himself. Yet a little desperate at the same time. Was he desperate for love? Was he desperate for sex? She didn't know. He wouldn't want to have sex yet. Would he? He said he was Catholic.

No, this dancing and necking is still innocent, she thought.

She would never describe herself as desperate for love. Yet when she thought about it, she did spend an exorbitant amount of time thinking about, if given the opportunity, who she would marry, what kind of wife she would be, her future children, and if they would have proper names. Their father would be someone highly intelligent and well educated. And, if blind, well, that would be an added bonus in her mind. It would be exhilarating to show how they got along being blind and raising their sighted, well-rounded, well-mannered children.

They would have a little girl or two. Or maybe a boy or two. Although she didn't know much at all about boys. They would learn to play piano, read and write braille, dance, sing...

Well maybe she was a little more desperate than she realized. Longing for a more conventional marriage and family than she had thought.

As Alice and Alan progressed through the evening and the bottle of Cabernet emptied, the kissing became more intense. No one had ever kissed her neck and ran their hand across her figure before. Never, for a girl in her twenties, did she feel the touch of a man like this. This feeling was foreign. She felt herself beginning to rationalize how it could be that she was still in this man's apartment. She wasn't a baby anymore. She still despised her family's smothering. If her mom only knew what she was doing right now, she would be beside herself. Possibly even faint. Or, even worse, have a real heart attack. None of it mattered in that moment. And even more so, the thought that she was resisting their hold on her was exhilarating. As they danced, doing their box step, and turning with each set, her body was suddenly stopped by a hard surface pushing up against her right calf. She gently moved her foot to test if there was an opening under the solid surface. Sure enough, *this is a bed,* she thought.

In an instant, she felt panicked. She wasn't ready for this. The couple fell onto the bedspread. He swiftly unzipped her yellow polyester dress. Things were moving much too quickly now. She began to feel frightened. Suddenly disappointing her mother and Marnie wasn't so funny anymore. God was watching her. She had to get out of there. This wasn't right.

She couldn't... She wouldn't... She was failing the test of strength horribly. And with one swift holler, she belted out, "No! Stop! I can't! I have to leave! I shouldn't be here! My cab! Let go of me!"

Alice pushed Alan away. She fumbled for her shoes. Surprisingly, it didn't take long at all to find them. She grabbed her bag and cane, which she remembered leaving by the door as she didn't have her guide dog with her that evening. She quickly unraveled the tie to the cane and the parted sticks fell quickly into place as she clicked the cane back and forth down the hallway, tears streaming down her face.

Alan did not follow her. He did not say or do anything. Would he at least holler out to her that he was sorry and that he didn't know what had come over him? But nothing. Was he ashamed? Angry? She didn't care. She was too emotionally fragile to have let that happen. And oh, if only he had asked her to marry him and would wait for the wedding night. A flurry of thoughts and emotions filled her little mind. As she made her way to the elevator and felt the braille numbers on the wall, finally finding the ground floor button, she fell back against the wall inside of the elevator. Still with tears streaming, she thought again that lasting love would not happen for her. Why did she get her hopes up and actually think that true, respectful love would come her way?

"Are you kidding me?" she said to herself. When she got to the door and exited the high-rise apartment, she hollered out, "Taxi!"

"Right here, Miss," said the door attendant as he opened up the door of a taxi. Alice took his arm as they walked to the cab, and he placed her hand on the outside of the door so that she could find her way to the seat. And off she went.

Before she knew it, she was back at her apartment. She was exhausted. She wanted to call Marnie or her mother. She just couldn't do it. If she could even work up the gumption to tell Marnie, her sister would make some sarcastic joke, making Alice regret the fact that she ever said anything at all. What's worse was that her sister wouldn't even have stood for having the knowledge of such a thing. Her mother would tell her what a sin it was to have even entered the man's apartment. She would be instructed to go to confession immediately and atone for her sins. Alice already knew this. It was her intention to see Father McHenry on Saturday. She would be the first penitent at 4:00 p.m. sharp. That night, Alice's hands started wringing. She scratched them sore. She felt so terrible about her behavior with the young suitor that she knew she must repent. She grabbed her rosary off the bedpost. Before she knew it, she had recited fifty decades. Two hours had passed as if it were twenty minutes. Her eyes danced as if she was actually searching for her sight. She was terrified. And then the voices started. She felt the devil was talking to her. The voices became increasingly sinister. She pictured herself burning and what hell must feel like. She pictured faces of monsters. But then, what did monsters really even look like? Sometimes she felt like people thought that she herself must look like a monster. It was all relative anyway. She couldn't make it stop. Eventually she cried herself to sleep as she always did when problems got the better of her. She wasn't going to think about it anymore. She would repent and stay with the life she knew. Being a good Catholic and turning her obsessions back to showing the world what the blind could do best and breaking the cycle of prejudice. That was where her purpose was, after all. She would decide, once again, that it was not in God's plan for her to be a wife and mother. Even though that was what she truly longed for the most.

From that day on, she never heard from Alan Dooley again. From time to time, she would wonder if he thought about her, and she would think back to the romantic way things first felt when they met at the seeing eye. She wished it could have been different and worked out in the storybook fashion that she had painted in her mind. Nevertheless, she had made her decision. She was strong, independent, and focused. There was no turning back now.

She did not expect, however, for Charlie to come back into her life.

CHAPTER 13

Charlie did like the pretty ladies. He was nervous around women and insecure in many ways, but confident in others. He didn't know the first thing about flirting or trying to act suave or macho. Even if he did, he wouldn't want to act that way. Most women found him very handsome, but whenever there was a possibility that one might be interested, he seemed to subconsciously do or say a little something shocking to make them lose interest. Such as wipe his nose with his fingers or talk about how funny it was that his sister's kid threw up on him. And because the only type of women he was attracted to were sophisticated types, they quickly turned their noses up at this gentleman. Alice would one day coin a pet reference for him, which he seemed to hold with reverence. He thoroughly enjoyed his nickname because he knew it was true. She would call him her "diamond in the rough."

Charlie decided that he would ask Mrs. Collins to arrange a private meeting with Alice. This way there wouldn't be any onlookers and it would make it a much more comfortable situation for them both. Initially Alice denied his request. But after some persistence from Charlie and Mrs. Collins, she finally agreed to a date. He also decided that he would wait for the right time to let Alice know that he was the boy who had those few encounters with her as a child. Mrs. Collins knew nothing of this history either.

After all, Mrs. Collins vouched for what a good man he was. She told Alice of his character, the way he cared for his mother, and the volunteer work he did at the church. Alice did want to know about his education, and it did not sit well with her that he had not been motivated to seek out a college degree. Maybe she could convince him to go to college if their relationship took off. However, she was getting ahead of herself. She hadn't even spoken with him yet. Nevertheless, she eventually decided to give him a chance.

Since there was great disappointment in the man that she thought would have been the perfect match, perhaps she should go a different avenue this time.

Charlie drove a 1939 Chevy pickup truck, which he felt did not seem at all appropriate for a first date with this classy lady and assumed, if all went well, he would be driving her home. Not even thinking about the fact that she wouldn't know it was a truck or what it looked like, except that she would have to step up into the cab. Besides, he wasn't underestimating her intuition about things. He smirked and thought to himself that she could probably sense much more than a "normal-sighted" person did anyway. Therefore, he borrowed his mother's somewhat newer Cadillac. That car also wasn't in the greatest shape, but it was much better than his pickup truck.

Alice was reluctant to meet with him privately. So, the couple decided that an appropriate first date would be to go to the Fat Tuesday dinner at church to start off the Lenten feast and sacrifice. Charlie really didn't like this idea because he would have to deal with the parishioners' nosiness and stares and gossip. He eventually decided that this time, he would not allow this to scare him away and he compromised.

Charlie arrived at the church cafeteria long before Alice. When she walked in, she helped herself to a seat closest to the door and sat down. Suddenly, Charlie wasn't apprehensive at all and had no problem approaching her this time. Probably because he was so tired of waiting and watching without acting.

Charlie walked up to where she was sitting, introduced himself to her, and took a seat beside her at the round table. By now, most of the regular parishioners knew of Charlie's romantic feelings for Alice, and instead of reacting the way Charlie had imagined, they steered clear of the couple, giving them their privacy leaving Charlie and Alice alone at the big table set for eight.

Charlie and Alice both understood the significance of the feast, and the religion was, of course, their common ground. It was awkward at first. Charlie kept clearing his throat in a tick-like manner, trying to put his words together eloquently so as to impress her. Alice could sense his nervousness. She knew the feeling all too well, but she had grown so tired of not speaking up when she wanted to and subsequently missing out on opportunities. She would not allow her insecurities to control her when conversing with others.

"So, Charlie," Alice said. "What made you want to go on a date with me?"

He blushed and would have stuttered if any noise had come out of his mouth. He was shocked at the question. After a moment, Charlie suddenly gained an unusual amount of confidence and responded back, just as shockingly, toward Alice.

"Well, when you walked into the church that first Sunday last year and told Mr. Wilson not to touch you or your dog without asking, I just knew I had to meet you."

Charlie couldn't believe what just came so deliberately out of his mouth.

That was all Alice needed to hear and suddenly, boom! She answered right back.

"Aha! I don't even remember that particular day because it seems I'm always having to remind everyone everywhere I go.

People grab me like they think they are helping," she said. "I want to say to them, 'Would you like it if I just came up to you and grabbed you?'"

They both laughed at this. And that was all it took to spark a most comfortable conversation.

They talked for hours. Or rather, she did most of the talking and he listened. She told him how she left her overbearing home to go to Northern Pennsylvania to instruct blind children and then moved to her apartment here in New Jersey. How she traveled with a private driver, paid for by the state of New Jersey. She told him how she now advanced all over the state and went out to children's homes. He learned about Davey Riley, Alice's first student. He was blind and deaf. She talked about how she remembered being so nervous as she arrived at his home on her first day of work. She didn't have a driver at that time and had to take public transportation to the children's homes. The bus often dropped her at the nearest crosswalk to her destination. She would simply step off the bus and head in the direction to where she thought she should go, listening for people to come by and then asking them if they could direct her to the appropriate address. Admittedly, she would accept the occasional ride or walk to the residence, even though she hated to concede her need for help. She went on to describe how she climbed the rickety steps of Davey's home on her first day of his lessons. How she felt the wobbly handrail and could hear dogs barking, coming from the side of the house. She didn't have a dog guide at the time and would use her cane to guide her. Davey's mother opened the door and was truly kind and gracious. Her name was Helen. Alice told Charlie how she first interviewed Helen before meeting with Davey to see what kind of life he lived. His mother proudly reported how she did everything for Davey. From preparing all his meals to literally feeding her ten-year-old boy, bathing him, and dressing him. It was a dreadful reminder of

Alice's own childhood. She reminded herself that Helen thought she was doing the right thing by meeting all of her son's needs and certainly not intending to keep him from growing. Alice tried her hardest to be professional and not let her emotions show. But she knew from past experiences that her expressions were a looking glass into her feelings far too often. However, she was practicing making a stone-cold expression and felt that she was getting better at mastering it. She quickly reminded herself that it was her job to teach the child, but the education really needed to start with the family. She knew if she came on too strongly with Davey's mother, she may never even get to meet the child. Then she would never be able to help him become an independent member of society. Finally, she went on to describe to Charlie how she fixed her composure and completed her interview, trying to be as unbiased as possible toward the well-meaning mother.

As Charlie listened, he watched her every move. From the way she reached out in front of her plate to grab the water glass, how she picked up her fork and knife, to how she cut the pork into tiny, bite-size pieces. She was doing it all so effortlessly. Not at all like anyone would imagine a blind person sharing a meal with someone would behave.

At that moment, all the memories of the blind school and meeting Alice and watching her over those years came rushing back. He had forgotten that Alice didn't know who he was and that it was he who had encountered her as a child. Would she even remember? He decided he should tell her now because if too much time went by, she might find him incredibly creepy. Also, he knew how she responded to him as a young boy, which he felt was quite favorable and might add to her comfort level.

Mrs Collins had filled in Charlie and Alice about each other prior to their date. However, they knew little else about one another up to this point.

As if it were the perfect setup for him to introduce their history, Alice took a sip of her water and placed the glass down on the table.

She then said so matter-of-factly, "I knew a boy named Charlie when I was a young girl. Of course, I didn't know him well. I think he worked at my blind school or possibly was a student. I never really had a chance to find out why he was there. It seemed like he came along when I was in trouble or in need of assistance. Then it seemed like he disappeared because I never saw him again after the seventh grade. I wondered over the years whatever became of him."

Charlie couldn't believe that she just said that. It was so co-incidental.

Charlie did not know how to respond and prayed to himself that he would say or do the right thing so as not to scare her off.

Charlie then took Alice's hands in his. He opened up her left hand and made the "L" shape with her thumb and pointer finger.

Alice was so shocked at first that she yanked her hand back. Then she said, "Are you that Charlie?"

Charlie responded, "Yes! I am that Charlie. I moved to New Jersey as a teenager. I did work at that blind school with my brothers. And I often wondered whatever happened to you. Until that day in church when you came walking through the doors. I almost immediately recognized you and thought that fate had brought us together once again."

Charlie went on to tell her about their very first encounter taking place in first grade. Alice had no idea that he was the little boy that sat next to her that she handed a pencil to. She remembered the day so clearly. She told him that her heart was breaking while he stood in front of the class unable to form his words and speak in appropriate sentences. She remembered him running through the doors, and she cried for him that day. She also didn't know that he was the boy in the doctor's office who picked up her yo-yo and placed it into her hand. He told her all about his speech problem as a little boy and the arrangement following his surgery, how he and his brothers repaid their debt by working at the blind school. He told her that the reason he left the school so abruptly was because he and his brothers were asked to leave following an incident at the school. He told her how a new principal, a man, was hired. Charlie saw him peeking through a hole in the girl's bathroom while they showered. Charlie had accidentally stumbled upon him when he had forgotten that he left the janitor's case on the radiator in the main office and ran back up to get it. As he turned the corner, he saw the principal peeking through the hole in the wall. Charlie knew it was the girl's bathroom, and he knew what the man was doing. He ran as fast as he could to Sister Gwendolyn's office and told her that the principal had taken ill and that she must go right away. He told her she would need the help of two orderlies and Father Giles. Naturally, when they all came bursting through the door to help, the principal was discovered and with that many people as witnesses, there would be no way the headmaster could get away with it. Charlie couldn't resist attacking the man and started kicking him repeatedly in a rageful fit. He had to be pulled off him, and everyone felt it was best that the boys no longer work at the facility. Charlie and his brothers left the school not long after the incident. The family moved to New Jersey, and he never thought he would see Alice again.

As they sat at the table following the Fat Tuesday dinner, it was now time for the chocolate parfait and decaf coffee. He watched her effortlessly unsnap the clutch of her little black purse and reach in to grab a tissue. It brought him back to the first day of school when she was a little girl when she reached into her bag and handed him the pencil. The girl with the beautiful hazel eyes. The same hand that he held that day on the bleachers and the same hand he held on to and offered the sign of peace at Mass that Sunday last April. It was always her. It came rushing over him like a tidal wave. He never forgot about their encounters but had buried them away until now.

Alice replied, "I remember our meetings all so well. My brother gave me that yo-yo. That time you helped me when I was locked out in the cold rain, I felt so foolish for acting like such a scared little baby."

Just then her expression changed. "I never saw you again after that," she said. Her eyes welled up at this.

"And here we are!" Charlie exclaimed.

They sat quietly for a moment as he took her hand again. She squeezed his hand back. It was now becoming so comfortable. So relaxed. So surreal. He wiped her tear with his handkerchief. Suddenly they were both jarred by the microphone sound as the metal hit the stand, making a horrible ear-piercing noise!

Sister Margaret announced to all in the cafeteria, "Okay, folks! Thank you everyone for your contributions to the Fat Tuesday dinner. But now it is time for cleanup."

Alice stood up and started helping by pulling the trash can around to each table, gathering up the tablecloths, and huddling the used plastic cups, plates, forks, and knives into a giant ball and throwing them in the trash. Charlie followed behind her, folding each table and chairs, gathering them up against the wall until the room was cleared. He helped Alice with her jacket and the two made their way back to Mother's car that he borrowed for the date. On the way back home, they continued on with their conversation. They told each other all about their families and growing up. They compared stories about the blind school. She told him how she lost her sight by falling from the swing and hitting her head. She told him how this had happened only a few weeks after that first day of school when Charlie was humiliated in class.

He told her all about his operation and how he learned to talk in such a way that people could understand him for the first time ever when he was just shy of his seventh birthday. Alice allowed Charlie to drop her off at her apartment. As they sat in the car outside her place, he simply asked her what she would prefer in terms of walking her to the door. Alice turned toward him and said, "It would be nice if I took your arm, and you walked me to my door."

Charlie did just that. They said their goodbyes and Alice pulled out a pre-typed small piece of paper with her phone number on it and handed it to Charlie. As Alice put her key in the door, Charlie watched it close and heard the lock secure.

He slipped the number into his wallet. He placed it right in front of the cash that he had lined up so perfectly in the order of one-dollar, five-dollar, and ten-dollar bills. All the faces were front-ward. He would use his hands to perfectly iron out any wrinkles in the bills prior to placing them in his wallet. This was Charlie's way of showing appreciation for every dollar that he had and treating his hard-earned money respectfully.

Charlie and Alice would see each other two to three times a week after that. Sometimes they would just go on long walks, and other times they would go for drives in his car. They would get ice cream and walk along the boardwalk at the seashore. Although he loved country music, Charlie appreciated Alice's classical music as well as the popular artists of the day. They both enjoyed listening to Perry Como, Dean Martin, Tony Bennett, and Andy Williams. And, of course, Frank! Charlie knew Alice loved to dance. And though not a dancer himself, he took to learning with her as his teacher since he knew this would make her feel respected and important. After all, dance was something that sight really wasn't needed for, especially if you had a partner. Also, this could be his way of being close to her without coming on too strong or physically scaring her. Alice graciously and excitedly accepted the invitation to teach him to dance. They learned to move their bodies in unison to the waltz and the foxtrot. They even mastered the jitterbug. She was a moderately good dancer, but her body was somewhat stiff, and she never allowed herself to be in a position of pressing up against him, so as not to give him the wrong idea. Alice was very nervous around any man. Charlie knew this about her but got so excited every time he got the chance to be with her and go dancing.

Charlie was not the man that she expected to be with. He wasn't blind. He wasn't professional. But he was good, loving, caring, and responsible. And she found herself feeling safe, happy, and calm when she was with him.

It was so frustrating that, quite frankly, no one in the outside world really cared about what she was trying to prove and took pity on her no matter how hard she tried to make others feel differently. Charlie used to think to himself that it was a good thing that she couldn't see others' faces when they were not looking at her in awe the way that she longed to be looked at. He was glad that she couldn't see the people gazing at her with such empathy.

At the same time, he felt sad that she couldn't see him and the way that he did look at her with a purely mesmerizing adoration, and that she might never appreciate his intense love for her.

Charlie told her how unfortunate it was that he would be leaving for the Navy in the next several weeks. He didn't set out to join the Navy originally but had tried to be a state trooper and was not tall enough. So, when he thought about the next best way to live a life of service, the Navy appeared to be a good idea. At first, he applied to be in the submarines but failed the physical due to his childhood operation and his throat scar tissue. The physician feared that it might open up under the pressure. So, the regular Navy was the next best choice. After all, it was peacetime, and there would be some potential opportunities should he decide that he wanted to make a military career of it. Besides, Mother had squandered all his brother's money, so somebody needed to help her out financially. He would arrange for his brother Rich to hold on to his money and give it to Mother as needed to avoid another situation like what happened with his brother's money. Rich never knew that their mother squandered all his savings, and Charlie preferred that it stayed that way.

Upon hearing this news, Alice was disappointed and sat quietly for a moment. She felt sad and happy at the same time. At first, she thought to herself, *Well of course I have met this wonderful person, and of course now he is going away. Just like that.*

Then again, her worries about his career choice and lack of education were now changing, as well as her opinion about this gentleman's life choices. It made her feel happy that he would want to branch out and explore the world. Besides, this would give her time to work on her teaching career. She was also in her late twenties and there was still time to do so much. They saw each other almost every day for the next several weeks. Charlie learned how to walk with Alice on his arm while Tusi walked alongside them. Tusi walked like a normal dog when not in her harness as Alice held the leash in her other hand while they strolled. She gave Charlie a slate, stylus, and little card with a braille alphabet on it to take with him and practice while he was away. Writing braille was hard enough, but then you had to master the task of turning the paper upside down and backward to place it on the slate to make sure the bumps pushed through to the other side so they could be read after flipping the paper back to the right side again. He accepted her gift and promised to practice while he was away so they could write letters to each other.

He promised Alice that he would come back and that he would not forget her. She promised him the same and told him that she would wait for him and pray for him every day. Which she did, without fail.

CHAPTER 14

Charlie was stationed in Boston for basic training. Once completed, he was transferred to the ship almost immediately. The Navy ship was larger than he had ever imagined. He couldn't believe his eyes as he walked up the plank to enter the massive vessel. He took well to the routine. He had no problem dealing with the physical exhaustion involved with boot camp and training. However, he never could understand or get used to the emotional pressure of being humiliated and screamed at. He often wondered how that made a boy a man, like they always said it was supposed to.

But nevertheless, he took it in stride. The bunks were down in the bottom deck, and the men were situated in them like sardines. It became so claustrophobic for him sometimes that he felt like he was stuck in a basket with no air and thankful that he never did make it to his first choice in the military which would have meant he would be stuck in a submarine.

One hot June evening, around the third week at sea, Charlie snuck up on the top deck. As he lay on his back, elbows up and hands folded behind his head, he looked at the stars. He thought about Alice and her wonderful little guide dog and her pretty clothes and hair ribbons and hats. He thought about watching her read her braille books and the how her high-heeled shoes clicked as she walked down the sidewalk.

Was she missing him? He thought so. They hadn't even kissed yet. He would save it for when he returned. They would have to date a while longer before he would be so bold as to try such a gesture. He wondered if she was now teaching a new little child how to secure a handle on being blind in the sighted world. Probably. And he was certain she was loving every minute of it.

Alas, the night was clear, and the only sound was that of the waves gently splashing on the sides of the ship as it cut through the sea at what seemed like lightning speed. The next thing he knew, he was awakened by a shadow of a man standing over him at 0500 hours. It was the captain. For the infraction of sleeping on deck, he landed himself on KP duty. And there he stayed. Serving slop for breakfast, lunch, and dinner. Scrubbing pots and cleaning dishes. He watched as the others had purposeful jobs like observers, radar controllers, and deck hands. He thought to himself that it could be worse. He was rarely assigned to clean the head.

He started to enjoy working in the kitchen. He was able to talk to his fellow sailors as he served them their food. He listened to their jokes and stories about their girls back home. He never shared his story about Alice, though. He reverently kept their newfound relationship to himself. He hadn't even told anybody about her back at home yet. However, he wasn't thinking about the town gossip and how the parishioners and Mother had already known all about it but never said a word. This was odd for his mother. She always had a hard time keeping her mouth shut. Especially when it came to her children. And especially when it came to her Charlie. She was probably so happy that he found love, and she was practicing self-control with not saying anything to him about it.

Navy life was nice for Charlie. It was peacetime when Charlie enlisted. But it was also the 1950s, right smack dab after the Korean War ended and right before the Vietnam War began. And there they were, in the middle of the Pacific. Sometimes it was so eerily quiet at night, and he never stopped sneaking out to sleep up on deck. But at least now he was smart enough to get back into his bunk before sunrise.

It was a dark, beautiful, clear sky, lit up with the Big Dipper in sight. He thought to himself that no matter how many thousands of miles he was away from home, from Alice, the sky was the same for everyone. She probably knew more facts about the stars and the sky than he did.

How very sad that she was never even able to look at its beauty, he thought. He decided he would learn how to describe it in such detail so that she would feel like she was actually experiencing it right there with him.

Though he normally didn't allow things to get him down or make him worry, there admittedly were times when he would lie on the hard steel surface of the hull, digging up all kinds of scenarios of what might happen to their massive ship. From pirates to North Koreans who were still angry at the Americans, to the ever-brewing Vietnamese tension—he was never really sure exactly where the enemy was lurking, but he knew they were out there. The last he heard, their ship was somewhere around the Philippines, but that was days ago. Maybe even weeks. The crew always had to be on standby and ready for anything. He could feel that they were being watched and wasn't sure how much of it was in his imagination or how much of it was real. Charlie often thought about what he would do if he were faced with actually having to kill another man. They were trained, and he was a good shot and liked handling a gun. But could he actually kill someone? At point blank? He was fairly sure he would rather be killed than have to kill. Sure, he would want to protect his country that he so loved, and he would protect his fellow sailors in a heartbeat. But no one ever knows what you would actually do when faced with this situation. He was a strong believer in the Ten Commandments and being faced with having to kill would be a struggle that he prayed about daily.

It had been a long, hot day in June. There were a lot of hearsay reports whispering about an area of submarines and foreign ships nearby. This wasn't that unusual. After all, the US was at the end of one armistice agreement with Korea and was already sending supplies and ammunition to the South Vietnamese government to help fight the communism spreading from the north. He knew that North Korea was not at all happy with the US interfering with taking over the southern region.

As he lay there, he remembered that Delilah's birthday was the next day. He wouldn't be able to contact her but knew she would know he was thinking of her. He heard that she and her husband, Bill, were expecting again and was sure she was happier than ever to be bringing another soul into the world to do God's work. The large vessel was slightly rocking but swished through the water with its continuous cutting speed.

Suddenly there was the loudest crash that Charlie had ever heard. It felt like ten lightning bolts in unison had hit the boat. It struck so fast that he couldn't think for a moment.

"We've been hit! We've been hit!" The screams came from the watchtower. Men scurried everywhere. The sailors took their posts. Charlie was left starboard. Then another crash. He never even realized that the boat was capable of turning to its side so abruptly, sending everything sliding at warped speed. Including Charlie. His body was thrown like a rag doll straight up against the metal side rail of the ship. He managed to grab a rope and held on for dear life, when suddenly a third and final crash came upon them.

The next thing he knew, he was in the water watching the ship go under. What felt like hours to him happened in a matter of minutes as the top of the lookout tower disappeared into the dark night. His head was killing him. And he couldn't feel his right foot.

After a few minutes of wading in the water, wondering how he would find a shoreline, a raft then came upon him, and a bunch of arms swooped down and pulled him in. The guys in the raft were Larry, Chip, and Buck. Larry was always a funny guy who reminded Charlie of his brother Rich, in a way. Chip was quiet and humble. Buck was just a big mouth. He never stopped talking. He controlled every conversation and sometimes, even though Charlie understood how irresistible getting your point across could be, he still wanted to punch him in the mouth to make his incessantly loud gibberish stop. It was jet-black dark on the open sea, and no one had a flashlight. They couldn't see anything or anyone. They could hear distant screams and yelling, then it all fell silent after about thirty minutes.

Quietly, with a dark, sullen tone, Charlie asked, "Where do you think we are?"

"The Pacific," replied Larry. As distraught and exhausted as they all were, this sent a contagious chuckle through the foursome. Even Chip let out a laugh. They soon fell off to sleep as the raft rocked in the treacherous waves. Their clothes were drenched. And they shivered as the night air got colder. They really had no idea where they were headed and who or what might be nearby.

They drifted for what seemed to be about four days. In and out of consciousness. Charlie could feel his ankle burning. His head still pounded. He was tempted to hold his foot over the raft so the sea water could clean out the wounds, but he knew it might draw sharks. Soon, however, there was enough water collecting in the little raft to soak his foot. They were starving and slowly dying of thirst. No land was in sight through the thick fog. Their bodies were scattered about the raft, like rats. Corpses, waiting for the vultures to start nipping away. Was this really going to be it for him? Would Alice wonder whatever became of him? Would there be someone else out there who would realize what a wonderful little lady she was and swoop her up and love her the way he longed to love her? Or would she end up all alone, never having a man to give her the beautiful children she so longed for?

He prayed, *Please God, don't let her be alone. She doesn't deserve that.*

He then thought that he saw her sitting next to him in the raft. Only she was looking at him and appeared to have her sight. She smiled as if to give him the message that everything was going to be okay. He drifted away into a coma-like sleep, as his body just couldn't take any more sun, dehydration, starvation, or hallucination.

CHAPTER 15

Charlie was awakened by cold water being thrown on him. It felt like an astringent against his sunburned, blistered skin. Yet it quenched his salt-pruned layers at the same time and sent a chill through his bones. Startled, his body jerked, yet he was too weak to jump up. The sun was shining straight into his eyes. He was just beginning to open them but could see a figure standing in front of him. It appeared to be a large woman with a straw hat. She was carrying a bundle on her back that he assumed was some sort of sack of grains or with whatever she was working. She was speaking in some language that sounded like it was probably Korean or Vietnamese or Japanese. He really didn't know. He had often thought to himself that he should prepare and at least try to educate himself on the culture and understand some different languages in the event that something like this happened, so he could at least tell what region he wound up in. It might have given him a better understanding of their fate if they at least knew where they were. Or maybe it was a good thing that he didn't know. Either way, it was too late now. He would have to do his best to communicate with these people. The other fellas were now waking up to the cold-water splash as well and surely felt much like Charlie was feeling. He knew that Chip probably knew some of the language and could shed some light on with whom they were dealing. Chip was smarter than them and had a much better ship's job, which was to learn to crack enemy codes in the code room.

They quickly learned that the people in the village didn't seem hostile toward them. They pulled them out of the boat and gave them water to drink and rice to eat. They tended to their wounds and applied fresh bandages.

The villagers didn't talk much among themselves nor to the four of them, but Charlie was pretty sure these people meant no harm. He watched the woman working with the big satchel on her back, wondering what must be inside. Just then, she turned her back toward him and he noticed a little tuft of black hair sticking out of the top of the satchel. He wondered at first if it was some sort of animal. Then as she turned again and bent over to clean the rice bowls out with the ocean water, he saw a little baby's hand poke out from the satchel and the baby let out a small cry. The woman rolled the satchel off her back, reached inside, pulled the little one out, and put it to her breast while sitting on the edge of the beach, dangling her feet in the water. It appeared to almost be a part of her work schedule. Just like taking a bathroom break or getting a drink of water during a work shift. Another task to complete about the needs of the day.

As they sat, recuperating, and hydrating themselves, Charlie pondered. *What a simple, beautiful life this is,* he thought to himself. He wished he had his camera to capture how this was one of the most magnificent sights he had ever seen. He decided he would photograph it in his mind and tell Alice all about the clear blue sky, the green fields, how you could see through the water straight to the ocean floor, the soft warm summer rain, and the mist and fog over the mountains in the distance.

He could even see slight snowcaps on the tops of the mountains that looked like a mural against the baby blue sky. *Almost every imaginable scene of nature all in one place,* he thought. *I will tell her about it if I ever see her again.*

The four men were handed bags to carry. The villagers pointed and hand gestured and talked in their native language. Charlie still wasn't completely sure but decided it was probably Korean. The villagers didn't make eye contact and appeared to be watching them with some suspicion, but the quad of men could tell these people needed their four able bodies for work. They tried to exchange smiles with the people but didn't get much in return at first. They were hand gestured into the back of the trucks and transported back to the village on the hay field flatbeds. Bags of rice and wheat served as places to rest their backs and heads. They arrived at a camp of straw huts. The huts were made into a circle with a large makeshift boiling pot in the center of the little community. There were farm animals in a pen next to the boiling pot. It was all very prehistoric looking, yet so pleasantly free and community like. The men were served broth and more rice. The women stripped them of their clothes and gave them fresh linens to wrap around their waists as the younger the girls washed their clothes and hung them to dry. They were directed to four straw-filled mats, where they quickly escaped and fell off to sleep within minutes.

The next morning, they were given their clothes, some more rice, melon, and green plums. The men knew that this was a friendly place, and they were more than willing to start in with work. They watched the people as they started their daily chores and set right in, learning how to work the fields, fetch water, and cook in the giant center pot. They had gatherings at night around the fire. There was dancing and games. The eldest man in the village told stories about North Koreans. Charlie could figure out some of it. The older boys and young men listened carefully, as it appeared that things were still bad between the North and the South. They figured they must be in the South, or they likely wouldn't have been treated quite so kindly.

Several months went by as the men settled into their roles in the village. They would try to speak with the elders in order to formulate a way to communicate with the United States military. However, it did not seem that these people were willing to cooperate in that sense. Chip, Buck, and Larry each settled in with a little woman of their own. Larry seemed especially taken with this one girl.

They spent all their time together. When the men weren't working, they played stickball in the field. They made a bat out of a large branch and a ball out of rolled-up tumbleweeds. Larry brought his girl flowers picked from the nearby plains. Charlie watched their relationship and likened it to how he hoped for his to be with Alice once he returned home. The women often made gentle advances to Charlie. He was, after all, incredibly handsome with his movie-star blue eyes. But Charlie was not interested. Of course, if he did accept their advances, no one would ever know or even mind. They were, after all, in a whole other country and may never get home again. He considered it on occasion, but he was used to controlling his sexual urges. He had done this his entire life. Ever since the nuns in school and Father Felix came and talked to the boys in seventh grade about the sinfulness of acting on their sexual desires and how self-control was of the utmost importance. Abstinence until marriage was the way of the Church. Charlie took this very seriously and was sure he would one day be back at home and would make Alice his wife. Yep, she would be well worth the wait! The men and the villagers grew trusting relationships, and the men became growingly protective of the group that had saved their lives and allowed them to live with them in their simple community.

It was now January, and they had been in the village for six months. There was still a lot of tension in the country, and they could hear the enemy getting closer to the village. The guys had a fairly good comprehension of the language at this point and what they didn't know, Chip would explain to them. They could hear the sound of gunshots from afar, and many of the young boys in the village were still away in the southern army. The enemies were moving in, and the four American men's lives were in greater danger with each passing day. Larry had married his girl by then, and she was expecting a child.

The men had decided that they should probably help the villagers prepare as much as possible for an invasion but that they should leave the village, as it did not appear at this point that anyone from America was going to find them.

It was a particularly dreary day at the end of January when the men planned and got their little boat ready for departure to head toward the Philippines. While the four of them were down by the shore, a small group of North Korean men snuck into the village. Charlie and his companions suddenly heard screams coming from the village. The intruders had pillaged, raped, and killed some of the women, children, and elderly already. It happened so quickly that they hardly had a chance to help. The men ran toward the village and were able to fight some of them off. Chip and Larry killed two of them. Charlie ran to the tent of the woman who first helped him that day when they arrived on their sinking raft. She lay there dead with a knife wound in her chest. Her little baby was crying and lying in the straw bed that was placed under an opening in the hut for sunlight. He stood and stared. He never really looked at the baby before. She was beautiful. She was staring off in a familiar way that he couldn't quite place initially. He walked toward her and gently smiled in spite of all the commotion going on around him. She didn't seem to make eye contact with him but quieted down with the sound of his whispers. Just then, Larry busted into the shack. He started grabbing apples and anything else he could find to shove in his satchel to prepare for escape.

"Charlie! We gotta go!" Charlie snapped out of his trance, and without realizing what he was doing, he grabbed the baby girl and the satchel that her mother always carried her in and ran for the shore as fast as he could. He didn't think about anything else. He never considered how he would care for her on a small boat that the group would jump into and sail off in. To who knows where. It could be headed toward a place far worse than the predicament they were just trying to get themselves out of. The men were launching the boat as Charlie and the baby approached. As he ran through the shallow waves, he felt a sting shoot straight through his left knee. He dropped the little girl into the water, and she sunk so fast that he started to panic. Diving in, he grabbed her little leg and swooped her up into the boat. The guys then pulled Charlie in over the port side to safety. The gunshots continued but they were able to get far enough away, rowing as fast as they could and ducking any stray bullets.

Larry's bride grabbed the baby, placed her in a swaddling cloth, and laid her on the floor of the boat under the seat for protection. They realized at this point that Charlie had been shot. Larry's wife wrapped Charlie's leg and stopped the bleeding while he paddled vigorously until the village was out of sight. The men did not stop rowing for a good hour to ensure they were far from the shoreline before taking a break and looking at one another to take in everything that just happened. Larry wrapped his arms around his bride, making sure her shawl was draped over both shoulders, then kissed her forehead. Buck threw his head back and took a deep breath as he rubbed his hands down his sweaty face. Buck knew they were traveling south, which was a good thing. Somewhere in the Sea of Japan probably. They tried to stay where they could see some shoreline and after several days luckily made their way to a port along the coast of Japan.

As soon as their little boat docked, they were flooded by villagers trying to get them to buy their goods and services. They walked through town and came upon a group of American soldiers in the distance. They ran, hollering and waving. Charlie was holding the little doll-like baby with her arms wrapped around his neck. The soldiers brought them back to camp. Once at camp, the sergeant caught wind that Charlie had a baby with him and ordered him to send her to an orphanage in Beijing.

Charlie couldn't bear to part with his little rescue. As Charlie stood in the officer's tent, he saluted him and said, "Sir, I wish to request to take this child with me."

The officer would hear nothing of it. He said that Charlie would be sent to the camp medic and that the child must go. "That is enough! The answer is no!"

"But sir!" said Charlie.

The officer put up his hand and while walking out of the tent, he said, "And get that knee taken care of!"

He then turned and looked Charlie straight in the eye. "Now I need to see the transport helicopter back to Hawaii. It is taking luggage and army personnel back. It is leaving at 1400 hours, which is now, and is unmanned by supervisory personnel."

Charlie stood, still in his saluted position, as a slight grin ran across his face. He was careful not to let his emotions show, however. "Yes, sir!" Charlie said.

He couldn't believe that the sergeant had basically given him permission to cast away the little girl onto the transport jet. He waited until the sergeant left, grabbed the little bundle with the baby girl stuffed inside, and swiftly shuffled as fast as he could, his leg dragging all the way toward the helicopter. There was no one to stop him. He figured they really didn't care that much. It's not like they could use him anymore, as he was sure his knee would be busted forever. The bullet was still in it, and he had reinforced pressure on the wounds with torn pieces of his clothes for the fifth time by now. As the helicopter took off, Charlie didn't let on what was in the satchel. The baby surprisingly slept through the whole takeoff and landing as they reached Pearl Harbor. When they descended the helicopter, Charlie and the baby sought medical attention for his knee. There was another soldier in the bed next to him. He was sleeping, so Charlie grabbed the bowl of oatmeal that sat on the guy's bedside table and stashed it in his satchel for the still sleeping little girl. Charlie abruptly obtained his medical papers, took his service pay that was handed to him upon arrival at the base, and was scheduled for transport in the military helicopter. Once in the States, Charlie and his little comrade started their journey and made their way back to New Jersey.

Once away from military supervision, he was finally able to unbundle the baby and hold her up in front of his face in an attempt to communicate with her. It was then that he realized, as unbelievable as it was, that the little girl was blind. The buses traveled for several days. He got off at the first stop in the main area of a small town in the middle of Iowa to stock up on baby supplies and food.

CHAPTER 16

Charlie initially told no one of his arrival home and made his way straight to Alice's apartment.

Charlie, with baby basket in hand, gently knocked on Alice's door. Alice opened the door without hesitation. She was so trusting of strangers. As if she knew that God would never let anything dangerous happen to her.

"Hello," said Charlie. His words were delivered in "a nice to meet you" sort of way.

Alice's face lit up instantly and she spontaneously went to throw her arms around Charlie's neck when her body was stopped by the little bundle. The baby whimpered, and Alice froze.

"What? What is this?" A look of complete serenity came over her face. She was quiet for a moment. Then so gently ran her fingers across the little one's nose, lips, and eyelids. She swaddled her out of his arms so naturally, as if she had handled the baby a million times before. She walked inside, cuddling her and speaking softly to her. Alice hardly asked any questions. She didn't care. She was falling instantly in love. The baby was soothed by Alice's voice and presence. Charlie limped to the kitchen and prepared a bottle for her. He brought it to her and watched as Alice pointed the nipple toward the baby's mouth.

At first, the bottle nipple bumped against the baby's cheek, then Alice felt for the baby's lips and with natural ease, inserted it into her mouth. The baby drank the bottle down within minutes and fell fast asleep. They placed her into the little basket that Charlie bought on his way over to Alice's house. Charlie took Alice's hand, sat her down, and told her all about his experience and about the first time he saw the infant in the woman's satchel. He told her how the woman helped him and cared for him. He finally told her how he discovered that the baby was blind and that he knew she needed to have a mother.

A mother just like Alice.

A tear streamed down Alice's face. She listened intently to his every word. She wasn't angry or shocked in the least bit. This act had touched her in a way like no other emotion she had ever experienced. She didn't question anything. She never gave a thought as to how she would care for the little one day in and day out. It didn't matter. It would work, and it would work perfectly. She sat for a moment and in a soft, childlike questioning voice, she said, "Am I her mother?"

"Yes, she is yours," said Charlie. "I-I-I in fact, was hoping she could be…ours. I was hoping as well that you would be my wife and we could give her a last name. You can teach her how to read and write braille, and we can raise her together."

He knelt down on his right knee, took her hand in his, and said, "Miss Alice Stiller, will you be my wife?"

Alice smiled and squeezed his hand so tightly. She was beside herself with emotion. She instantly responded to Charlie. She threw her arms around his neck again and he enveloped her tiny body in his strong arms. He had gotten two of his upper arms newly tattooed since being away: a ship on the left arm and an "A" tattooed on the right.

"I would love to be your wife. And I would love to be this baby's mother!" said Alice. "I can't believe all this is happening. And becoming a wife and mother all at once. Neither of which I had decided would happen to me in my lifetime. Charlie Aldridge, you have managed to change my life forever and have made me the happiest person alive."

The couple sat, hugged, and cried while the baby slept peacefully at their side.

Charlie decided he better visit his mother so that he could drop these giant bombshells to her in person. The couple called Mrs. Collins and explained the current situation. Mrs. Collins came and stayed with Alice and the baby for a couple of days while Charlie took care of things.

Charlie contacted a family friend and previous teacher, Sister Adrian. Sister Adrian now worked for Catholic charities. She made arrangements through her connections to obtain a birth certificate and grant the little one US citizenship. Charlie knew this was likely illegal, as it happened quite effortlessly, but he was not going to ask any questions. They officially adopted her and named her Matilda Alice Aldridge. They reluctantly had the support of both their families but had to remind them frequently, especially Charlie's mother, that Alice could do things for herself. This did cause a bit of tension between the women, but eventually Mother caught on and took her proper place as grandmother and mother-in-law, allowing Alice to mother without much interference.

Alice's family was not at all keen on the idea and continued to be quite suspicious of Charlie's intentions despite witnessing the way he cared for Alice and Matilda. Nonetheless, they did what they needed to do to make Alice happy.

The wedding was absolutely beautiful. Marnie made sure that Alice had the prettiest gown, made from the best silk material, imported from no other than South Korea. It was simple and practical enough, not too fluffy or extravagant, to make handling the dress less cumbersome for Alice.

To Charlie, Alice was still the most beautiful woman he had ever seen. He just knew he could take care of this girl and show the world how different a life they could lead. As she stood, facing him at the altar, she was petrified and overjoyed at the same time. Here she stood, with a steel factory worker who had a wild group of unruly friends. None of whom knew anything about the Republican political party or had ever even picked up a novel. But he was also the kindest, most giving person she had ever come across.

Her feelings of doubt made her feel like a terrible person. She pushed them away because she knew that marrying this man was good. He was good. He loved her. He wouldn't hurt her. He would take care of her. But she didn't need taking care of, she thought to herself. Later on, this would become a constant struggle for her, especially after marrying Charlie. The demons that would fill her head at night and keep her awake would almost take over completely at times. Sometimes it would go on for days at a time without sleep. The anxiety of thinking about all she wanted to accomplish and the whole world was holding her back. But at least for now, at this moment in time, those behaviors were kept at bay. She hadn't had an episode since long before Charlie came home from the war. In fact, Charlie knew little about this side of Alice at this point in their lives.

Alice did know that she loved Charlie and their new little baby girl.

Charlie was always thinking of things that they could do that other normal couples did that didn't require Alice having her sight. They rode their first bicycle built for two while in Niagara Falls. Later, Nat King Cole's song would become one of their favorites. Alice didn't enjoy it as much as Charlie did in the beginning. Mostly because it was scary. Also, although she was a woman of many gifts and talents, coordination was not one of them. Charlie liked to walk holding hands. Sometimes she would concede, but sometimes she couldn't shake the idea that people then couldn't admire the blind girl walking independently. Charlie tried to get her to understand that not everyone was watching her and not everyone cared that Alice Stiller Aldridge was blind and looked independent of her husband. People would pass unknowingly, just with the regular smile, looking pleased at the newly married couple walking along hand in hand.

Charlie worked the day shift at the factory so that he could be home during the evenings and nights to help out with Alice and the baby. They bought a charming little Cape Cod house in the southern New Jersey woods. Charlie was the happiest he had ever been. Alice appeared to be quite happy as well, but Charlie was beginning to notice some strange repetitive habits that started to concern him. She would tell him stories of people watching her and spying on her. She started scratching her hands at nighttime. Sometimes to the point of bleeding. Charlie couldn't understand how she could possibly know such a thing, as she didn't have her sight. He tried to listen and be understanding, but sometimes she didn't make any sense at all. She would normally be okay again by the next day or so. Therefore, he didn't give it much thought in the beginning, but it did linger in the back of his mind.

CHAPTER 17

As the 4:00 p.m. whistle blew at Henry's Iron Powder Mill, Charlie was finishing up his shift as he always did. Shoveling steel and loading barrels. Working as if he was a slave in a work camp with whips above his head. So caught up in the constant feverish shoveling, enjoying the pain of torn muscles as his shirt dripped with sweat. In a trance-like working mode until every piece of coal was emptied into the bucket. He was unaware of his surroundings; the black soot ran into his eyes. So much so that he could barely see.

"Yo, Charlie! You can stop working now! Charlie! Snap out of it! Shift's over!" said his best friend, Leon, with a smirk. "Are you in there, Char?" he said.

Charlie stopped and stared, somewhat confused. Like when waking up from a deep sleep and wondering where you are. Slowly a smile ran across his face.

"Of course I'm here! I'm here! Ready? Let's get out of here!" he said.

Leon was very close to Charlie. He stood six feet four inches tall and weighed about 260 pounds. Charlie stood at about five feet four inches tall and weighed about 150 pounds. But Charlie had the body of a steel fireplug. The mill was full of every bar-fighting, law-hopping, ex-con, baby daddy, wild man in the county, and Charlie had a way of making friends and gaining the respect of each and every one of them. The guys, all wearing green pants and matching work shirts, were completely covered in a reddish-brown hardened dust by the end of their shift. They all poured into the locker room, showering and fooling around as if they were a team of football players after a big game. The shower floors would be left in a pool of iron ore that looked like old blood flowing down the center drain. Charlie was getting dressed into a new set of clean work clothes that he would wear home that night.

Johnny and Sam were shoving each other around in the locker room, getting ready to, as usual, spiral out of control and start throwing punches. Charlie thought about the time that his car broke down at the end of his evening shift. He had noticed that Bobby Worchowski's car was unlocked so he borrowed a pair of jumper cables out of the car. Bobby had the temper of a lion released from captivity. When he found out that somebody took his cables, he flew through the locker room, growling like a bear, looking for the culprit. Once he found out it was Charlie, he grabbed Charlie, threw him up against the lockers with his fist up, ready to clock him in the face. As he drew his arm back, he looked straight into Charlie's trusting blue eyes that seemed to say, "go ahead and hit me." Bobby just couldn't do it. As he gently lowered his fist, he gave Charlie a little shove and walked off. Bobby knew, after all, that he still had his job because of Charlie. Charlie had covered for Bobby when he was late one day after violating parole and driving to Florida to "make a delivery for a guy." What everyone understood was that Charlie would give the shirt off his back for anyone...once!

But they knew not to put him in the position a second time, of having to be dishonest or clean up after you. If so, Charlie would no longer be your friend. Pure and simple. Everybody knew what Charlie was about. It was the stuff you couldn't teach. It was natural. Charlie was attracted to the underdog, the poor guy, the guy that made mistake after mistake, the law pusher. This was fascinating to him. Not that Charlie would ever compromise his values or ever in a million years live his life like these guys did. But he felt comfort, nonetheless, being around them. He told himself they were all good deep down. They all had troubles and he liked them for it. The guys, in turn, felt this vibe from him. And they knew he wasn't really afraid of any of them. The bosses also took a big liking to him. Sid Wilson was the director of finance. He trusted Charlie with anything. If Sid had a job at his house, he asked Charlie to do it. Charlie would work for free if you asked him to, but most didn't have the heart to not pay him. He was everyone's friend. Until a person gave him a reason not to be. He was sly as a fox when reading people. If you got one over on him, it was because he allowed it to happen. He practiced living the way he was taught to live. If someone needed something, you gave it to them. It wasn't for him to judge if a person made life errors one after another. If someone needed money and Charlie had it on him, he would give it. If you didn't pay him back, you wouldn't get it again.

As the guys all headed out to the Polish American club to throw back some cold ones on the steamy early summer's eve, Charlie checked himself in the small mirror inside the locker door, tucked in his clean shirt, glanced at the white cloth name tag with red stitching around the oval patch that was sewn into the left chest, and headed home to the quiet three-bedroom home in the wooded town of Mill Ridge. It was raining out. And since he loved to walk in the rain, today he would walk home. He would leave his car in the parking lot and just get up a little earlier in the morning and walk back again to work. He could never understand why the guys would prefer to go to the bar over returning home to their wives and children. There was nothing more heart pounding than pulling up to the house and watching little fat-faced Matilda run out to the driveway in her bare feet with dirt on her clothes, face, and hands. She would be dressed in her bloomers and sun top flowery outfit. She always turned the shirt around with the opening that was meant to be in the back now in the front to show off her outie belly button. She had giant brown eyes and long, straight black hair. Her skin was a light Asian tone. Her hair was usually unruly but somehow fit her, and she always looked beautiful nonetheless... and she was in love with her dad. The highlight of her every day was when he came up the drive and she would leap into his arms. Alice would be in the kitchen, making meatloaf and listening to the Mills Brothers' greatest hits.

Alice wore a red maternity dress. Her unpainted toenails peeked through the open-toe white slippers that came in the mail from Marnie last week. Her hair was pinned back to the side. She had ear-length curls that never seemed to fall. Her milky white skin and rosy cheeks were glowing, and she had a light tint of pink lipstick that would sometimes have little remnants on her two front teeth. The meat was formed into an uneven, poorly molded loaf. The ingredients weren't completely mixed throughout. However, to Charlie, she had created a usual masterpiece for dinner. Charlie didn't notice the imperfections as he walked through the door with Matilda in his arms. He still felt a surge of wonder when he would see Alice as she moved about the kitchen with the greatest confidence. The puddle of water in front of the sink, the little pieces of ground beef scattered on the counter that she dropped during dinner prep onto the floor did not matter. None of it mattered. Their life was completely and utterly perfect.

Later, Charlie would quietly sneak in around her in the kitchen as he always did and clean up any spills or food droppings. If Alice ever knew, oh how furious she would be. He made sure nothing was out of place when Mother made her surprise "stop-ins," as no one ever knew when that would be. He knew how Alice despised her mother-in-law's tisking and meddling and head shaking with concern about the appearance of the house and the children. This would only add to Alice's paranoia about the outside world judging her.

It was bedtime for Matilda. Alice and Charlie sat on either side of her while Alice read her the story *The Little Engine That Could* in braille. Matilda would always choose to lean her little head on Charlie's shoulder because Alice's shoulder would repeatedly move up and down while she was reading. Alice's arms would move from side to side as her hands read back and forth, changing each giant page every thirty seconds or so. Her arms never stayed still enough while she was reading, and when lying on her mother's shoulder, Matilda's head would bounce up and down as her momma's arms ran across the page as she told the story so expressively. Alice always made the books sound extremely exciting, as she had perfected the pronunciations and exclamatory remarks. Matilda's eyes would fly open in expectation as the little engine would climb so desperately to the top of the mountain, and then she would clap her hands in pure glee as he came flying down the track. She felt like she was on that train with him. She would jump up and down and hug and kiss Charlie when the little underdog made it. Charlie sat quietly as the two enjoyed the wonderful ride through their nightly bedtime stories. As Alice got Matilda ready for bed, Charlie would clean up the kitchen, removing any evidence of sloppy mealtime prep. He would go over the counter, the floor, fix the refrigerator contents. But being careful not to move the order of Alice's things, as she would remember where she put it, and if out of place, would surely know he was the culprit. As Alice lay sleeping in bed, he approached her. He removed his clean set of work clothes that he put on every day after his shower at work, to be donned the next day for his next shift. He neatly draped them across the back of the chair, climbed into the cold crisp sheets in his dulled white T-shirt and Fruit of the Loom briefs, and wrapped his arms around her petite little body, smelling the lavender in her hair. She didn't stir as he watched her quietly dreaming with a hint of a snore. He then clicked off her talking alarm clock to avoid the hourly update of what time it was. He drifted off to sleep to the sound of the ticking of her gold braille watch that sat on the nightstand.

CHAPTER 18

It was two short years later, and day after day, no matter the shift, Charlie stopped first at the first convenience store nearest to their home for a small coffee and grabbed a gallon of milk. He made a turn onto Charleston Road in the somewhat newer station wagon that he had purchased when they had a growing family. He watched as a miniature U-Haul passed by, sending an uncomfortable, unexplained chill down his spine. As if there were some dark attachment to the contents of the vehicle. As if he should follow it to its destination. The driver, who had scruffy hair and a dirty long beard, locked eyes with him as he turned the corner. The U-Haul soon faded into the busy Route 138 traffic and was out of sight within moments. As Charlie waited for the light to turn green, he thought about his childhood. The U-Haul truck reminded him of the time his family packed up and left their daddy sitting on the curb with nothing but a sandwich and a cola.

Charlie drove up to the driveway of their beloved little home. The car puttered a bit before turning off. Charlie never believed in buying new cars. In part because he wasn't a rich man. But mostly, a new fancy car in his mind would be making a statement of a pompous, social climber. A person that he would never in a million years want to be. He felt that things of the world were for the sinful. Not for hard-working manly men. He felt that God didn't intend for people to indulge themselves. That you should get by on simple means. Just enough to provide food, clothing, and shelter for you and yours. He didn't see any type of masculinity in the latter type of living. Men with bright sweaters and smoking jackets were unmasculine in his mind, as they cared too much about fussing over themselves, and this was the right reserved only for the ladies. Charlie had no bones about a woman dressing nicely, fixing her hair and makeup just so, because women were made to be beautiful beings and had every right to fuss.

This was exemplified in the way that he would so carefully pick out Alice's dresses at the store, trying to think of what Marnie would pick out for her. After all, he had to admit, Marnie did have great taste, and Alice had the prettiest clothes, hair accessories, and jewelry when he first met her.

Charlie also felt that for a man, admitting illness and pain was only for "sissies." Real men didn't get colds and didn't feel pain. In fact, Charlie enjoyed making himself suffer a bit. He truly felt that if he experienced physical discomfort, it was something to overcome and would make him stronger. Something humanly deserved and something to be tackled as a character builder. A true testament to manhood and purpose in life.

But on this day, something was different. Matilda didn't come running down the driveway that he painted with black tar the summer before to make it smoother for Alice to walk with her cane or Seeing Eye dog without tripping. This was quite unusual, as Matilda seemed to have the circadian rhythm to know to jump up on the glass coffee table and be on the lookout for Charlie through the big bay window when 4:15 p.m. came around.

He exited the car and walked ever so cautiously. He had an overwhelming feeling of eeriness at this point. He turned the doorknob to their green Cape Cod home. As his right shoulder pressed against the door, he was met with the stop. He shuffled for his house key in his left pocket. It wasn't unusual for Alice to lock the front door, especially anymore and if she was having one of her "paranoid" days.

He opened the heavy green door with the top triangle decorative windows and the brass knocker with the engraved cursive "A." The knocker made a clinking sound with the opening of the door the way it always did. He was immensely proud of that initial on the knocker. Names and initials had great meaning to Charlie. It was a sort of confirmation of belonging. An affirmation of being something, of living that something.

As he opened the door, there was an empty, hollow sound. There was no music playing, no sound of the scattered little voices of Matilda teaching her new little sister, Michelle, her letters, and Michelle's little efforts at repeating Matilda's words in response. As he walked through the empty house, looking at everything that represented the normal life they'd built, it was all gone. All that was left was the TV on its unsteady stand and the green couch with the intentional pools in the polyester material that he bought at Gimbels with the wedding money. As he looked to the left, their bed with the brown headboard and built-in bookcase with drawers was gone. The only memory of where they spent their nights were the marks in the carpet that shaped the frame of the bed. He had always loved how the two pillows represented their union and evened out the bedspread when the bed was made each morning. It took a while for him to realize what had happened, even though it was clear that they had gone. Charlie slumped against the wall, slid down onto his bottom with his head in his hands. He thought how someone had finally gotten to her. They convinced her to leave him. In spite of it all. Everything they'd worked for.

She couldn't handle things after all! he thought.

Her fragile state was much too much.

Ever since last June. The pain of Michelle, slipping away on that fateful day. Though still unbearable to think about, he reflected on it as he sat in the dark, cold, echoing room.

He thought back and ran the whole scenario through his mind again.

It had been another unusually sweltering summer day in the beginning of August. Michelle and Matilda were napping in their shared bedroom. Charlie's mother was away in Pennsylvania visiting with Delilah. Charlie was not home from work yet, and Alice was in the kitchen. Michelle had somehow climbed out of her crib. Her little shoes with the mini bells weren't on her little feet because she was always taking her shoes off and running around barefoot. Alice didn't hear her as she pushed open the metal door that never quite latched closed, and she didn't close the storm door because it was ninety degrees outside and Mrs. Butler from down the street had recently dropped off some produce that she had picked up for Alice while the girls were sleeping. The occasional breeze that came through the house because the front door was facing north was as satisfying an experience as the lemonade that she was perfecting and had chilled in the fridge. Unbeknownst to Alice, Michelle had made her way down the three front steps and around the side of the house and was out of sight just as Charlie pulled in to the half-circle driveway that his brothers helped him construct just before Rich passed away in a car accident the year prior. Charlie dropped his keys on the table just inside the door. He took his shoes off and picked up Michelle's little shoes. The bells jingled while he put them in the rack next to his. He found Alice in the kitchen as she was in her apron, putting the rub on the chicken thighs. He gave her a kiss on the cheek. She told him the girls were still taking their naps but should be awake very soon. Charlie had gotten off a little early that day because he had finished all the work in his usual lightning speed. The little ones would be waking soon. As he tiptoed into the room to check on the girls, he saw Matilda sleeping like an angel. Then he turned to the crib. His heart suddenly sank to his stomach. Where was Michelle? Her crib was empty. He remembered that the storm door was open when he came in and that the metal screen door flew open without him hardly touching it. He knew it right away. Panic struck him. He could only see spots in front of his eyes as he ran out the door, across the street, and looked side to side under every parked car, behind every tree, and down the street as far as his eyes could take him. Looking everywhere, he ran from house to house, banging on every door.

He even tried to elicit the help of Mrs. Martino by knocking on her door, but she didn't answer. Mrs. Martino was always so mean to Charlie. She wasn't shy about commenting on how dangerous it was to have a blind woman raising young children. And how strange it was for a man to want to marry a blind girl and that he probably took advantage of her and had her do weird things for him in the bedroom. She never had children of her own, and Charlie excused her behavior for that reason. He felt sorry for her instead, as he knew she must wish that she had a child of her own.

As the neighbors all came out of their homes to help, Mrs. Martino pushed her side curtain over ever so lightly to peer at the commotion. Then let the drape hang back down again covering her window. The rest of the neighbors all searched, calling Michelle's name. Charlie ran back to the house. He knew he had to tell Alice what had happened. That Michelle had disappeared. He hoped that Alice would have some explanation as to where Michelle was. He prayed that she would tell him that a neighbor or friend picked her up and took her to their house for the afternoon. Even though he knew this would never happen, as Alice always liked to be the only caregiver of the children. He ran through the door and didn't have time to worry about protecting her psyche and just blurted it out.

"Michelle is missing!" he shouted.

When he saw the look on Alice's face upon hearing the news, he knew immediately that she would never recover from this. Not only was their little baby missing, but this was going to send Alice into a complete frenzy.

Knowing that she, the woman who prided herself on the ability to do anything a sighted person could do, including raising children in a safe and secure environment, had let her baby slip out of sight.

He couldn't worry about that right now but still his heart broke for Alice too. Charlie could not allow himself to let Alice bear the responsibility of losing Michelle. The words came rushing out of his mouth before he could even think about what he was going to say.

"I lost Michelle," he said. Knowing that she was certain Michelle was sleeping in her crib when Charlie came home, she assumed that Charlie must have taken her outside and would have been responsible.

Alice's eyes grew large as she flew into a fit of screaming, punching, and crying!

"What? How? How could you? What have you done? She was in her crib sleeping with her cowbell shoes on! How could you lose our baby? How could you let that happen?" she cried.

Charlie tried to hug her, but she punched and pushed him away. He ran back out the door, feverishly yelling and searching through the woods, down to lake one, lake two, lake three which were all man-made lakes in the town. He dove in repeatedly. By that time, the whole police and fire departments were in the neighborhood. The search went on for hours as they were flashing their lights into the night. Through the thick forest, scouring all three lakes. Michelle was nowhere to be found. The search went on through the night and into the morning. Sergeant Cook questioned Charlie.

Charlie's story was good, well thought out as he told the officers that he had been home for several hours while the children slept in their cribs. He told them that Alice was sleeping, and he'd been in charge of watching them. Everyone figured she climbed out of her crib and made her way out to the front door. Charlie advised he was out in the backyard cutting up the deer meat that he had gotten from one of his brother's hunting excursions and didn't hear the sound of the aluminum doors swinging open and shut. Surprisingly, No one questioned Alice, as they assumed it was all under Charlie's watch, and that was how he wanted it to remain. He feared if anyone knew that Alice lost one child, then child protective services would certainly not trust her with mothering another. He could not bear seeing this happen to Alice knowing it would surely send his wife into a state of no return. The search went on the following day. No body was found. Not in the lakes, not in the woods. Nowhere. Michelle seemed to have vanished into thin air. Charlie never told anyone his secret that Alice was alone with the girls when Michelle had disappeared.

From that day on, Alice wasn't the same. She rarely spoke and would sit for hours in silence. She stopped singing, playing the piano, and even dancing with little Matilda. Matilda would try pulling Alice's arm to get her up out of the chair, but she wouldn't budge. Mother had to move in to help care for the house and Matilda while Charlie, in his grief, had to return back to work. He took Alice to a psychiatrist, and they trialed different medications, but she became increasingly withdrawn. She started to imagine all sorts of crazy things. Charlie would come home, and she would tell him that the refrigerator repairman was there all day working on the freezer door or that a group of military officers came to the house asking for her paperwork from the reports she had written up about the blind and deaf children she was teaching. Her behavior escalated even more. He came home one day to find that she had shaved her eyebrows off because they were so itchy that she couldn't stop pulling at them. She would wake up in the middle of the night, terrorized, reporting that the devil was talking to her and telling her she needed to change her evil ways, or she would never see her loved ones again. She began acting as if she didn't recognize Charlie and would carry on as if he weren't even present. He felt that she will hate him forever because of what she thought he had allowed to happen. Her hands were so broken up and scabbed from the constant scratching. Charlie finally decided that it was the dreaded time to talk about hospitalizing her. He had made arrangements with Alice's doctor for some time the following week.

But now she was gone, out of his life…and so was Matilda. And so was Michelle.

He sat in their empty living room. His thoughts returned back to the present. His once young, movie-star face was now a little wrinkled and worn-looking. His piercing blue eyes suddenly weren't so bright anymore. He thought to himself about what had probably taken place with Alice after their loss. She clearly had fallen into a deep psychotic state due to the inability to accept that her baby had disappeared. Alice's family, more than likely, took advantage of the opportunity to get her away from him. He thought that maybe they knew exactly what had really happened on that fateful day when Michelle went missing, but they were probably all in denial as well. And this would be their chance for the family to get her in a place where they could take care of her because they felt they knew best what she needed. They felt she never should have married and were always worried about her fragile emotional state. They took his Alice and his little Matilda. He knew even then how hard it would be to find them. And if he did find them, Alice would probably never come back to him anyway and never forgive him for what she thought he had done.

Not after how it appeared that her grief had turned to hatred toward him. His emotions flowed. He punched a hole into the brown paneling that Rich and Rob helped him put up around their living room when they first bought the house just before the wedding. He began ripping the paneling off the walls in a fit of complete rage. Soon the living room was torn apart. It was in pieces all over the floor. He sobbed out loud as he lay in the rubble, flat on his back. He surprised even himself that he was capable of such a profound outburst. He lay there until the next morning, when he was awakened by the sun peering through one of the holes, he had made in the wall the evening before.

CHAPTER 19

Almost two years had passed while Charlie tried to put himself back together after they left and he had moved in with his mother. He did not miss a single day of work while he devised a plan to find out where Alice and Matilda were as well as continue his search for Michelle. He was torn between leaving their home in the hopes that one day he would find Michelle or she would return while he was away, while looking for the other two. He never stopped thinking about his three girls for one minute.

He decided, at least for now, he would start by looking up Mrs. Robertson. Mrs. Robertson was the only friend that he knew to be true to both Charlie and Alice and the only one that would tell him if she knew anything about their whereabouts. She had moved away to Pennsylvania.

She wasn't hard to find, as she was a popular person when living in town who had many friends. She had a lovely demeanor and was kind to everyone. As it turned out, she did know where they were and felt a responsibility to tell Charlie their whereabouts but did not know how to contact him and assumed he had known where Alice was. She told him that Alice received psychiatric hospital care and had been granted custody of Matilda. The exception was, as long as she had a live-in nanny and housekeeper. Charlie wondered how this could have been done without his knowledge. None of it made any sense.

She also told him that Matilda had surgery to her eyes and was able to gain enough vision to read large print. She had an eyeglass prescription that enabled her to see quite well enough to perform her daily routine as an almost completely sighted little girl. Charlie's heart sunk upon hearing this. His little girl had her vision. She must be flourishing. And how cute she probably looks wearing her little eyeglasses. He thought perhaps he might be able to reconnect with both of them. Mrs. Robertson told Charlie that, because of her mental collapse, Alice didn't remember anything about Michelle and had no recollection of Charlie or any history with him. The doctors felt the overwhelming trauma was too much for Alice's mind to accept. Therefore, these memories were completely blacked out. Charlie was heartbroken by the news that Alice would not have any memory of their years together.

Charlie thought long and hard about this, and as much as he wanted to reunite because of his undying love for Alice, he decided that he would not attempt to reenter her life so as to keep her in a homeostatic psychiatric state of mind and would not remind her that their sweet Michelle was gone.

Mrs. Robertson told him that Alice and Matilda were in an apartment in the city of Pittsburgh where Alice had access to public transportation and sidewalks. She had a job now and was back to teaching blind children and adults.

Upon hearing this news, Charlie decided that he would quit his job at the steel factory, move to Pittsburgh, and settle close to where Alice and Matilda lived so that he could keep an eye on them and ensure their safety.

Charlie was lucky with the sale of the house because the town had decided to build an annex road right where their property stood, and he was offered three times what it was worth. He knew he would be in decent shape until he found a job that would accommodate watching over Alice and Matilda while allowing him time as well to return to New Jersey for his search for Michelle.

Charlie took the address from Mrs. Robertson and found the apartment where they were staying. He stood outside and watched and waited all day. Once it was almost dark, a bus pulled up to the corner and out stepped Alice with a pretty new little German shepherd. His heart sunk the same way it did every time he saw his girl. She seemed well and just as he had remembered her when she was in her twenties before he had witnessed any mental breaks. This made his heart leap.

"Elsa, forward," she said. Then the two traveled up the concrete steps to the brick apartment building on Somerset Avenue. The front door opened, and there was Matilda!

She had become more adorable than ever. Charlie could not take his eyes off her. She wore coke bottle glasses and looked incredibly cute as she jumped up and down waiting for her mommy to come to the door. She was holding hands with a tall, attractive Black woman with a very lovely looking face. The woman smiled and held on tightly to little Matilda's hand, making her wait until Alice got closer to the front door before rushing toward her.

"Mommy!" shouted the little girl. The two of them hugged, and Matilda patted Elsa on the head as they all entered, with the heavy glass door closing behind them.

Charlie couldn't believe that he just got a glimpse of his girls. He felt such a sense of relief that they looked so happy. Matilda had sight now!

In no time at all, Charlie was able to get an apartment right down the hall from Alice and Matilda. Charlie was fearful that someone in Alice's family would recognize him and didn't want to risk stirring up any problems. So, he dyed his hair and grew a mustache. He wore glasses and a hat every time he left the apartment. Even though it had already been well over a year, and Matilda had actually never been able to see much at all before.

She had the operation and hadn't been around him in person since. And Alice certainly did not know what he looked like. However, he did not want to risk Marnie or any other family members coming to visit and noticing him. Besides, he knew how smart little Matilda was and couldn't make himself known to her. He would look through the peephole of his apartment door before leaving to ensure that no one was around. He wondered if Alice or Matilda might recognize his scent or something. He was so very fearful of Alice sensing anything that would send her into an emotional spiral. Yet he needed to be near them. He could not accept the fact that she truly did not remember him. Rather he decided that he and the memory of Michelle had been suppressed by Alice, and he felt that it was best to remain this way.

Charlie was able to find a three-to-eleven shift at the Westerly Power Plant. It worked out perfectly. He would get to work by 3:00 p.m., home by 12:00 a.m., up at 5:00 a.m., walk to Henry's flower shop and home in time to watch Matilda walk to school with Miss Janice every morning. Then he would perch himself at his favorite table across from the school and watch Matilda play on the playground at lunchtime.

The nanny, Miss Janice, was very kind and loving and took wonderful care of Matilda. She looked out for Alice as well but understood Alice's ways and made sure not to overstep her boundaries. Miss Janice never married and did not have any children. She worked as a home health aide until stumbling upon this role as a live-in nanny with the pair.

Miss Janice became very curious when bunches of lily of the valley flowers started showing up by the front door every morning. Miss Janice would open the door, look around, and ask passersby who had dropped them off. One day, Charlie was walking by.

Miss Janice quickly opened the door and asked Charlie if he knew where the flowers had come from. He shrugged his shoulders and said, "Nice day, ma'am," as he lifted his baseball cap to gesture her and walked on. She stood, watching him stroll down the hall, and then looked down to his door. Perplexed, she had a strange feeling about this man. She had seen him around a few times now. With every sighting, he did some sort of kind act for someone else. Like helping Mrs. Williams get her cat out of one of the trees that lined the front of the building. Or clearing the snow from the steps leading up to the door. He would sit out front and talk to the older men while they played chess in their chairs and table that were set up on the sidewalk. She wondered if it was him, what he was all about, and if it was him, why he was giving flowers to just them.

A month passed on and every morning, Miss Janice would collect the lilies from in front of the door, bring them in, place them in fresh water, and place them in the center of the table. The scent freshened up the whole apartment. Miss Janice had to find out who the mystery person was. She stayed up all night one night and listened for footsteps outside the apartment door. She confirmed that it was Charlie after finally catching him through the peephole. She didn't let on that she knew and had decided that Charlie was just doing a nice thing for the blind girl and little Matilda. Miss Janice had always wondered if there had been a mister in Alice's life. Alice's family never talked about where Matilda came from. And Alice didn't seem to know or remember much at all about the past several years.

Matilda had three favorite stuffed animals. The first one was a white mountain lion with silky fur that she called Mommy. One was a big brown bear with soft fur and blue eyes. She called the bear Tada. The third was a little white lamb with a babyish-looking face and a tiny pink ribbon on top of her head that she named Shelly.

Matilda would tell all sorts of stories to Miss Janice about her stuffed animals. Miss Janice was very impressed with Matilda's imaginary stories, as at times they seemed so real. Sometimes Miss Janice wondered if the characters were actually real. Matilda would talk of how she would play with Shelly in her crib. And color in the big giant coloring books so Matilda could see the pictures and help Shelly to stay within the lines. She would talk about how Tada rode the red bike and mommy sat on the back, and Shelly was in a little seat behind Mommy while Matilda rode her very own bike with a banana seat and two little wheels attached to the back of the large double bicycle. Miss Janice wondered how Matilda knew so much about making up an imaginary family.

Where are the other characters from Matilda's stories? Miss Janice thought to herself. How did Matilda know what a crib was? She was in a big girl bed at her home here. And where had she seen people riding on a tandem bicycle? Miss Janice was very curious about Alice and Matilda's secret pasts and knew there had to be some circumstances around how they wound up in this situation, with the child's custody being dependent on Miss Janice being their live-in nanny.

As the months passed, Matilda stopped mentioning stories about her imaginary friends. Miss Janice had been warned not to ask Alice about her past, as it might upset her and send her swirling into psychosis. But she was so curious, she just couldn't help herself. As they sat on the couch in the evening, listening to the news on the radio while Miss Janice helped Alice pay some bills and read the printed mail to her, Miss Janice thought how she could investigate their situation. Miss Janice started asking Alice if she knew any Asian men. Alice replied that she did not. After all, Miss Janice felt that Matilda's father must have been of Asian descent given Matilda's beautiful light-brown complexion, round brown eyes, and jet-black straight hair, like many people of Asian descent. She began to ask Alice where she and Matilda had lived before coming to Pittsburgh.

Alice appeared confused for a moment, as if trying to put her thoughts together. Her eyes grew wide, and her facial expression appeared somewhat fearful for a moment. She started rubbing her hands together.

Miss Janice became a bit concerned with this and thought she'd better not press on.

"My dancing friend," Alice replied with a whisper.

Alice no sooner stopped rubbing her hands, and then calmness seemed to come over her. She then said, "I don't remember." Then Alice let out an odd little giggle, as if she were embarrassed that she didn't know where she came from before moving back to Pittsburgh. Alice was quickly distracted by the large-print braille magazine that her fingers stumbled upon as she fumbled around all the papers and books displayed out on the table. It was the newsletter from her alma mater. Along with it was a letter talking about this year's convention for the blind and that it would be hosted by the college the following June. They had invited Alice to give a speech on her postgraduate accomplishments and talk about her blind and deaf students that she taught and what those students were doing today. Surprisingly, Alice had excellent recall about all the students that she'd taught in the past, as well as her college days and her childhood. It was just that period of time when Charlie had come into her life through the time when Michelle disappeared that she drew an absolute blank.

Alice was so excited by the invitation.

"Oh, Miss Janice! I will have to tell the National Federation of the Blind that I cannot work the week of June 17 next year! Oh, and I want Matilda to come and see my speech and meet some of the blind children. She will be seven by then, and she can help be their guide now that she has gained more vision. I have taught her the braille alphabet, and she can read and write some braille. It will be a wonderful experience for her. And for you too, if you can join us," said Alice.

Alice chattered up a storm, like a little schoolgirl getting ready for the first big dance or something. Looking so forward to being on display and telling the whole world about her accomplishments.

As Alice got ready for bed that night, just like every night in their household routine, she knelt by the side of the bed as little Matilda swept in and knelt down alongside her. But not until first setting up Tada and Shelly alongside them to say their nighttime prayers. They would pray the Our Father, three Hail Marys, and finally "As I lay me down to sleep…"

And now it was story time. Matilda placed the little lamb in the tiny rocker bed that was next to Matilda's. While Alice read through the list of children's braille books, awaiting Matilda's choice, Matilda set up the big brown bear on the other side of her. The braille was imprinted on clear pages so that Matilda could see through to the underlying page where the illustrations and printed words lay. The little girl laid her head on the shoulder of the big brown stuffed animal while Alice read the story of Peter Squirrel as Matilda's little eyes grew heavy and fell fast asleep.

CHAPTER 20

As Charlie watched Matilda at school, he noticed that the other kids had sensed that she was different from them. She wasn't invited to play hopscotch with the other little girls. She could see the numbers, but the boxes were too small for her to focus on. He knew she loved playing hopscotch because Miss Janice was always chalking out giant boxes with giant numbers inside them and when completed, Matilda would play repeatedly until she was tuckered out from the game. Charlie's heart was filled with sadness as he watched her stare off with no one to talk to, as the girls were all huddled around the tiny hand-chalked game. The hopscotch games that Miss Janice chalked out would cause Matilda to have to jump so far to reach each box, but she was able to perfect it quite well after some time. Charlie was off the following Friday, as he was scheduled to work the weekend. He set out to Harper's hardware store, bought painting supplies, and got his level out of his silver metal toolbox that had his name painted in black numbers. He climbed over the tall chain-link locked fence at the Saint Andrew's Catholic School parking lot, painted a giant-size hopscotch with giant letters inside each of the boxes, and cleaned up any evidence of him being there long before school hours came around.

The next day, the principal, Sister Antoinette, was furious. She called all the parents and talked to all the staff about what had happened. As she was on the phone, hollering at the maintenance staff and questioning them to see if they knew anything about the incident, she peered out her office window at the mysterious painted game on the ground. She spotted little Matilda. Matilda was hopping and jumping away, throwing the little stone on to the next number, and so on. The kids were all so impressed with Matilda's ability to jump so far, skip over the block that held the stone on it, and on to the next. They started cheering and competing with one another to play the game as well as Matilda. But none of them were a match for her skills. Matilda's smile was priceless. Sister Antoinette had never seen her so happy. As she was yelling on the phone, her booming voice started to crack. She was so touched by this beautiful turn of events. Then her voice changed again into a gentle whisper, and she simply said, "Never mind." She then slowly hung up the receiver. The mysterious, giant-size hopscotch remained, and how it got there was never investigated again.

The months grew into the next year and Matilda was growing like a weed. Before now, she rarely noticed Charlie hanging around. But on occasion, she would catch his eye. She would look at him with her big brown eyes and give him a warm smile, almost as if she knew he was someone familiar to her.

As she started to outgrow her dolls and stuffed animals, her three favorite friends made their way up to the top shelf in her bedroom. There they would sit watching over her. She stopped playing with them and bringing them to bed for the most part but would sometimes still sleep with Tada when she was scared or sad about something.

Alice's long-awaited convention for the blind finally came around the following year. The bus arrived at the college. Alice, Matilda, and Miss Janice found their rooms, unpacked, and made their way to the dining room for dinner. The three sat at the main table. The maître d' approached the table to ensure that all their needs were being met. The maître d' was a handsome Black man with a charming smile and piercing chestnut brown eyes. He was about the same age as Miss Janice. Miss Janice was tall with soft, light-brown skin. Even little Matilda sensed the chemistry between the two of them, which seemed to spark immediately as he pulled Miss Janice's chair out for her to take a seat next to Alice. Matilda sat on the other side of Alice. Her little head peered forward as she flashed a sweet, devilish look toward Miss Janice. She let out a giggle and covered her own mouth up to hide her giddiness. Miss Janice nodded and grinned.

"Hush, child," said Miss Janice. Miss Janice was having a tough time keeping herself from giggling like a child as well. After the president of the National Federation of the Blind said the grace, they all dove into their meals. Matilda looked around at all the blind people in the room. There were so many. Young and old, men, women, and children. They outnumbered their sighted guides by about ten times. She watched as they tucked their napkins and bibs into the tops of their shirts, fumbled with their utensils, and dug in. Many of them were sloppy eaters. They didn't look at all like her mom. Alice was always so neat about everything. Her food never fell off the side of her plate or dropped on her lap. For the first time, Matilda became aware of her mom's dedication to appearances. She thought about how her mom must have spent hours mastering the art of picking the right food from the menu that would be the neatest on her plate and the easiest to navigate. Then cut and pick up in small little morsels. Matilda wondered if that was why her mom liked soup so much. It was easier to scoop and easier to learn to steady the spoon and send down the chute. It would be much less complicated than stabbing around the plate in hopes of catching a piece of meat on the prong of the fork and longing for it to stay there on the journey from the plate to the mouth. Matilda learned so much about blind people on this trip. She never gave it a thought with her own mom and had been taking it all for granted. Alice had made everything seem so normal. As far as Matilda knew, her mom had a handle on adapting to life with being blind. Matilda was beginning to appreciate her mom's style and class. Her mom was an obvious cut above the rest.

Matilda grabbed her mother's hand and caressed it. She then gently held her mom's hand up to her own chest, cherishing this very moment of being with her. As Matilda sat in amazement, looking at her beautiful, strong mama, a tall, stately looking woman took to the microphone and introduced herself as the secretary of special affairs at the college. She welcomed all the members of the National Federation of the Blind. She talked and talked about community services and thanked what seemed like hundreds of people for their contributions. Matilda's eyes grew heavy as she slumped down in her seat and played with her napkin on her lap. Miss Janice repeatedly looked over, giving her a watchful eye to remind her to sit up straight.

Then the woman made an announcement.

"And with no further ado, I introduce to you, Ms. Alice Stiller. Class of 1947."

The woman went on to tell how Alice completed her four years at the college, obtained highest honors, graduated magna cum laude, and went on to the University of Pittsburgh to obtain her master's degree. The woman mentioned the many volunteers, such as Mrs. Masterson, who transcribed all the written books into braille for Alice. She spoke of how Alice still worked with the blind and deaf children and adults, teaching them the skills for independent living, and empowering the deaf and blind to become productive members of society. She went on to tell how she advocated for braille literacy and was currently working with the governor's office to pass a mandatory bill that all blind students be given the opportunity to learn to read and write braille.

"We present you with the Sisters of Mercy Award for Steward-ship and Community Service."

Alice and her guide dog, Elsa, with minimal assistance from Miss Janice, took to the pulpit.

Matilda watched as her pretty mommy talked into the micro-phone. She watched her read the braille notes from her prepared speech as her mom ran her fingers across the little index cards. Her voice was so eloquent sounding, and she enunciated every consonant with perfection. Matilda thought about how nice her momma's hair looked, as they had just gone to the hairdresser yesterday. Her mom usually bobby-pinned her parted hair over to the side, but on this night, she put it in soft curlers and let Miss Janice help with styling it to look like one of those ladies from *The Lawrence Welk Show*.

Matilda thought about how her mom must have really loved Miss Janice because she never allowed any grown-ups to help her with anything and was deeply insulted any time anyone tried to. Her mom had so much hairspray in her hair that Matilda thought it almost looked like a wig. Her lipstick was a brighter pink than her mom usually wore, and Matilda thought about how she would try it out on her own lips once they got back to the hotel room. Alice had a silk pea-green-and-yellow scarf tied around her neck and was wearing a blue dress with a belt that matched the yel-low in the scarf. Even at her young age, Matilda felt proud of the way her mom looked. And even more proud that she could pull it off being a blind person. Matilda realized that she really wasn't even paying attention to what her mom was saying, as she was so distracted by the fact that she was like a celebrity on this day. All eyes that could see, and ears, were on this woman that Matilda only knew as her mom. The person that spoke softly and kindly to her and told her how wonderful she was on a daily basis. The one who's lap she would sit on as her mom's arms would envelope

Matilda whenever she spoke. The one who read her books at night and taught her about manners and how all things are possible when you trust in God.

Alice finished her speech by thanking everyone who had been fighting for children's braille literacy and announced the names of several children from her success stories that at one point in their lives might have had future or contribution to the world, and now through learning to read and write braille would be able to communicate, move on to higher education, and obtain willful employment where there would have otherwise been no opportunity.

Matilda watched as the children, who were more recent students, approached the podium to stand alongside her mother. They were each accompanied by one or both of their parents. Her mom gave awards to each of them. She fashioned her speech about each one so as not to let one appear to be better than another and mentioned the strengths of each of them. Matilda reflected on how good her mom was at doing that. She never wanted anyone to feel less than what they had the potential to be.

Therefore, her mom took the time to study what would be an asset of each child that could be highlighted, for quite possibly the first and only time in many of their lives. She used words like "determination," "strong will," "perseverance," "faith," "support from their parents," and so on. They held on to each of their awards that were presented to them with their names brailled into the gold-plated placard. A statue was perched on top of each wooden stand of the trophies. It was a figure of a child with its eyes closed, holding a book under its arm and a cane in the other hand.

They held their trophies like brand new toys on Christmas morning. But it was more than that. Matilda noticed that they all wore expressions of great pride. They stood with straight postures, chests held high and shoulders back...no doubt taught to them by you-know-who.

They were all holding their symbol that made them feel like accomplished young men and women, who now, no matter what obstacles would be set in front of them, would be able to conquer anything from this moment on. Matilda watched as the children's parents, grown adults, fought to keep the tears from flowing as they watched the praise their little loves with special needs were receiving from her mom. It could have been the first time in many of the parent's lives that they felt their children were recognized as purposeful human beings and not poor little blind children.

"My mom is doing all of this," she thought. "She is changing lives! Forever!"

Of course, Matilda had always loved her mom and thought she was wonderful. But this was the first time that she realized what a magnificent person she really was and how she contributed to society in so many ways. She couldn't fathom how she had spent every day with her for the last seven years and not realized this before. How could she be so lucky to have her as a mother? Matilda completely forgot about the time period where her mom would go days on end spent in her room, crying and talking about monstrous people and how there were men outside waiting to take her to jail. How she had to go back and forth to the doctor for weeks until her medication was straightened out.

That woman was not this woman, standing in front of this room full of admirers.

After the ceremonies were over, Matilda was no longer intimidated to approach the young children. Some had odd-looking shaped eyes. Some had their eyes closed, and some had prosthetic eyes. She now saw them as just like her and any other child. Although a fading memory somewhat, Matilda recalled what it was like to not have good vision and the fear of needing to hold on to someone due to the unexpected of what was in front of you. It had been almost four years since her vision was corrected, but she could still relate to that distant feeling of the past. She ran up to the group of children that were milling around and giggling, as they were still elated by the recent recognition like little graduates at an after-party.

"Hi, I'm Matilda. My mom is Ms. Alice," Matilda said with pride. "I used to be blind too. Until the doctors fixed my eyes," she said.

There was a silence for a moment. As if her intention to belong was met with resistance, as she would no longer be considered one of them since she was now a sighted person. She began to feel embarrassed by what she just said. Mom taught her what the word "pretentious" meant, and she wondered if that was the way she appeared at this moment. That wasn't at all what she was trying to do. On the contrary. She was trying to relate to them.

She then felt compelled to add, "But I still can't see really well, and I wear very thick glasses!" She still did not get the response from the group that she was looking for, as she hoped her statement might make the group want to include her.

Finally, the little girl standing in front of her with long, curly blonde hair and a red checkered dress with a white Peter Pan collar, red tights, and black Mary Janes spoke up. Matilda remembered that her mother coined this little girl with the adjective "industrious."

"Hello, Matilda. It is very nice to meet you. We are just getting ready to do a spelling bee. Would you like to join us?"

Matilda breathed a sigh of relief. She was incredibly happy to participate in the game. After the third round, she realized that her spelling was not as good as many of the others. Albeit many were much older than her. Nevertheless, this sparked a new competitive interest in her to work on her spelling and vocabulary. Another little boy pulled out a giant braille Scrabble board. Matilda recognized this, as they had the same one at home. Her mom had been teaching her how to play, which made her feel very comfortable with this game. The printed letters on the board had a braille covering. The board was colorful for the sighted yet had a hard plastic covering over the top with each block perimeter raised so the tile could be snapped into place and not moved around as the children felt to read the word puzzles and figure out their next spelling move. The inside of the blocks had clear braille over print describing each spot for the number of points they were worth. Matilda thought what a clever setup this was so that the sighted and non-sighted could play.

The children played for hours. They laughed at the words that some had spelled out. And some argued that some of the words were made-up just to gain points. They would have votes to determine if the accused would be knocked out of the game or allowed to stay. The night came to an end with ice cream and a piano recital by one of Miss Alice's students, Anna Isabella.

Matilda thought that Anna Isabella's face was somewhat de-formed looking. Matilda was trying to look at the wall instead of at the girl, as her mother always told her how impolite it was to stare at people. Especially she was told not to stare at blind people because they couldn't stare back and give you a dirty look and make you look away. But she couldn't help herself. The girl's odd-looking face was distorted with scars. One eye was closed and the other looked wide open, and all you could see was mostly the white part of her eyeball. Matilda felt fear, then felt guilty for feeling fearful. What must have happened to her to make all that? Did she fall off a bike or something? Just as the little girl put her fingers on the piano keys, there was a resonating sound like a symphony. She played like an angel. It was a familiar song. One that she had heard her mother play many times before. Matilda's eyes suddenly shifted to follow the little girl's fingers as they so effortlessly moved across the keys. It almost didn't seem real. It was as if she were faking it, and they would soon discover some music player behind the curtain or something. But no, it was definitely real. Matilda had taken that song for granted all this time as it was constantly being practiced by her mom at home. Alice had taught this little girl to play it. Matilda started to feel a little bit jealous that these children, exhibiting all these skills at the spelling bee, scrabble game, and now the piano, were all taught by her mom. Her mom was spending time with these children perfecting their skills and making them a bunch of little prodigies. Matilda thought how she took for granted and dismissed her momma's requests to learn some songs on the piano or practice reading more. Even the dreaded task of learning braille. She did learn a lot of braille when she didn't have her sight. But why should she learn it now that she could see relatively well and learn printed material? It was this night that taught Matilda how little she had seen of the world and the remarkable clarity that the blind visualized of the world, every day of their lives.

CHAPTER 21

Matilda, Alice, and Miss Janice had grown into a comfortable little family over the years. Matilda spent little time with anyone else.

She was used to having the daily deliveries of the lily of the valley flowers as well but had never thought much about where they were coming from. Opening the front apartment door to find them sitting on the ground each day was as normal a routine as eating breakfast. It was as if she thought everyone had flowers delivered to their house each day.

Miss Janice had become distantly friendly with Charlie down the hall. It was nice to talk to the neighbors on occasion. Charlie would carry Miss Janice's bags whenever he saw her with the groceries. He did not say much but was always kind and continued doing small favors for others in the building. She did notice that he never had any visitors and wondered if he had many real friends or family.

When autumn came around the following year, Matilda was turning eight, and she was becoming more beautiful every day. Her piano skills were improving, and she looked forward to the daily lessons that she now accepted, full heartedly, from her mom. She was a naturally gifted player, and Charlie would often stand outside the apartment door with his ear up against it, eyes closed, listening to her magical little fingers while they played the most magnificent music he ever heard.

One particular evening, after walking from the bathroom, Alice tripped on Matilda's shoe that Matilda had left on the floor in front of the bathroom. Alice fell forward and hit her head on the corner of an end table that was sitting in the hallway. The blood was gushing, and she was howling in pain. Miss Janice frantically jumped out of bed, ran to the freezer, wrapped ice in a towel, and applied pressure to Alice's forehead. She instructed Matilda to hold the towel tightly against Alice's head as she instinctively ran down the hall to Charlie's apartment. She frantically pounded on the door. As he opened the door in his nightclothes, she grabbed his hand and pulled him down the hall into Alice's apartment. Charlie was taken by surprise and his hands were shaking because he hadn't been this close to Alice in years. He was concerned about her ability to instinctively know things that others would not. He worried that she would recognize his scent and remember who he was. Miss Janice asked if Charlie would stay with Matilda while she took Alice to the emergency room, as the bleeding was not ceasing. Charlie was trying not to speak in fear of Alice recognizing his voice. He stood far back toward the corner of the room. He just shook his head vehemently, cleared his throat, and in a whisper said, "Sure, sure."

Miss Janice didn't realize his bizarre behavior as she was so preoccupied with Alice's injury. Alice did turn her head toward him, as if she had heard something familiar, but was distracted by Miss Janice as she was carrying on about how the bleeding wasn't stopping. Miss Janice helped Alice hold the towel on her head to help control it.

Charlie noticed the stuffed animals on Matilda's shelf and remembered the bear from when his little girl was just a baby as they would cuddle up with their nighttime stories. He had actually won that bear for her at the church carnival years ago playing the kick the can carnival game. Charlie picked up her little furry friend on the shelf, brushed it off, and handed it to Matilda to comfort her while her mother was bleeding so profusely. She looked up at him with her big dark eyes. He stared back into them, savoring the moment as she hugged Tada. He had never seen her really look at him up close because the last time that he was with her, she hadn't had her surgery yet and was still blind like her adoptive mother.

Miss Janice and Alice hurried out the front of the building where they waved down a taxi to take them to the hospital. For some reason Miss Janice wasn't at all concerned about little Matilda being in the care of Charlie. They had been neighbors for several years now, but he, for all intents and purposes, was still a stranger. He just had such a peaceful, loving, way about him. Miss Janice would see him crossing the street to Saint Joseph's Cathedral every morning for daily mass and just knew in her heart that he was a good man.

After the two women left, Charlie stood in front of Matilda in the quiet apartment just looking at his little black-haired baby girl growing up so quickly before his very eyes. She walked over and took his hand in hers and said, "Can I see your apartment? I bet it looks just like ours."

Charlie instantly replied, "Of course."

He then thought for a moment if there might be any clues about the history of the little one in his apartment that would give him away. Any pictures that he had of the family were not out on tables or hanging on the walls. All his keepsakes were tucked away in his Navy footlocker that he kept under his bed. He would pull them out every week and look back at the wedding photos, the girl's baby pictures, and his Navy friends. But he was incredibly careful not to have any evidence lying around for this very reason. His apartment was fairly generic. He was very neat and orderly.

Everything was kept in its place, and it was quite charming for a single male person's dwelling.

He decided that it was safe to bring her to his place. Charlie found a slip of paper and pen in the drawer next to the sink. He jotted down a little note telling Miss Janice that they were up the hall if she happened to come back before they returned from Charlie's apartment. They grabbed the stuffed bear and locked the door behind them.

As they entered his apartment, Matilda could smell an almost overwhelming scent of the lily of the valley flowers. She immediately thought to herself that this was a familiar place to be, as she found so much comfort in that smell.

"Hey, do you get flowers placed at your front door every day too?" she said. Charlie's face became flushed, as he was not expecting that giveaway. He forgot that every day, before delivering the flowers to his ladies, he first brought them into his house, cut the stems, and fixed them up in a pretty bouquet. He hadn't realized that there was any evidence left behind.

He just shrugged his shoulders and said, "Do you like fish?"

Matilda shook her head. Then he brought her over to his fish tank. He told her how he named the fish after his three best friends from the Navy. That one was Buck. That one was Larry. And that one was Chip. He realized at that moment that he hadn't seen any of them in years and wondered where they might be as he and Matilda watched the fish swimming around without a care in the world. He thought about how Matilda had no idea that she was part of that family of men on that shoreline so many years ago, and that she was completely unaware of where she had come from and how she got to America.

Matilda loved the fish and loved the scent of his apartment. She started dancing and holding on to Tada, swinging him like a dance partner, round and round and round.

Finally, she collapsed on the couch. "Can you read me a story?" she said.

He looked around the room and thought for a moment. He did have some of the braille children's books from when she was a baby tucked away in his footlocker. However, that would definitely give him away. So, he found one of his mother's old cookbooks and sat down next to the little girl on the couch. As he opened the book and started reading to her about how to make chocolate cupcakes, she gently rested her little head on his shoulder just like she did years ago. Tears filled Charlie's eyes as he repeatedly cleared his throat so that he could pronounce the words without choking up.

Matilda said, "That sounds yummy. Can we make cupcakes together?"

Within minutes, Matilda was fast asleep. Charlie slowly slipped away and gently placed her head on the pillow on the couch and covered her with the afghan that he kept draped over the back of the couch that his mother had made for Matilda when she was just a baby.

After returning home from the hospital, Alice allowed Miss Janice to give her the pain pills that the doctor prescribed and help her get into her nightgown, assisting her to bed. Miss Janice found Charlie's note, then walked down the hall and lightly knocked on Charlie's door. When he opened the door, Miss Janice too noticed the scent of the lily of the valley. She glanced over at the couch at the little sleeping beauty covered in the little afghan.

Charlie rushed toward her with great concern and asked if Alice was okay. Miss Janice was a little taken aback by Charlie's eagerness to know about Alice's current status. She paused for a moment and looked into his face.

"I know you are the one bringing the flowers. I saw you through our peephole."

Charlie blushed.

"Do you bring flowers to all the neighbors or just to our apartment?" She looked at him with a suspicious but thankful, curious grin.

He let out a little giggle and said, "But is she okay?"

Miss Janice, still with that investigative look on her face, replied, "She is just fine. A few stitches but shouldn't leave a scar."

The look of pure relief on Charlie's face made Miss Janice even more curious about him. She just knew there was something more here than neighborly concern.

"I'll be back to get her at 6:00 a.m. You have a blessed night now," said Miss Janice.

Charlie couldn't believe that Miss Janice had presumptively decided to leave little Matilda in his care overnight. He responded, "You have a blessed night as well."

As Miss Janice turned to walk down the hall, Charlie added, "Thank you."

Miss Janice whispered to herself under her breath, "Hhmmmff, there is something about that boy. What is he thanking me for? Hmm hmm hmm." She shook her head, paused for a moment, looked back at his door, and let herself back into their apartment.

Miss Janice started watching Charlie a lot more after that day. She was convinced that something was secret but couldn't put her finger on just what it was. Why the daily flowers? Was it coincidental that he lived down the hall? Why did it seem that he was always available when the trio needed something? She would catch him watching Alice come off the bus, walking down the hall, fiddling with her bags, and talking to Matilda. She began to notice that Charlie offered help to everyone except for Alice. But she would watch him when he looked at Alice. She could see pain mixed with longing in his eyes.

He seems like he loves her, she thought. Miss Janice never thought much about Alice having a male friend before. And Alice had never expressed any interest to Miss Janice. She figured she better leave well enough alone given Alice's history and did not want to be responsible for sending her off the edge again with introducing some new situation into her life.

But maybe. Just maybe, she thought.

Matilda had made a new friend in Charlie and was excited to spend time with him. She would visit him on Saturdays. He taught her to play gin rummy, solitaire, go fish, and crazy eights card games. They would do crossword puzzles together. Matilda was very smart and would help him figure out the trivia answers to make the words fit into the boxes. She was now becoming a terrific speller and would find herself correcting Charlie sometimes. They would go across the street to Mass. Charlie told her that his favorite song was "Make Me a Channel of Your Peace." He told her that this was how we should try to live our lives, and if we can accomplish this, we will have true happiness. He even baked chocolate cupcakes with her, as promised, following her grandmother's cookbook recipe. Charlie was so happy to spend time with Matilda. Everything was falling into place so naturally. Matilda would spot him in the cafe across the street during school recess and send a little wave. She didn't think that it was odd to see him there day after day. In fact, she started to look for him every day at recess. Just so the two could exchange a smile and a wave.

CHAPTER 22

Alice's sister Marnie liked Miss Janice a lot and trusted her dearly with her little sister. Miss Janice set out to visit Marnie, as Marnie was now getting older and forgetting a lot of things. Miss Janice wanted to know more about Alice's past. She brought Marnie her favorite sticky buns from H&L Bakery. When she arrived, she put on Marnie's favorite big band record on a low volume and sat down next to her to talk.

Miss Janice filled Marnie in on Alice's latest NFB trip and told her how Matilda attended with them. And that Alice gave her speeches and awards to the little ones that she taught. Marnie still held on to her sarcasm and commented on how Alice must have loved getting all that attention. The two of them laughed out loud.

"Marnie," said Miss Janice. Her tone quickly changed to a more serious one. "I have been wondering lately about Alice's past. Who is Matilda's father? Why isn't he in the picture, and were they ever married? Is he of Asian descent? What happened? If you don't mind my prying," said Miss Janice.

Marnie sat quietly for quite a while. She then gave her reply.

"Matilda is adopted. Alice got her from Catholic charities, and because Matilda had a vision issue, they allowed Alice to parent her. After Alice had her last breakdown, the courts did let her keep Matilda, but that is where you came into the picture and that is why you are a live-in nanny. It was a requirement in order to keep the two of them together."

Janice knew all this, except for the adoption part. "I mean no disrespect," she said. "I am just growing ever so curious about what happened before I came along."

Marnie's admonishing tone became quite apparent to Miss Janice.

"Alice was married at one time," said Marnie. "My dear, don't go stirring up her past. She has forgotten all about them, and it should stay that way. She is happy now with just Matilda. She has a routine. She doesn't need anything coming back to haunt her and send her into a tailspin all over again! Leave it be!" said Marnie.

This statement sent a chill down Janice's spine.

Them? she thought. Now she was more curious than ever.

Just then, Marnie's nurse came in and announced that it was time for Marnie to go to therapy and that she was sorry to cut their visit short.

"No problem!" said Miss Janice. "I have to leave anyway so that I can get home in time for Matilda coming home after school." Miss Janice gave Marnie a hug as she made her way out of the building and down to the bus stop.

While on the bus ride back to the apartment, Miss Janice ruminated over what Marnie had said. Who was she referring to? What had happened to Alice? How odd was it that Alice had never mentioned "them" from her past? She wondered what Marnie meant by telling her to leave it be. She had so many questions. Miss Janice couldn't help it anymore, and she just had to know.

The following day, Miss Janice and Alice were going through Alice's mail, bills, and letters as usual. As Alice was brailing away with her slate and stylus, making sure that every piece of mail was labeled for her reference, Miss Janice lightly tiptoed around the subject. She tried so hard to choose the right words and say the right things so as not to upset Alice. She wanted so desperately to figure it all out. Miss Janice knew it wasn't her business but had become such an integral part of Alice and Matilda's life that she felt it was becoming her business. And if Matilda had a father out there, she should one day know.

Miss Janice knew that Matilda's father could not have been monstrous. After all, Alice was married. Somebody had loved her, at some point, enough to adopt a little girl with her...

As they sat, writing up birthday cards to everyone that Alice had on her monthly birthday list, Miss Janice came out with it.

"Alice, were you ever in love?" Miss Janice said.

Alice appeared startled by the question. She stopped labeling and pushing her stylus through the slate and paper.

Alice did not answer at first. It was almost as if she was confused by the question. Like she had to arrange her thoughts first before answering. Not as if she were trying to avoid the question. But more like she wasn't sure about it herself.

Finally, she answered again with the same answer as the last time Miss Janice had touched on the subject. "I had a dancing friend." A smile lit up Alice's face as she went on. "We would dance to Nat King Cole, Doris Day, the Mills Brothers..."

Then Alice started to sing.

"When I was just a little girl, I asked my mother, what will I be? Will I be happy? Will I be rich? Here's what she said to me..."

"My dancing friend was always there. I met him when I was a little girl. He taught me my left hand from my right. See?" Just then, Alice placed her hands on the table, palms down, and with her left hand made the shape of an "L" with her pointer and thumb fingers.

"Where is he now?" said Miss Janice.

Alice's smile quickly turned to a look of bitter sadness.

"He let her go," said Alice so matter-of-factly.

"He let who go?" replied Miss Janice.

"I can't remember. I don't want to talk about this!"

Alice started wringing her hands as she scratched them. Her eyes started dancing. Miss Janice knew what these behaviors meant and thought she'd better stop prodding or she would have a disaster of a mental frenzy on her hands.

"We better get these bills taken care of and let me read the birthday card that you are sending out to your niece so you can braille the message to her as well," said Miss Janice.

This seemed to redirect Alice. She responded in turn and resumed brailing away.

This had only prompted even more questions for Miss Janice. *Who is the dancing friend? Who did he let go? Why is this so secretive, and why can't anyone know about him or talk about him?* Miss Janice thought to herself.

Miss Janice decided, at least for now, to try to put it out of her head and just carry on, leaving things to her imagination about what had happened in Alice's past. She would occasionally try to jolt Matilda's memory. Although Matilda was just a little one when Miss Janice came into her life and was blind until the age of four, she wouldn't remember much about her history. Nevertheless, Miss Janice tried.

As Matilda was in the tub playing with her rubber dolls, Janice knelt down on the floor in front of her as she washed her long black hair and sprayed the detangler in it.

"Matilda, where did you get the names for your stuffed animals?" asked Miss Janice.

"Because they are my family," said Matilda as she squeezed the washcloth's soapy water over her dolls' hair.

Miss Janice flopped down on her buttocks, and her legs were stretched out on the floor. She just sat there, stunned.

The next day was Saturday. It was time once again for Matilda to visit with Charlie for the morning. Charlie and Matilda were sitting out front of the breakfront steps and playing cards with some of the other fellows from the building. Miss Janice was walking back from the corner deli with her groceries.

When she was about a block away, she spotted Charlie holding up his hands and making the shape of an "L" to show Matilda which hand was her left. Miss Janice stopped in her tracks. Her jaw dropped, and the groceries slipped from her hand. The milk spilled and the cans went rolling down the street. Charlie and Matilda ran over to help her. She just stared at Charlie.

She couldn't believe what her suspicions had told her was now seemingly real.

He is the dancing friend! He is the man that Alice had in her life ever since she was a little girl! He is Matilda's father! she thought to herself.

"Dancing friend," she said in a whisper, still taking in her revelation as she approached Charlie.

"What did you say?" said Charlie.

"You are the dancing friend," she said.

Charlie's face turned bright red, as he knew what that name meant. He was speechless.

"I-I-I…Why did you have to…Don't tell Alice…She can't…"

The look of fear and disappointment on his face gave Miss Janice a pit in her stomach.

Charlie turned and quickly ran up the breakfront steps.

"Charlie! Wait!!" said Miss Janice. "Come back!"

The following morning, as Miss Janice was leaving the apartment, there were no flowers by the door. She spotted the building superintendent leaving Charlie's apartment. Miss Janice asked where Charlie was, and the super shrugged his shoulders and told her that Charlie had paid the next month's rent, turned in his keys, and left.

Hearing this, Miss Janice felt terrible. And just like that, Charlie was gone. What would she tell Matilda about her friend? Would they ever see him again?

Matilda would ask about Charlie every day. She looked for him from the schoolyard every day at lunchtime. Miss Janice told her that he went away, and she wasn't sure when he would be back. Matilda eventually stopped asking, but she never stopped looking. She just knew he had to be close by.

CHAPTER 23

As Matilda grew, she became quite headstrong and independent. Miss Janice allowed her to now walk the last block to school on her own. She wanted so desperately to walk the whole way like the big kids did. But Miss Janice would not hear of it, as Matilda was only ten years old at this time.

It was a Wednesday in October. Matilda told Miss Janice and Alice that she had made a new friend at school. Her name was Dawn. Dawn invited Matilda to walk to her house the following day with her after school. Miss Janice and Alice were both excited for Matilda to go on a playdate given that she didn't have many friends to play with outside of school. They quickly agreed. Miss Janice asked for the little girl's address so she could pick her up at dinner time. Matilda already had it all written down and handed it to her. Matilda was so excited that night that she could hardly sleep. The next morning, Miss Janice helped her get her things ready for school and off they went. All day, the two girls talked about their playdate and how they were going to play with Dawn's Barbie Dream House when they got to her house and how she would meet the dog named Maggie. It seemed to take forever to get to the end of the school day. When the 3:00 p.m. bell finally rang, Matilda ran down the hall and out the front of the building. She waited on the front step for her friend to come down and meet her. The kids all filed out and left with their parents or with their friends to walk home or to their buses, which had now filled with students and pulled away. It didn't take long for the front schoolyard to empty out. Matilda decided to wait on the front steps as agreed.

Dawn was nowhere to be found. And Matilda was left all alone, standing on the top step of the old school building. The teachers had all gone inside too.

Matilda started to think that perhaps she was confused about the plan.

"Maybe she meant for me to walk alone to her house and meet her there," Matilda said to herself.

Dawn told her she was only three blocks from the school. Something inside Matilda told her that she shouldn't journey out on her own. She felt a little bit scared. She thought about it for a few moments longer. She knew Miss Janice would say no if she asked her.

I'm ten years old now, she thought to herself. She rationalized her choice by thinking about the twins down the hall from their apartment, who were only nine, and they walked everywhere by themselves. Matilda believed she could find Dawn's house and get there soon so that there would be plenty of time to play before Miss Janice came to get her. She decided to set out, as she was pretty sure she knew where Dawn's house was, as she remembered passing it before. Since Dawn lived pretty close to the school, Matilda assumed she would just ask people and figure out how to get there like her mom always did when she was out with her Seeing Eye dog. She had been longing to walk to the after-school destinations like the big kids did for so long. And now was her chance.

Matilda took off on foot down Bentley Street. She passed the first block, then the second. She reached into her pocket and pulled out the paper that Dawn's address was scribbled on. It read 41 Stonehaven Lane. Alice looked up at the street sign. It certainly wasn't Stonehaven Lane. Her heart started to pound ever so slightly. She didn't want to be scared but suddenly found herself feeling more alone. The sun was going down too, and it didn't seem that any familiar faces were around.

She walked another block. Now she knew she was going the wrong way because Dawn had told her she lived three blocks from the school. *Was it one block, turn, then another block, or was it two blocks, then turn?* she pondered. She was starting to feel panic, which was making her become more confused. She thought to herself for a moment that this was how it probably started when her mom got in one of her frenzied episodes. But this feeling never happened to Matilda before. She was beginning to feel a sense of doom.

What she didn't know was that Dawn never even asked her mom if Matilda could come over, and when her mom came to get her after school, Dawn tried to tell her mom of the plan, but her mom wasn't listening. Her mother whisked her off, as she had a dentist appointment, and they were already late.

At this point in Matilda's journey, she decided she better go back to the school. She suddenly turned and ran back the other way.

Oh no! she thought. *Is this the same direction back to the school?* Her eyes were getting fuzzy, and she was getting more and more confused about her surroundings. She started spinning around, looking for someone who looked trustworthy, but she was afraid to approach anyone. She tripped and fell to the ground. Her knee was cut. She sat and cried, holding her scraped knee. She put her hands together in the praying position.

"Why did I go off by myself? Oh God, please let Miss Janice come looking for me."

She sat there for several minutes, sobbing and shaking.

As she sat on the sidewalk with her head in her crossed arms on top of her bended knees, she noticed a shadow on the ground in front of her.

Quivering, she slowly lifted her head and looked up. There was still some sun remaining, and it was shining straight into her eyes. She could see a silhouette of a man standing there, peering down at her. The shape of the man looked somewhat familiar, but still she was afraid. The figure bent down on crouched knees in front of her, placed their thumb and index finger under her chin and lifted her head up.

It was her friend, Charlie. She couldn't believe it was him. Yet in that moment, she realized that she almost expected it to be him. She thought about how much she had missed him and how incredibly happy she was to see him. She leapt into his arms and hugged his neck so tightly as if she would never let go. She never even thought to ask him why he left or where he went so many months ago. She never even thought about how he knew to find her there. The two stood on the corner hugging for a minute or two.

She whispered in his ear, "I missed you." Charlie's eyes welled up, and he gave her an extra little squeeze before letting go of her and putting her hand in his. Charlie quickly composed himself and told her that they had better get back home before Miss Janice called the police. The two walked hand in hand back to the apartment building. Charlie dropped Matilda at the door and rang the bell for Alice's apartment. He looked at Matilda and told her he had to go.

She then responded, "Oh, please don't go. Please stay!"

Charlie's heart was filled with pain at the look on her sweet little face as he gently pushed her away and told her to wait for Miss Janice to come to the door.

He was walking backward as he left and said to Matilda, "I am always nearby. You never have to be afraid."

And off he went, just before Miss Janice came to the door to find Matilda standing there all alone.

Miss Janice looked so surprised and confused, as she was just getting ready to go pick up Matilda at Dawn's house and had no idea that Matilda had been lost.

Miss Janice looked all around, both ways, up and down the street. She looked at Matilda, and Matilda simply said, "Charlie."

Miss Alice shook her head. "Umm hmm," she said.

And into the apartment they went.

The following Tuesday, Alice and Miss Janice received word that Alice's sister Marnie was in the hospital and was not expected to live much longer. The hospital was about an hour from them, and since there hadn't really been anyone reliable to watch Matilda anymore, they took her with them on the bus to Lourdes Hospital on Camac Street.

Matilda had never seen anyone look as old as Marnie did in the hospital. She was fond of her aunt Marnie but didn't spend an awful lot of time with her anymore, as she had been getting sick for some time now. As they entered the room, Miss Janice assisted Alice over toward her sister. They hugged and cried when she met with her sister at Marnie's bedside. They whispered to each other and reminisced about their mother and their past. They talked about all their siblings that had now all passed on and that Alice would be the last surviving member of the family. They held hands tightly as they told each other how much they loved one another.

Marnie then asked to see Matilda. Matilda was reluctant to go toward her, as it was a bit frightening to see the old woman lying there looking so different from what she remembered from the last time she saw her.

As Matilda approached, Marnie's hand grabbed hers and she whispered, "Always take care of your mother. You are a special child and will do great things with your life," Marnie said.

Matilda couldn't help but be bothered by the strange odor coming from the bed. She was distracted and somewhat pulling her hand away. Anxiously awaiting the appropriate moment to move back from the awkward close encounter with her aunt, Matilda replied, "Thank you." She then reluctantly kissed her on the cheek and backed away from her as quickly as possible.

Matilda thought to herself that she was probably too young to be standing in this room right now and was surprised that Miss Janice allowed it because she was always so concerned about protecting Matilda. She realized Miss Janice probably didn't want to let her out of her sight given the situation after school just a few days earlier.

Then Marnie motioned for Miss Janice to come toward her. As Miss Janice approached her, Marnie shooed Alice and Matilda out to the hallway with a wave using the back of her hand.

Matilda was thrilled to get out of the room and swiftly went over and grabbed Alice's hand as she walked out and sat on the bench just outside the door along with her mom.

"Janice," said Marnie. "The house and everything in it now belong to Alice."

Marnie had never gotten married and didn't have any children. Marnie's home was extravagant. It was along the lake, about an hour from Alice's apartment in the city. The home was built in 1851 and had several rooms and annexes. The first thing that Miss Janice thought about was how much work it would be to clear everything out and organize all her things. It seemed that Miss Janice would inherit that part of it, as there wasn't anyone else at this point to take it on.

Marnie went on to tell her about all the money that would be left to Alice and Matilda. Then she paused. In a whisper she said, "There is more to their life than you know."

Before even realizing what word was slipping out of her mouth, Miss Janice replied in a sharp, surprisingly confident tone, "Charlie!"

Marnie's eyes flew open with a painful, almost piercing stare for a moment. Marnie gasped, as if she was going to say more. She then took a deep rattling breath in. Her exhale truly sounded like all life was being let out of her body. Then Marnie fell completely still. Her eyes were almost fixed on Miss Janice's, in a most chilling way, as she took this last breath.

Miss Janice closed Marnie's eyelids as she sat back, helplessly wondering, needing to know more about where the answers lay.

The answers must be in that house somewhere, she thought to herself.

In no time at all, the three of them had moved into the old home. It was more beautiful than Miss Janice had even imagined. She had no idea that Marnie had so much money that she was sitting on all these years. It became apparent now that the plan all along was to care for Alice after Marnie's passing. Miss Janice was not privy to all the contents stated in the will and wasn't sure if there was anyone else involved in the inheritance, but it did not appear so. On top of the inherited money that Miss Janice was entrusted to handle for Alice and Matilda, Miss Janice was also given a handsome sum for herself.

All the services remained in place to care for the home. They even had a butler and a housekeeper.

The butler was none other than the man that Miss Janice had met at the convention a couple of years prior.

This would eventually blossom into a relationship for Harold and Miss Janice.

Alice continued to do her work with the blind and deaf but now had agreed to accept having a driver to take her from place to place again, as she too was getting a bit older and less stubborn over the years.

Once settled into the home, Miss Janice made it her business to once and for all finally find out what the big secret was involving Charlie. There had to be something somewhere. Papers or pictures. Miss Janice went through everything. The items in the attic were put together so meticulously. There were albums, newspaper clippings about Alice, baby pictures, and every event at the blind school. Including graduations, piano recitals, an interview from the guild about being a teacher of blind and deaf children. It seemed that every moment of Alice's life was captured in these books and albums. However, there was a portion of Alice's life missing.

All of Alice's late twenties to thirties. No baby pictures of Matilda. But slews of pictures of her after the age of three. Where was everything in between? There was a big part of Alice's life missing in Marnie's collection, and Miss Janice tirelessly searched for years without coming up with a single clue.

CHAPTER 24

Over the years, Matilda had grown into an exceptionally talented, driven young woman.

After high school, she went on to Berkeley College and majored in music. She was an accomplished pianist, thanks to her mother, but always kept her interest in and volunteered with blind children. She would help her mother every chance she could with fundraisers, conventions, getting bills passed for blind literacy, and promoting an appropriate ADA education for blind and deaf children. She was very actively involved in the blind and deaf community.

It was a brisk October evening. Matilda was putting on a concert at the Pittsburgh musical theater. Miss Janice and Harold, along with Alice, attended. The theater was full. Matilda's performance was breathtaking. The crowd applauded with three standing ovations. There must have been five hundred people there. Everyone was so proud. As Matilda stood and took a bow, the stage lights were shining into her eyes, but she could see a very familiar figure in the audience. She couldn't see the face, but she knew it was him. Her face lit up and she gave a giant wave as if she were ten years old again. Miss Janice took notice of this and quickly scanned the audience to see who Matilda was so excited to see, and she spotted Charlie. He was older looking, and his hair was now white as snow. He was still incredibly handsome. She remembered the way he walked. It was him! Miss Janice jumped out of her seat, pushing through the legs of those seated near them. Not even having the wherewithal to say, "excuse me."

Her determination to get to him was certain. She had to catch him and talk to him. She needed to know who he was and why he always showed up in their lives. Yet always so mysterious about keeping himself at a distance and not making himself known to Alice.

Charlie no sooner slipped out of the crowd as Miss Janice ran through the lobby doors and out the main entrance. She ran down the sidewalk. He was out of sight. Just then, she looked around the corner and saw him swiftly walking with his old familiar bounce in his step toward the 903 bus to Ohio.

She hollered, "Charlie, stop!"

Charlie started walking faster.

"Charlie! Your wife and daughter need you!" she said.

He stopped dead in his tracks, his back toward her. He cocked his head to the side and paused again. The bus came along, and Charlie hopped on. As it pulled away, he looked out the back window of the bus at Miss Janice and shook his head from side to side, slowly, with a serious stare at her, as to let her know not to delve any deeper into what she might know.

She sighed, threw her hands up, and headed back to the theater.

The following week, Miss Janice contacted Matilda and requested that they talk the next time Matilda came to the house. Matilda was concerned that there was something wrong with her mother, and Miss Janice assured her that it was nothing like that, but she wanted to talk to her about her young life and if she had any information about where she came from. She was clearly a different nationality than her mom or Charlie. But everyone was always told that Matilda was adopted. It had always been accepted, however strange sounding it was, that a single mom adopting a child from another country was on par with Alice's desperate attempt to prove her independence in her young years. So, no one had really questioned it, including Miss Janice.

Until now.

Miss Janice rummaged through any old box she could find looking for clues. She asked Harold, the butler, if anyone came to visit Marnie regularly before she'd passed away, or if he knew of anyone else in Marnie's life. Harold could only remember an older couple with a little girl coming to the house on one occasion. Many years ago. There was some type of argument that had taken place, but he couldn't make out what was being said, and he never saw them again.

Miss Janice had recently found a letter from Alice that she had sent to Marnie when she first moved to her apartment after getting her first job. It had a return address of a little town in New Jersey near the Delaware River.

Now it was the second Saturday in November. Each month, Matilda and Miss Janice set aside a Saturday to go through a different room in the old house and clear out anything that could be given to Goodwill. Until now, Janice had never mentioned anything about her suspicions of Charlie and his involvement in their lives.

When Matilda arrived, Miss Janice grabbed her arm as soon as she came through the door. She decided to spill the beans and tell Matilda about all her thoughts over the years about Charlie and Alice and Matilda and how she knew that there just had to be a connection. Miss Janice told her about the flowers every morning at the doorstep and talked about what a coincidence it was that every time they needed help, Charlie miraculously appeared out of nowhere to save the day.

"Like a father would," Miss Janice said as she shook her head ever so slowly up and down.

Matilda tried to take in all this information. She slumped into one of the old parlor club chairs. It was a beautiful antique that had clearly been reupholstered several times but was starting to lose its shape, and Matilda's frame sunk deeply into the center of it. Her knees were knobbed together as she thought back. Matilda too had always found it strangely coincidental how Charlie always happened to appear at the most convenient times. He was always there in the nick of time, whenever they needed him. It was as if he was always waiting and watching.

"You don't really think…," said Matilda. The look on Matilda's face was a dead giveaway that she already knew the answer to that. Miss Janice continued to shake her head up and down. "But I am Asian. Mom adopted me because she always wanted to raise a child with a visual disability. I don't even look like him! Or her!"

"Now child, you know as well as I do that no one in this whole wide world would give your mama a baby to raise on her own with no pa and no one else to help her. No matter how hard she could kick and scream to get her way!" said Miss Janice.

"I suppose you could be right," said Matilda. "But why be so secretive? Why couldn't he just tell us who he was? Why live down the hallway all those years and never say one word to Mom, you, me, or anyone?"

"Well, I don't know. But we are going to find out! I just know there's a whole lot more to your mama's story than we know. Your aunt Marnie knew. I can bet you that. And someone went far out of their way to keep your mama and you away from it!" replied Miss Janice.

Matilda took the address label with the New Jersey address written on it and slid it into the pocket of her overall jeans. Matilda was now quite lovely. She had a clear, beautiful Asian complexion. Her long, straight hair looked panther black. She wore it in pigtails. Her bright red lipstick complemented her unusual big brown eyes.

Her thick-lens glasses made her look studious and complimented her look. She had a boyfriend now that she had met in her orchestra group, and they were becoming quite serious. She wouldn't dare tell him about this preposterous story that she and Miss Janice had come up with. He would think she was crazy.

CHAPTER 25

It was Thanksgiving the following week and in between performance schedules. As money wasn't of much concern anymore since she received her inheritance from the will, Matilda set out alone to find out about her and her mother's past, where they had come from, and how they had ended up here.

Matilda's vision was still not good enough to be able to drive, so she too took public transportation everywhere she went.

Matilda sat on the bus, looking out the window, and reminisced about Charlie and when he had lived down the hall. She remembered how she loved him and trusted him with her life. She thought back to her conversation with Miss Janice and grinned.

"Like a father would." The words ran through her mind over and over again.

Was this wishful thinking? She thought back to her favorite stuffed animals. Why was she so attached to them for so long? She had those stuffed animals ever since she could remember. Why were there three, and how did Shelly and Tada get their names?

She now realized that Tada probably stood for Dada, and the second was obviously her mama. But what about the third one? Maybe that one represented Matilda herself, she thought. But where did this name Shelly come from?

Matilda's cheeks suddenly became flushed, and her heart dropped. As she studied her thoughts, she had some semblance of a memory of a big mustard-yellow chair with a lady sitting in it, reading braille, who must have been her mother. She could barely remember but felt that there had been a baby there too. Or was there? She couldn't decipher what was made-up in her mind versus what was reality as her sight was very minimal before the surgery.

After all, Matilda's blindness at that age clouded her visual memory even more. The picture in her mind of the baby was quite real, though. After all, she could remember the chair. And the TV. And the piano. The piano seemed exactly like the one that was in their apartment in Pittsburgh and now sat in the parlor in the big old inherited home.

Why didn't I remember this before? she thought. Maybe it was just someone visiting that left a mark on her mind. Or maybe this baby was who she named the third stuffed animal, Shelly, after.

The bus stopped in the little town of Willing Heights. Once she stepped down on the curb, it was much less built up than Pittsburgh. However, there were still about four taxicabs lining the curb in front of the grade school. She grabbed the first one she saw and showed the driver the address in Riverdale. The driver told her it was only about ten minutes up the road and set the fare tab going.

As she approached the street, it appeared that the houses that may have once been there were all torn down, and they were building new construction. She didn't think about where she would go from there now that she got to the address. Nonetheless, she paid the driver, got out of the car, bundled up her turtleneck collar, buttoned her top coat button, pulled the fuzzy hood up over her head, and started walking.

She stopped an elderly woman on the street who was walking her dog and asked what had been at this site before the new homes started being built. The woman told her it had been a block of apartments. Mostly studios or one-bedrooms for singles. Matilda asked the woman if she remembered a blind girl living there about twenty-five years ago or so. The woman shook her head and said she did not remember.

Matilda then asked if there was a Catholic church nearby. If so, Matilda just knew that her mom would have frequented the church and someone there might remember her. The woman told her that there were six Catholic churches in the area. Matilda then asked if there was one along the bus line, and the woman told her that Sacred Heart would be the easiest one to get to from the bus line. She pointed her in the right direction, and Matilda walked down Washington Street to 5th Street, down to River Road, where she caught the bus heading south. When she got off at the stop, the driver pointed her in the direction of the church. It was just about time for the five o'clock Saturday evening Mass. Though Matilda hadn't really attended Mass for several years, she felt some nostalgia setting in, even though she had no idea if her mother ever even set foot in this place. There was something about it that felt so warm, and something extraordinarily strong pulled her in through the front doors. She had an overwhelming sense of a spiritual presence in this place. She didn't remember ever having such an experience in her life before this moment. Matilda walked all the way to the very front pew. She didn't know why she chose to do this, as in the past several years, and in the off chance that she did go to Mass, she would always just grab a seat in the very back corner and slip out before it was time for Communion.

This Mass was particularly interesting to her. The priest was noticeably young and announced that he was newly assigned to the parish. His sermon was about doing virtuous deeds and not for the purpose of showing others that you were good. But rather to help others and do right by all of God's children but not brag or boast. To be humble and only let the Lord see your acts. The priest asked the congregation if they were so lucky to know anyone like that.

Matilda immediately thought of Charlie. And then she thought of her mom. And then she thought of Miss Janice.

Wow! How lucky I am to know three selfless people. And they all took part in raising me, she thought.

Even though her mom did revel in getting attention for her accomplishments, she was still very selfless at heart.

After Mass was over, Matilda rushed to the back before the rest of the people started to file out and stood outside while they exited. She pulled out a picture of her mother from around the time that she may have lived there. As the parishioners shuffled out the door, Matilda asked each of them if they knew this woman. Some ignored her completely. Some took a closer look and shook their heads as they walked on past. One woman seemed to peer at the picture for an unusually longer period of time but then also moved on.

The crowd shuffling by became smaller and smaller until no one was left. Matilda sighed, then turned and walked away.

"Honey, wait!" a voice called from behind.

A woman who looked to be older than her mother approached her. It was the woman who had peered a bit longer at the picture but had moved on.

"Can I see that picture again?" said the woman.

Matilda held up the picture, and the woman grabbed it from her hand and studied it.

"That's Alice," she said in a whisper. "I wondered what ever happened to them," she said.

She then looked up into Matilda's big brown eyes.

The woman placed her hands on her cheeks and said, "Oh my stars! You are the little Asian girl. I can't believe it!"

Immediately, the woman threw her arms around Matilda.

"Yes! Yes! I knew your mother well!" said the woman.

"My name is Jean Collins. I introduced your parents! Oh, and what a shame about the little baby. I'm sure they were never the same after that!" she said.

Upon hearing this, Matilda's face turned white. Her jaw dropped. Jean looked at her with a confused look on her face.

"My dear, what did I say to upset you? Why are you asking if anyone knows your mom?"

Matilda's words were broken. Her lips quivered.

"I didn't...I didn't know...I didn't know I had a father. And the baby? I think I am going to be sick. I need to sit down." Just then, Matilda fainted.

She woke to the sight of a ceiling fan spinning overhead. She was lying in a strange bed in a strange room. She could smell beef. Like a soup or a roast or something. The room had pretty, pink-flowered wallpaper on the walls. It smelled kind of nice too. Like a mixture of perfume and mothballs.

Mrs. Collins came rushing through the bedroom door to check on her.

She clasped her hands together and brought them up to her chest when she saw her awake. She rushed over to grab the wet cloth that she had placed on Matilda's forehead. Then went over to open the window.

"This room gets so hot in the winter, we have to run this fan and occasionally open a window to let the room cool down," said Mrs. Collins. "I will bring you some dinner. You can stay with us as long as you need to until you feel better," she said.

It was at that moment when Matilda remembered the conversation before she blacked out.

"Wait! I need to know who you were talking about." Matilda threw the covers back and jumped out of bed.

"I only know my mother and Miss Janice. It's just the three of us. I came to find out more about where I came from." Then, in a sheepish whisper of a voice, Matilda said, "Was my father's name Charlie by any chance?"

Mrs. Collins looked at her with pity that she might not have known who her sweet father was.

"Oh dear! Yes! Yes! Charlie was a nice young man. He was so in love with your mother. And he was so in love with you. And your little sister!" said Mrs. Collins.

Upon hearing this, Matilda once again felt nauseous and fell back down again onto the bed.

"Oh dear, you're fainting again," said Mrs. Collins.

Matilda stared at the ceiling fan as if in shock.

"No, no. I'm okay. This is a just a lot of information, and I have so many questions. But I have to get up and out of this bed."

"Come, we will eat. I will start from the beginning and tell you everything I know." The pair shuffled down into the tiny, warm kitchen. Matilda was still processing what she had just heard. She did not know where to start with the questions. Mrs. Collins lived alone since her five children grew up and moved away. She only had her two cats for company but was still regularly active in the church. She was moving about the kitchen so nonchalantly. Matilda wondered how this woman could be delivering such world-shattering news in such a calm, everyday, matter-of-fact fashion.

Mrs. Collins served up the soup as Matilda sat there. She felt stunned and numb. Mrs. Collins took a seat right next to Matilda and draped a little knitted shawl over Matilda's shoulders as Matilda took a sip of water, trying to wet her parched mouth.

Mrs. Collins told her all about the first time that Alice walked through the church doors of Sacred Heart, like gangbusters, in high fashion with her guide dog. How she put the people right in their place and gave them a rather harsh talking to about how to treat blind people. Matilda definitely knew she had the right person after hearing this.

Mrs. Collins told her how Charlie lived right up the street with his mother and sisters and brothers. She told her how his mother and brothers had all since passed away. She talked about how Charlie was a little odd but such a good boy. And how he was completely starstruck with her mother. She talked about their love affair and how he joined the military and went away for a while.

Still, she was speaking so off the cuff. She told her how Charlie came back from the Navy with Matilda in his arms. Then knocked on Alice's door and asked her to marry him.

Matilda almost fell off her chair again as she was hit with more incredible news. Mrs. Collins grabbed Matilda's shoulders and propped her back up to her regular sitting position as if she were a doll. She was behaving as if she was pulling a falling sack of potatoes back up on the chair.

It was as if Mrs. Collins didn't have a filter and hadn't given any thought to the fact that she might consider breaking all this news a little more softly to Matilda.

At this point, Matilda didn't care anymore about the blunt delivery of information. She was now getting used to being hit with shocker after shocker and just wanted to hear more.

"So, then they moved out to that little country house in the woods of Milford Lakes, and I didn't see them much after that. Then of course the baby came along," she said.

"Yes! Yes! What baby?" said Matilda.

"I don't remember her name," responded Mrs. Collins. "But she was about two years younger than you. You know your mother was very emotionally unstable, and I heard she was having a challenging time. The people in her new neighborhood didn't know them like we did. There were some that thought the couple was very irresponsible for having two children with Alice being blind and with her emotional fragility and such."

Mrs. Collins looked off somewhat pensively. She told Matilda that it would have been better if they just stayed in this town instead of moving out to the woods. Here everyone knew them and could offer more support.

"What happened to the baby!" Matilda shouted. "Sorry. What happened to the baby?" she repeated in a calmer tone.

"Well, as the story goes, Charlie was watching the baby and he lost her, and they never found her again. Everyone assumed she drowned in lake one. But no one ever found her body, and the lakes weren't very big. And it was man made. It didn't make sense," she said. "Your mother lost her mind and never forgave him. I heard she went away for a while, and they split up. But then I lost touch with both of them after that. I often wondered over the years what became of them...and you!"

Mrs. Collins looked off into the distance, as if she were once again forgetting who she was talking to and providing all this life-altering information to. "No one ever believed the story as it was told because Charlie was always so cautious with Alice and the children. It didn't make sense," she said.

The next day, as the taxi waited outside for her, Matilda hugged Mrs. Collins and asked if there was anyone she might know that would have any information about where they lived in Milford Lakes and anything else after that. Mrs. Collins shook her head and for the second time appeared to take pity on Matilda.

This time, it was because of everything that Matilda had just learned about her past in a matter of a few short hours. The two hugged and Matilda ran out to the taxi with her duffel bag thrown over her shoulder. The taxi drove down the snow-covered street toward her next destination. Matilda asked the driver to take her to the center of town in Milford Lakes, New Jersey.

CHAPTER 26

As she stepped out of the taxi, Matilda looked around the little wooded country town. It was charming.

Now she understood why Charlie would have wanted to live here. There was a gas station, a post office, a library, and police station all lined up in a cute little row. Right next to one another. There was an inn on the corner that had a giant statue of a Native American out front. There were very little sidewalks, and she wondered how her mother ever got along in such a place as this. Her mom loved city streets lined with sidewalks and activity. It seemed odd to her that she would have enjoyed this kind of life.

Matilda looked up the street a bit, and there appeared to be a small coffee shop ahead. She decided to grab a little bite and possibly run into some retired folks that might remember her mom and Charlie. She grabbed the seat by the window and ordered her black coffee along with a blueberry muffin. She pulled the picture of her mom out of her pocket and spoke to it.

"You are so mysterious, my beautiful mom," she said. "And you really don't remember any part of this life that I just found out all about? I had a sister, and she disappeared without a trace," she said.

It seemed ridiculous to Matilda too that Charlie would lose a child under his care.

Matilda knew how attentive and loving he was toward her. It didn't make any sense. Maybe he was that attentive toward her because he had lost her little sister? It still did not add up. She walked throughout the coffee shop, showing the picture to everyone there and to anyone coming through the doors. She reminded the passersby that this woman would have been blind and probably had a guide dog, a husband, and two little girls. They all studied it and shook their heads.

One gentleman looked at the picture and actually listened to her description of her family. He seemed to recall the family and said he thought that they lived on Wawa Trail but wasn't quite sure.

She presumptuously gave the man a big hug. "Thank you so much!" she said. Then she ran out the door. She stopped in her tracks, turned, and ran back inside.

"Where is Wawa Trail?" she said. The man drew the directions on a napkin and handed it to her. It was only a few blocks away. Matilda hurried down the road, took the second left and then the right. She walked until she came upon Wawa Trail. This did not seem familiar to her at all. Although she reminded herself that she had been blind at the time and only three years old, or maybe even younger, when she'd lived there.

Matilda knocked on almost every door on the street. Some weren't home, and others, when answering the door, had no recollection of the woman in the picture or of Matilda's depiction of the woman and her family. She wondered which home may have been theirs and tried so hard to remember something about their house or its surroundings but just couldn't identify with anything that would be even remotely familiar. Matilda thought it was very strange that no one would remember such a tragedy happening in such a small town just 20 years earlier and that so many wouldn't know of their family.

After growing tired of the arduous walking and knocking, she decided she would go to the library and look for the article on the missing child. She would read up on what happened to her little sister.

"That is a crazy thought. I have a little sister," she mumbled to herself.

Once at the library, she situated herself in the microfilm room and started her search. She imagined it was spring or summer time, since Charlie reportedly lost the little girl, and it was thought that she had drowned. So, it was more than likely during a warmer season. She typed in keywords and looked through article after article until…There it was!

"Husband of blind woman and father of blind child loses baby. Baby thought to have drowned."

The article was written in a bizarrely cold, judgmental manner and was to the point.

For such a small town, you would have thought there would be a lot of interviews with various neighbors and police officials, pictures of manhunts and community uprisings. Instead, it seemed more like a report about a missing dog or something. Matilda found this to be very odd.

She printed out the article and shoved it, rather sloppily, into her satchel and hurried out the door.

She was on her way to check into the hotel across the street. She was walking rather swiftly and was very distracted with her thoughts as she bumped shoulders with a passerby who was carry-ing a bag of groceries. The groceries flew out of the person's arms and all over the little dirt road. Oranges rolled down the trail.

"Oh, I'm so sorry. I-I-I…"

She bent down and began crawling around the dirt road. She frantically picked up the oranges and placed them in the hands of the person whose palms were open with arms outstretched to accept the oranges.

"Please forgive me for being so rude. I just received some rather overwhelming news, and I-I-I…"

Matilda looked up into the face of the person she just basically assaulted and was once again left speechless.

There she was…It was like looking at her mother, Alice. Only twenty years younger. She was a beautiful girl. Her hair, skin, and eyes were just like her mother's. Her mouth was just like her mother's, but this girl's eyes were open. Bright and beautiful!

They were hazel green as well.

The two just stood there and stared at each other for a moment.

The girl clearly became uncomfortable as the gaze went on for too long to be your average eye connection.

"Shelly?" said Matilda.

The girl looked back at her with a look of disdain.

"No," replied the girl. "I think you must be mistaken."

Matilda already noticed a stark difference in the girl's personality than that of her mother's. This girl did not hold her head up high with confidence and appeared to be very shy and nervous with this encounter. She was dressed rather homely, in a black jumper with black tights and black rainboots. She wore a white hat and matching scarf. She didn't look very happy and had a flat affect about her.

The girl quickly looked away, grabbed the rest of her groceries off the ground, and made her way back down the trail as if speed walking to get away from Matilda as quickly as possible.

Matilda just had to follow her. "Wait! Wait!" said Matilda.

The girl sheepishly turned around to look at her. Her head was down, looking just over her shoulder at Matilda. She had a look on her face that was perplexed, a little scared and a little creeped out by this person. She started walking even faster in an effort to lose Matilda. Once realizing that she was frightening the girl, Matilda decided to back away and stopped in her tracks while the girl walked on down the road until she was almost out of sight. She could see the girl in the distance, periodically looking over her shoulder to ensure that she was not still being followed.

Matilda made her way to the inn and sat down at the bar. As soon as she walked in, the bartender was taken by the sight of her. Her coke bottle glasses seemed so fitting to her look and personality. She wouldn't have looked nearly as cute without them. She plopped her purse on the bar and the two locked eyes for just a moment.

"I'll have a whiskey sour," she said quite confidently. She didn't let on that she thought the bartender was incredibly attractive as well. He was not quite so shy about his interest as he smiled and didn't take his eyes off her as he handed her the drink. She had never had a whiskey sour before but didn't know what else to order. It was really the only alcoholic drink she knew the name of because sometimes Miss Janice would order it when they would be out to dinner on special occasions. She took a sip and started coughing and gagging and trying to catch her breath. The bartender let out a little chuckle but thought it was the cutest reaction he had seen in a long time.

"I'm sorry to laugh at you, but clearly you don't drink much, do ya?" he said.

Matilda's face turned red with embarrassment.

"No, I don't. But what a couple of days I've had!" she responded.

In the usual, bartender cliche manner, he bent over onto his elbows where he could come closer to her and said, "Why don't you tell me about it?"

As she brought her coughing and gagging under control, she started in with the whole story about how she came here from Pennsylvania, looking to find out more about her mom and where she came from. She blurted out the whole story with incredible speed and hardly stopped to catch her breath.

"You see, there was this guy, Charlie, who I just found out is my father. And I pretty much knew him my whole life as the neighbor down the hall, and then he disappeared and came back whenever I was in trouble. And this lady just told me a couple of days ago that he is my dad, and there was a baby who I think might be my sister but apparently she died, but nobody ever found her body, and then I ran into this girl just a short while ago who looks just like my mother and then I scared her away and…"

She stopped as she noticed the look on the bartender's face. He was pleasantly amused but bewildered at the rush of words flowing from her lips. His jaw was somewhat dropping as he listened to the jibber-jabber.

"I'm sorry. It's just that all this news has been overwhelming for me. And I always talk too much when I am upset."

"It's okay," said the handsome lad. "Do you have any pictures of these people about whom you are talking? I've lived around here for a few years now and pretty much know everyone in town."

"No," said Matilda. "I came here just with a picture of my mother. My mother! Yes! I have a picture of her! The girl I just saw looks just like her."

She fumbled for the picture that was now down in the bottom of her bag. As she pulled it out, it was a bit crinkled up with folds in it.

The bartender took a good look at the photo.

"I think I know a girl that looks very much like the woman in this picture. She walks everywhere. Keeps to herself and doesn't seem to ever be with anyone or really have many friends. I think she works at the Lucky 13 store just up the road."

"Thank you. You have been so helpful," said Matilda.

She didn't take another sip of the drink, laid her money down on the table, and left.

"Good luck!" hollered the bartender.

Matilda waved her arm while walking out the door with her back toward him.

The next day, Matilda headed straight for the ironically named convenience store as soon as it opened. She entered the shop, and there was an elderly man behind the counter. He wasn't very friendly. Matilda described who she was looking for. The man replied, "Oh, you must mean Rita. She won't be back until Wednesday," he said.

"Well, do you know where she lives?" Matilda said.

"Nope," said the man. "She will be back on Wednesday." With this, he turned and walked through the swinging doors into the kitchen.

It was only Monday. She spent the next two days walking around town and window shopping, walking up and down Wawa Trail and the surrounding area, looking for some semblance of where she came from. As she walked by a little log cabin, she couldn't help but notice someone opening the curtain slightly and looking out at her. As she started toward the window, the curtain dropped, and the person disappeared. Matilda wondered if that might be the mysterious Rita, aka Shelly.

Matilda continued walking nonetheless, looking over her shoulder, as she could feel that she was being watched.

When Wednesday finally rolled around, Matilda anxiously got up early, showered, brushed her teeth, and waited outside around the back of the Lucky 13 store until it opened. She didn't want to scare the girl off a second time but needed to see her again. Watching and waiting, sipping her cup of coffee from the disposable cup that she had her fingers wrapped around, trying to keep her hands warm.

It was approaching 11:00 a.m. when sure enough, the girl came walking up the road in her work uniform. Matilda could see that the girl even walked like her mother. Sort of a leaning to the left posture.

Matilda had always figured her mom's tilt was from walking with her guide dogs all those years but now realized it was a genetic feature.

Now that she was sure it was the same girl, Matilda went back to the library to try to find more information or news articles about the tragedy. She looked through microfilm all day and came up with nothing. Matilda waited until closing time at Lucky 13. As the girl turned out the lights and locked the door, Matilda hid behind the building and walked far behind, following the girl home. The girl's house was on the street behind Wawa Trail. Matilda stood behind another tree and looked on to see who would greet the girl. Once inside the house, she watched as the girl turned on the light in her little log cabin. It didn't appear that anyone was there to greet her. There were no cars in the driveway. She could see a calico cat jump up onto the windowsill and peer out as if it were looking right at Matilda.

After watching the downstairs lights turn off and the light turn on at the second-floor middle window, Matilda stood and waited. Waited to see if there was any other activity in or around the house. After about ten minutes, all lights were out in the house and darkness filled the street.

Matilda made her way back to the inn.

She could hardly sleep as she lay there, thinking of how to approach the girl without scaring her away this time.

Matilda still carried a rosary in her pocket, as her mother had taught her, and placed it in her hands and started to pray.

"Please God, help me to talk to this girl tomorrow and to say the right thing."

Matilda now knew, in her heart, that this was indeed her sister that disappeared so many years ago.

Again, so many questions. How did it happen that they became separated? How did this outlandish story of Charlie losing a little baby come to be? What happened in this charming little wooded town so many years ago? And why didn't anyone ever tell her mom or Charlie that the baby was found and safe? Who had raised her?

CHAPTER 27

The next morning, Matilda walked out of the inn, pushed the doors wide open with force, and walked straight down the dirt road. She was on a mission. She walked steadfast and determined until she reached the front door of the house where she had followed the girl home the night before. In the daylight she noticed that there was a knocker on the door with the name "Martino" engraved in cursive in the center.

Matilda paused for a moment, took a deep breath, and grabbed her hands to control them from shaking. As she grasped the handle of the knocker, she held on to it for a moment with hesitation.

Then with three swift knocks, she made her presence known.

The door opened ever so slowly, and there the girl stood. Her head was down, and it appeared that she was hesitant to make eye contact with Matilda.

Matilda's eyes grew opened wide and a huge smile ran across her face. The girl sheepishly looked up at her. She had a sort of longing expression on her face yet looked frightened at the same time.

"Why are you following me?" said the girl.

"Hello, I am sorry for just showing up unexpectedly," said Matilda. Her words were hesitant and choppy. "I wanted to apologize for upsetting you the other day. You see…I saw you, and… Well, I…I have this picture…"

She pulled the picture out of her front pocket and handed it to the girl.

"This is my mom. I recently found out that I had a sister that went missing in this neighborhood when we were very young, and I came here to find out more about her. When I bumped into you on the street...Well, you see, you...you look just like her," said Matilda. She tried to deliver her words in a more compassionate manner than the news had been delivered to herself just several days before. *But how do you break this kind of news to someone gently?* she thought to herself.

The girl stared at the picture for what seemed like a lifetime to Matilda. She wanted to say something but thought she should wait for the girl's response. Without taking her eyes off the picture, the girl opened the door and stood to the side as an awkward welcome for Matilda to come inside.

Matilda sensed that the girl was having the same kind of stunned reaction that Matilda had experienced just days before when Mrs. Collins so abruptly rocked her world.

"I wondered if we could talk a bit about who you are," said Matilda.

The girl still hadn't said anything else. The girl finally took her eyes off the picture of Alice long enough to say, "Wait here."

Matilda took a seat on the old musty-smelling couch and looked around the still house. There were pictures on the piano of the girl with a man and woman but no other pictures of any other people or family.

When the girl returned, she had a book in her hands.

"Your name is Rita, right?" said Matilda.

"My name is Francine Martino," responded the girl. "People call me Rita. I'm not really sure why, but they just always have."

"Did you grow up around here?" asked Matilda.

"Yes, I've lived here my whole life with my parents. They are both dead now, and it is just me and my cat, Whiskers. My uncle lives one block over. He was a county judge for years but now has dementia, and I look in on him every day," she said.

Rita told Matilda that she had found a book under the floorboards in her parent's room after they had passed away. It had her baby pictures in it and some articles about a missing baby girl.

Rita still held the book tightly to her chest with both hands, and Matilda had to control the urge to yank it straight out of her grasp.

"There is this picture of a woman who looks just like me and a man who I had seen around here and there ever since I can remember," said Francine.

"Charlie," whispered Matilda. "Is the man handsome with bright blue eyes and dark eyebrows?" she said.

"Yes!" said Francine. "He watches me. But no one else ever saw him. I told my mother about him once because he helped me when I fell off my bike. She said to never talk to him again if I saw him and to tell her right away because he would hurt me the next time. But I knew she was wrong because he always looked at me with love in his eyes. I have seen him a lot over the years but never told my mother again. You see, she loved me. But she could become terribly angry and fly off the handle frequently. She was extremely strict and could be very mean to outsiders. I wasn't allowed out much at all. I never really knew many people in town. I spent most of my time at home. After my parents died, my uncle got me the job at the store."

Matilda took Francine's hands in hers. She looked her square in the eyes.

"Francine, I believe that you are that missing girl from the newspaper articles and that you are my sister. And that man that you have seen over the years is our father. His name is Charlie. We have a mother. Her name is Alice. She is blind. And she is a lovely, wonderful lady who has accomplished so much in her lifetime."

As they looked through the book together, Matilda told Francine all about Alice and how Alice seemed to have no recollection of life from the time when she met Charlie until Matilda's life after the age of three or four. Matilda told her that she believed her mother suffered the traumatic event of losing her little baby, which caused her to lose all memory of that time period. She told her how she believed the baby's name was Shelly or Michelle.

Francine was a bit taken aback with the realization that the woman who raised her all those years must have somehow known all this and kept it from her.

Francine and Matilda seemed to connect almost immediately after this. They talked, cried, and laughed for hours. They shared their stories of growing up and talked more about each other's encounters with Charlie over the years. Matilda told her how much she loved him but how he mysteriously came and went from her life. They talked about how she too knew he was never far away and would always be close by to protect her.

Matilda asked Francine if she had any idea of why someone would take her from the family or what the circumstances might have been surrounding her disappearance so many years ago. Francine told Matilda that if anyone knew it would be her uncle. He had dementia but still had moments of lucidity, and they might be able to get some information from him.

The two girls decided to pay him a visit. As they approached his house, which looked almost identical to Francine's house, only one block over, Francine knocked lightly and opened the door to his home on Wawa trail.

"Uncle," she said.

"In here," he called.

As the two entered, Francine's uncle appeared to be in an alert state. He recognized Francine and asked her who her young lady friend was. He was very pleasant.

Francine introduced Matilda and because she knew she had caught him at a time of lucidity, she decided to come right out with it. She told him that her friend Matilda gave her news of a young girl that went missing years ago, and Rita and Matilda felt that it might possibly have been Rita.

Rita then said, "We think my friend here is actually my sister."

The gentleman did not hesitate for a moment. He turned to her unapologetically, and without any attempt to avert or avoid the topic, he said, "I was wondering when you were going to figure that out. It's about time. After all these years, a weight has finally been lifted from my shoulders" he said.

Her uncle started in. He told them that his sister had taken Francine from the family when she was very young. The baby had pushed through the metal door that was unlatched and crawled down the steps and around to the side of the house. His sister, Mrs. Martino, never approved of the couple and didn't feel that they were responsibly raising their children. And having no children of her own, she decided that the baby would have a better life with her and her husband.

He then turned to Matilda but could not look at Rita. He then said to Matilda, as if Rita wasn't sitting right there, "Your father found out about this and tried to get her back. But she blackmailed him and told him that she would get me to issue a court order taking you away from your mother, especially after her breakdown following Rita's disappearance. I also used my connections to help your mother get custody of you with the stipulation that you had live-in care to help you and your mother for the rest of your lives. We managed to keep it a secret in town for many years. Everyone assumed that my sister adopted a baby, and no one asked any questions. People tend to protect one another around here" he said.

Rita didn't have it in her to confront him in an angry way. She looked with pity on the old man who was confessing his misdemeanors without remorse. Her affect remained flat as she processed the information.

In fact, she said nothing. She simply stood up, kissed him on the forehead, and told Matilda that it was time for them to leave. As the girls walked down the dirt path toward Rita's empty house, Rita told Matilda that she did not wish to stay there any longer, as it was not her home.

They went back to the old log cabin so that Rita could gather her things. Matilda slouched back into the big old couch as the dust flew again. She then leapt forward with elbows on her knees.

"That's it!" said Matilda. "He is always there when you need him! Come on! I have an idea!"

Matilda grabbed Francine's hand, and Francine held on so naturally tight to her big sister's. They ran out through the screen door, leaving it to bang behind them.

Matilda started yelling in the street, "Charlie! Charlie!" She felt somewhat embarrassed to be yelling his name out in the middle of the town, but she kept on. "Charlie, we know you're out there!" she said.

Then Francine looked at her as if needing permission to join in the call. Matilda shook her head.

"Come on!" she said. The two girls, in unison, started excitingly chanting and calling his name in the streets. They were laughing and running. Their voices got louder and louder. They reached the main street and people stopped to look at them, trying to figure out to whom the two crazy-looking girls were calling out. The bartender came out of the inn. He leaned against the pillar, threw his head back, put his hands on his hips and chuckled at the two grown ladies acting like little girls skipping and running down the street. The townspeople looked at one another and shrugged their shoulders. Merchants came out of their stores to see what the commotion was. And before you knew it, the townspeople started joining in, and everyone was calling Charlie's name!

Crowds of people chanted his name and threw up their arms. None of them knew why they were calling him. They were infected by the joyfulness of the two lovely girls.

"Charlie! Charlie! Charlie!"

It became louder and louder as more and more people joined in.

The girls were running faster and hollering. Suddenly the girls stopped in their tracks.

At the end of the dirt road, from behind an old barn toward the end of town, he came walking out.

Slowly and purposefully. Their smiling, giggling facial expressions turned quickly to startled, then morphed to looks of pity, then to looks of pure joy at seeing the man that they now both knew as their father. Their eyes filled with tears as he walked closer. His hands were shaking. His face was flushed. He had tears in his eyes. He walked straight to both girls and fell to his knees, sobbing.

"My beautiful babies! My Matilda and my Shelly!" he cried out fiercely, as twenty years of pent-up emotion poured out of his body.

The girls fell to the ground and threw their arms around him as they all sobbed together, wiping each other's faces, laughing, crying, and hugging. They sat in the middle of the dirt road until dusk, without a care that cars might try to pass.

Charlie told them everything right then and there. Francine wasn't even angry at Mrs. Martino, the woman she knew as her mother for her entire life. Charlie explained how he loved Alice so much and couldn't bear to risk her having another breakdown and possibly losing Matilda too. Charlie explained that he didn't discover Francine's whereabouts until almost almost 3 years later.

When he approached Mrs. Martino, she threatened to have Alice committed, as she had the connection of her brother, who was a judge who knew lawyers all over the state. He couldn't bear to have two children taken from her. He confirmed that Mrs. Martino was behind the arrangement for Alice, Matilda, and Miss Janice. He thought it best to leave it this way so at least he could always watch both girls from afar and ensure that they grew up happily and safely.

CHAPTER 28

Francine sold the house that she had been living in all alone and was invited to move in with Matilda, Alice, and Miss Janice. They tried to convince Charlie to do the same. After all, it was a giant house with plenty of room for all of them. Miss Janice didn't mind at all and was thrilled that they would come full circle and be united as a family again. Charlie agreed to help Francine move in, but he couldn't bring himself to live in the same house for fear of upsetting Alice. He did agree to live on the property, however.

There was a small school that was built on the property as well and run by Alice and Matilda. Of course, for blind and deaf children. Some of them, who lived too far away, would stay on the property for a few weeks at a time, and others would come and go as their parents were able to bring them for lessons. Alice, though advancing in age, still enjoyed teaching the students to read and write braille.

Now, with the three girls that meant everything to him all in one place, Charlie felt so very content and was able to finally settle down a bit. The girls had a little cottage built for him so that he could always be close by. He would help with the grounds and maintenance of the home. He preferred that Alice didn't know that he was anywhere near, as he enjoyed watching her from a distance.

Alice, still very psychologically fragile, would have to be eased into getting to know Francine.

Or Michelle, as Alice named her and gave the nickname of Shelly.

As Francine entered the grand living room to the big, old pristine looking home, she looked to the far corner where Alice sat reading her braille monitor magazine. Alice always read it from cover to cover. Francine's mouth was dry. *My mother is still so beautiful,* she thought. Not that she could remember what she looked like before. But still beautiful. She was so nervous. She clasped her sweaty, shaking hands and plopped them on her thighs, still clasped.

"Hello?" said Francine.

"Hello," said Alice. "Who is there?"

"My name is Francine. May I come in?" she said.

"Of course," said Alice. "What brings you around here? Are you a friend of Matilda's?"

"Yes, I am. We met in a town called Milford Lakes, New Jersey."

Matilda stood in the doorway and started toward her to stop her from mentioning any trigger words to their mother. Then she stopped to watch Alice's reaction.

Alice sat quietly for a moment, as if she were thinking of something from her past. The look on her face started to become worrisome for a moment. Then she simply responded, "That's nice," and carried on with her reading.

"Would it be okay if I lived here for a while with you and Matilda and Miss Janice? You see, I don't have any family, and I would like to get to know you better," said Francine.

"That would be just fine," said Alice.

"Can you show me how you are reading that book?" said Francine.

Alice was more than happy to show her new friend how she wrote and read braille. She grabbed her slate and stylus out of her pocket as if they had been waiting there to be shown off to the next curious learner. She demonstrated how to write the first three letters of the alphabet and had Francine practice writing in return. The two had hit it off wonderfully within minutes, and Francine was a natural with her mother. They talked and laughed as if they had known each other their entire lives. Matilda and Charlie watched as the pair enjoyed each other's company.

Alice taught Francine the entire alphabet in just one week. They practiced writing notes back and forth to each other. Matilda would join in and play braille games with their mother as well. Alice was incredibly happy now and very calm. It was so comfortable being with Francine and Matilda together.

She would tell stories about her childhood, her sisters, her mother, and her accident. She talked about the blind school and the children there and how she learned to be independent as a young blind girl. She bragged about her college days. Every week they would sit together on Friday evenings and Alice would tell the girls another story about her life. Alice even told them about her past crushes.

One day, as they sat together to play a game of Scrabble with their braille cards, it was time for another story.

Alice suddenly blurted out, "You know, there was this boy that I met when I was very young. He seemed to come in and out of my life all throughout the years. He was always there when I needed something. He would just show up. It was rather mysterious."

The girls glanced at each other and shook their heads as they silently smiled and mouthed the name "Charlie" to each other.

Alice went on to say, "He taught me many things over the years. I can't remember his name, but I used to call him my dancing friend."

Both girls in unison responded, "Why did you call him that?"

Alice said, "Because we used to dance. We rode a bike together too. It was one of those built-for-two bikes. We did a lot of things that sighted people do. One of the things I liked most about him was that he didn't seem to care at all that I was blind. In fact, I think he liked it. He didn't treat me like I was blind either, which made him vastly different from anyone else that I ever knew."

Matilda and Francine looked at each other. "Whatever happened to him?" said Matilda.

"I don't know where he went. I don't remember much at all after that," Alice said.

Their mother looked sad for a moment, as she appeared to be trying to reflect and pull more from her memory.

Then, before they knew it, she snapped right back out of it and carried on with their games.

Over the next several years, Alice grew to love Francine just as much as she loved Matilda. She referred to them both as her girls. They felt that Alice subconsciously knew that Francine was her little baby that had disappeared and sent her into another psychological world that blacked out years of her existence. But no one would ever know. They were just happy to be with their mother. Charlie was still always around. He would even sit on the other side of the room while the girls spent their Friday evenings together. He would do crossword puzzles or read the newspaper quietly while his girls chatted and played the old albums from their parents dancing days. Charlie would tap his foot to the music while the girls sang and danced around the room.

Alice, who always had extremely advanced senses, never appeared to take notice that Charlie was in the room. This unconventional family time worked well for them for many years.

Matilda married the bartender, and they had a set of twins. A boy and a girl. She named them Charlie and Alice. They built a small cottage for Francine, and Matilda had a home built as well for her family. All on the same property. They opened up much of the house and maintained the miniature blind boarding school on their own. With Alice's guidance, the girls and Charlie ran a highly successful, nonprofit home for the students. They followed on with Alice's determination to help as many blind children as possible to live fruitful, educated lives, such as her own.

CHAPTER 29

No one was home one particularly cold December evening. Miss Janice, Harold, and the girls were out doing some Christmas shopping. Alice was sitting in the family room. She began to feel a chill. She decided to go up to her bedroom and fetch a warmer sweater to place around her shoulders while she read her books.

As she made her way up to the second landing of stairs, her foot got caught in the side of the spindles at the top step. Before she knew it, she went tumbling down the entire flight of stairs, hitting her head on the floor down below.

As she lay there, Charlie came rushing in. He instinctively ran toward her and called her name.

"Alice! Alice! Are you okay?" he said.

He slid on his knees across the marble floor until he stopped just where she was laying. He grabbed her and held her tightly in his arms. Her head was bleeding as he wiped off the blood, took off his shirt and wrapped it around her head.

"We have to get you some help," he said.

"No! No! No! Don't! I want you to stay right here with me and don't leave me. I have missed you," said Alice.

As she turned her head in his direction, he was sure that her eyes were looking straight into his.

She was breathing heavily but with longer pauses between each breath, and the breaths were sounding more and more rattled. She was smiling. At him! It was hard for her to talk, but in a soft, quiet voice with pressured speech, she said, "My dancing friend. I never forgot you. You made my life complete. You gave me my sight when I was with you. I knew you would bring us all together again."

With these words, she took her final breath.

Sometime later that evening, the family came through the door to find Charlie sitting in the middle of the marble floor at the bottom of the staircase, holding Alice's lifeless body in his arms. He was rocking her back and forth. He was singing to her.

The song was one of their favorites. They stood in the doorway and waited, allowing Charlie to finally have the chance to hold the love of his life in his arms once again.

They watched and sobbed, holding one another quietly as he sang to her.

It was their favorite song, from their favorite Nat King Cole album.

"Unforgettable."

The following night, Matilda had a dream. It was of Charlie and Alice. They were riding their red tandem bike with the lily of the valley flowers in the front basket. Alice was letting her feet spread out, and Charlie was pedaling away. They both looked noticeably young, and their laughter filled the air.

The dream was so real, Matilda jumped up out of her sleep. She ran out her door in her white nightgown and bare feet, across the property to Charlie's cottage. Francine was already there upon Matilda's arrival, as she'd had a dream as well.

Only hers involved Charlie and Alice holding hands at an altar and Francine was now kneeling down in front of Charlie's Navy footlocker that he had left open with a note sitting on top of all his beloved belongings. The note read: "My darling daughters. I will never stop watching over you and will always be with you. Love, Charlie."

Charlie was gone again but the girls couldn't help but feel that he might be back. They sat in Charlie's cottage and played his old albums that he had saved from his dancing days with Alice. They danced and sang along as the girls had learned much of the verses from their mother after spending all those Friday nights together in the big old house with Charlie sitting on the far side of the room.

THE END

JEROME M. ALLEN
1930-2008

I want to walk in the woods and look at the trees
watch the animals and feel the cool breeze
I want to walk in the rain without an umbrella
No golashes or raincoat because I'm that kind of fella
At a big fancy party I'm outside with the kids
Not inside with the grown-ups trying to hold open my eyelids
I rode my bike to the seashore and back
Had to prove I could do it without heart attack
The Native American history brings me great peace
How wonderful to live off the earth and not pay a lease
I want to sleep on the floor without any pillow
Or under the stars or a weeping willow
All I need is the shirt on my back
But if someone else wants it there's another for me on the rack
I if was given a million in cash
I would buy a cup of coffee and give away the stash
I tried to give my family the perfect life
We just couldn't make it happen, me and my beautiful wife
My daughters and grandkids mean more than the heavens above
But I will stay here now forever and pour down my great love
I tried to live as Christ lived except for temper and pride
But I always knew I had him by my side